Mrs. Oliver's Twist

Saralyn Richard

PALM CIRCLE PRESS

Other Books by Saralyn Richard

Detective Parrott Mystery Series
Murder Outside the Box
Crystal Blue Murder
A Palette for Love and Murder
Murder in the One Percent

The Quinn McFarland Mystery Series
Bad Blood Sisters

A Murder of Principal
Naughty Nana

"Teachers affect eternity; no one can tell where their influence stops."—Henry Brooks Adams

This book is dedicated to the memory of Marietta Allmond, my sophomore English teacher, who inspired me to become a writer.

And to the memory of my senior English teacher, Mary (Midge) Pennington, who believed in my talent and pushed me to use it.

And to the memory of Bill Zehme, one of the brilliant creative writing students I taught at Thornwood High School, who credited me with inspiring his writing life.

Praise for Mrs. Oliver's Twist: A Quinn McFarland Mystery

"From the captivating title to the first brilliant pages and beyond, this cleverly crafted mystery is a fabulous read. There's so much to praise in this book, it's hard to know where to begin. The characters, including the villains, are complex and compelling. The premise is delicious, and the twists (pun intended) are brilliantly executed. I found myself racing through the chapters full of fast-paced suspense. I love it when a story keeps me guessing until the very satisfying conclusion!

Though this is the second book in the series, the author does an excellent job of weaving in the necessary backstory from the first installment, so readers who are new to the series can jump right in. That said, I'm now absolutely picking up the first book!" —**Valerie Biel**, award-winning author of *Beyond the Cemetery Gate*

"The aptly titled Mrs. Oliver's Twist abounds in twists and turns that the author passes around like crumpets at teatime. A delightful mystery that leaves readers gasping for breath while trying to decide who to trust… and who to fend off with a ten-foot pole." —**Barbara Conrey**, USA Today Bestselling Author of *Nowhere Near Goodbye* and *My Secret to Keep*

"Quinn McFarland is back from her honeymoon and excited about her upcoming life changes. She didn't count on being called to the morgue to identify her high school teacher, though. Mrs. Oliver helped Quinn through tough times in high school, and now Quinn hopes to return the favor. But how well does Quinn know her beloved English teacher? Finding the truth about Mrs. Oliver pulls Quinn down a rabbit hole through a dark world of secret identities, drug trafficking, and other unspeakable crimes, threatening her safety and her marriage. The title whispers to the reader to get ready, as twist after twist turns the truth inside out and upside down. It's such a clever game of cat and mouse that readers will never know until the end who is leading the chase".—**Joy Ann Ribar**, author of the Bay Browning Mysteries

"Returning to reality after a heavenly honeymoon isn't fun, but when your parents guilt-trip you about family business suffering in your absence, and a policeman darkens your door, it feels like things can't get worse. Until you're asked to identify a body. Quinn McFarland hits the ground running in Mrs. Oliver's Twist. Everyone has a public and a private persona, but the deeper Quinn delves into her favorite high school teacher's life, she discovers more than she bargains for. And that information may get her or someone she loves killed. Jump into this fast-paced twisty novel that combines crazy family dynamics with heart-pounding action." —**Sharon Lynn**, Award-winning author of A Cotswold Crimes Mystery Series

PRAISE FOR BAD BLOOD SISTERS:
A Quinn McFarland Mystery

"Mortician Quinn McFarland may work with the dead every day, but she's never been so close to murder. A blood sister oath with dangerous repercussions, a warning delivered with a dying breath, a journey into the dark underbelly of coastal Texas…Saralyn Richard's BAD BLOOD SISTERS has suspense and surprises aplenty. A gripping story of a woman wrenched from the safety of her life, and her race to reclaim it."—**Tessa Wegert**, author of *Death in the Family and The Dead Season*

"A delicious five-star mystery served with a side of nail-biting suspense and a dash of romance for dessert. Genre-smashing goodness!"—**Avanti Centrae,** international bestselling author of the VanOps thriller series

"You won't be able to put it down until the last twist is turned."— **Terry Shepherd,** author of the Jessica Ramirez thrillers

"After one delectable taste, you'll devour the rest of this cleverly plotted, neatly tied-up book in one sitting. *Magnifique!*" —**Laurie Buchanan,** author of the Sean McPherson Novels

Chapter One

Quinn was done with death—or so she thought—until the day she returned from her honeymoon. But timing was everything, and she should have known returning to her job would mean trouble.

"We're swamped at the mortuary," her father said, while driving her and Josh back from the airport. "Your brother's been working eighteen-hour days, and your mother has had to do double duty while you were gone."

"Mom? You're kidding me." Quinn's mother ran the funerals, but she almost never set foot in the embalming room anymore.

"I kid you not. Of course, she'd never begrudge you your honeymoon, but she could not wait for you to come home. We've had a real circus these last two weeks, including a tragic golf cart accident—three family members killed."

Quinn shot a glance at her husband. She'd hoped to have at least one more day off before returning to work, but there was no way she could let her family down. She'd buy a jumbo pack of spearmint gum, take her iPod's new playlist into McFarland's tomorrow morning, don her plastic jumpsuit and apron, and carry on as if nothing had changed since she'd married Josh Brady.

She hadn't broken it to her parents that she'd applied to the school of allied health at the University of Texas Medical Branch hospital. Although wanting to work on the living side of things, she'd paused her education after her Bachelor of Science degree to work in the family business. Now she wanted to be a physician assistant.

After a great night's extension of their honeymoon in their own bed, their first as Dr. and Mrs. Brady, Quinn and Josh headed back to the real world. Quinn began the "beauty shop" phase of preparing one of the previously embalmed golf cart victims for funeral, when Police Sergeant Schmidt flung open the back door, as if he belonged there.

"Glad you're back in town." Schmidt was known for his loud voice and boisterous manner. "Another suspicious death, and I think you know the victim."

Quinn's stomach knotted, and she wished she were back at the Jamaican resort with Josh. After covering the body she'd been working on and taking off her gloves, she ushered the sergeant into the front parlor, where a comfortable seating area gave the impression of a friend's living room.

Schmidt lowered himself onto the edge of the padded wing chair. His open mouth revealed large teeth embedded in moist, pink gums. "You know how much I value your opinions. After last year, you're practically an unofficial officer."

Not easily flattered, Quinn resisted rolling her eyes. Last year, Quinn had been involved in the arrest of Lionel French, who owned an adult entertainment business, trafficked in humans, and had killed at least two women. Since then, Sergeant Schmidt had treated her like a colleague, instead of a private citizen. She knew something unsavory was coming.

"Dead woman's a former teacher at the high school. Mrs. Oliver. English, I think. Subject area—not nationality."

A chill flitted down Quinn's spine. Mrs. Oliver was one of her favorites. Sophomore year, when Quinn's boyfriend had taken up with her BFF and dumped her, in that order, Mrs. Oliver's wisdom had been a comfort. In a quiet, but firm way, the teacher had steered Quinn away from painful and embarrassing social situations and toward more academic pursuits. Quinn had become president of the school's new reading club, and that had introduced her to a different group of people. Looking back, Quinn wondered whether the purpose of the reading club had been solely to assuage her personal grief. She owed a lot to Mrs. Oliver.

"What happened?" she asked, not sure she wanted to know.

"We don't know much. Body was found on the west end of the island, floating on her back in the surf at low tide. No vehicle, no ID. Moved to the medical examiner's an hour ago. The medical examiner recognized her as his English teacher. Said she was something special, beautiful and charming."

"She *was*." Quinn muttered, still in shock that Mrs. Oliver had come to such an end. Doing a quick calculation in her head, Quinn figured Mrs. Oliver would be in her sixties now. Widowed and childless, the woman had continued to teach way past the age when most retired, even though rumor had it her husband had left her very well off.

Just a month ago, Quinn and Josh had received a card from her with a generous check as a wedding gift. The card said, "Best wishes for a happy life together. Perhaps you'll use this to start your home library— Trish Oliver."

Quinn brought herself back to real time. "What do you need from me?"

Schmidt grinned, flashing his gums. "We've got no leads. *Nada.* Chief Ramirez said you were close to the woman when you were in high school. I figured you might could tell me something about her—her affiliations, her politics, people she knew and cared about?"

Quinn bristled at the policeman's colloquialism. Mrs. Oliver would never have tolerated such. The image of Mrs. Oliver's rosy-cheeked face shimmered before Quinn's teary eyes. It had been sixteen years since Quinn had her for English. "She was my teacher. We weren't close in the way you might be to a contemporary. She knew me better than I knew her."

"How about you come with me to the morgue? Maybe if you look at her, you'll remember something."

Quinn couldn't say no. She owed it to Mrs. Oliver to help the police figure out how she died. "Okay. Let me clean up and change clothes. Give me five minutes."

Riding in the squad car brought back difficult memories, but Quinn concentrated on the wad of gum in her mouth, put there to mask the odor of poor Mr. Shaw, the corpse she'd been working on. When they arrived, the medical examiner greeted her with a bear hug. Paul Honey was a good friend of Quinn's brother, Jack. That's how it was on this Texas island. Everybody knew everybody, and they all knew each other's business, too. "Congratulations on your wedding—or should I say best wishes?"

Quinn shrugged. "Either way, thanks." The morgue smelled only slightly better than the embalming room at work, and she was eager to get out of there. "Sergeant Schmidt tells me you've got my teacher here."

"Yes, of course. Trish Oliver. She arrived with no identification, but I'd recognize that face anywhere. Come on in, and I'll show you." Paul led Quinn and Sergeant Schmidt to the storage room where the air conditioning was blowing at sixty-eight degrees. A wall of compartments held bodies awaiting autopsies and other procedures, a milepost before being transported to the funeral home and then to the gravesite.

Quinn's shivering began on the inside and radiated out, having everything to do with the person she'd come to see than the temperature of the room. As Paul strode to compartment number nine and rolled out the body, Quinn shifted her weight from one foot to the other. Her impulse was to run.

"Here she is. We haven't processed her yet." He opened the body bag and flipped open the top fabric with a swift motion, revealing the woman's bloated face and torso. She was dressed in a short-sleeved blouse and gauzy pants. Her legs and feet were covered. Sand and abrasions marred her complexion, and her arms were bruised. Her hair was tangled, untidy in a way that it had never been in life.

Quinn forced herself to stare at the body. Her work had trained her to focus on the details that identified the corpse as a unique human being, rather than a lifeless object. Through blurry eyes, she focused on one feature and another. The woman had aged since Quinn had seen her last, but she was still beautiful. Her cheekbones and chin, her slender figure, her graceful hands.

"Wait," Quinn said with an intake of breath. "Give me gloves." She donned a pair of blue nitrile gloves and held up the lifeless left wrist. Her eyes met Paul's and then Schmidt's. "This woman is not Mrs. Oliver."

"Wh-what?" the policeman said. "What are you talking about?"

Quinn laid the hand down gently. "This lady is Mrs. Oliver's identical twin, Elizabeth. See the small Greek letter, *epsilon* tattooed on her wrist? Mrs. Oliver had *pi* on hers."

Chapter Two

Quinn hated being dragged into another police investigation. Her brush with dangerous criminals last year had cured her of all cravings for adventure, and she'd promised Josh no more taking chances. But after hearing about the epsilon-tattoo on his victim's wrist, Sergeant Schmidt pleaded for her assistance. "You know the victim. Your insights could be valuable."

Quinn didn't know about that, but she did have questions, starting with this one—if the dead woman was Mrs. Oliver's twin sister, where was Mrs. Oliver? Quinn couldn't ignore the fact that Mrs. Oliver had been there for her, when she'd needed emotional support. Quinn couldn't turn her back on her teacher now. What if she was *also* in danger?

"How did you know about the tattoos?" Schmidt had asked.

Quinn considered the question. "I don't remember exactly. I think I noticed the *pi* on Mrs. Oliver's wrist one day, and I asked her what that was all about."

"Did people really tattoo their babies' wrists back in the day?" Schmidt muttered aloud, possibly not expecting an answer. "Seems cruel."

"These parents did. Mrs. Oliver said she and her sister couldn't be told apart otherwise. The tattoos were tiny originally. As the girls grew, so did the marks."

"You seem to know a lot about Mrs. Oliver. Mind if I take you to her house for a look-see? Far as I know, no one's reported this lady missing or anything. If she's visiting her sister here in town, you'd think we woulda heard from the real Mrs. Oliver by now. All attempts at contacting her have failed."

Quinn shuddered at the thought that something untoward may have happened to Mrs. Oliver, too. She was surprised by Sergeant Schmidt's desire to include her in this early investigation. An inner voice warned her not to involve herself, and if she hadn't seen the *epsilon* tattoo, she might have begged off. Knowing that the victim wasn't Mrs. Oliver helped, but what if her teacher was lying unconscious in her house—or worse? "I'll go with you, but I need to get back to the funeral parlor soon. I've been away, and there's a slew of clients waiting for me."

Schmidt ushered Quinn back into the passenger seat of the squad car, where she squeezed herself between the computer screen and the door. The policeman repeated the word, "slew" with a chuckle.

As he drove west on Seawall Boulevard, Schmidt waved at several people who were walking, running, or biking. His police radio sent staccato messages into the space between him and Quinn, but none that required action from him. "Do you think Mrs. Oliver's sister was murdered? Maybe she had a heart attack or something." Quinn worked with dead bodies, no problem, but crime put a nasty taste in her mouth.

"We'll know more once the medical examiner has had a chance to examine the body and run toxicology, but based on first impressions, I'd say foul play is possible. She's basically a good-looking corpse—you know, fit, healthy-looking for a senior citizen. The bruises and abrasions might be defensive wounds, or they might have come from erosion on the beach. You know, sand, shells—the medical examiner's report will tell us a lot."

Quinn agreed with Schmidt's assessment. Having seen more than a few corpses, she understood the need to wait for evidence and expert examination. "I've been thinking about what I know about Mrs. Oliver's twin. Not much, really, but I think she lives in New York or used to. She came to Texas before Thanksgiving, the year I had Mrs. Oliver as a teacher. She visited our class and performed Lady Macbeth's soliloquy. She was a talented actor."

"What's her name? Elizabeth what?"

Quinn rubbed her head, trying to remember. The woman's name was something peculiar, flamboyant—*a color. Fuchsia, purple, indigo? No, lavender.* "Everyone laughed when Mrs. Oliver introduced her. Obviously a stage name—Elizabeth Lavender."

"You gotta be kiddin' me. Lavender? Like the flower?" The sergeant's lip curled, revealing his trademark gums. "Well, I guess you gotta give her points for originality." He pulled into the driveway of a large brick home in one of the nicest neighborhoods on the island.

A tall, skinny guy jumped out of the Alert Alarms truck parked at the curb. He carried a metal clipboard with papers attached.

"That's our keyholder. Give me a few minutes," Schmidt said, as he climbed out of the car. He met the alarm guy on the pebbled concrete leading to the front door. Quinn unfastened her seatbelt and leaned her forehead on the window of the squad car, while Schmidt showed his badge and signed the papers. Afterwards, he motioned for her to join them on the porch.

Schmidt tapped Quinn on the shoulder and nodded. "Tell Frank here that you've requested a welfare check, because you're concerned about Mrs. Oliver's safety."

Not entirely sure what she was getting into, she understood the police couldn't enter the house without a warrant, unless there were exigent circumstances, one of which was a welfare check request. Quinn muttered. "I *do* have reason to be concerned about Mrs. Oliver. Please check to see if she's okay." Frank asked her to sign the same paper.

Schmidt rang the doorbell and Quinn held her breath, a stone in the pit of her stomach. After no response, Schmidt readied his weapon, and Frank used his key to open the front door.

He tapped Quinn on the shoulder. "You stay here until I make sure the house is clear."

Frank nodded. "I'll be in my truck."

Schmidt hollered Mrs. Oliver's name several times with no response and closed the door behind him, leaving only a crack open.

Left on the porch alone, Quinn experienced a wave of bladder urgency, and she realized she hadn't been to the bathroom in hours. On the theory of asking forgiveness rather than permission, she nudged the door open and scooted in.

Darting into the flagstone-paved foyer, Quinn tiptoed around, until she found a powder room off the entry hall. Relieved, she closed herself in, locking the door behind her. While she did her business, she examined the décor and accessories in the room. The glimpse into her teacher's tastes and lifestyle registered as surreal.

A basket next to the toilet held reading material. Curious to see what her English teacher might find suitable for bathroom reading, Quinn lifted the contents of the basket and spread the items out on her lap. Not magazines, but paperback books. *The House on Mango Street*, *The Scarlet Letter*, and *Catcher in the Rye* were on top, all three taught in the Ball High School curriculum. The fourth book, however, stuck at the back, caused Quinn's mouth to plop open. *Fifty Shades of Grey*. There was no way Mrs. Oliver would read that book, no way she would purchase it or display it in her powder room. Not the Mrs. Oliver that Quinn knew.

She replaced the book and finished up, turning on the tap to wash her hands.

A second later, Schmidt banged on the door. She eased it open to find Schmidt, pointing his pistol right at Quinn's chest. "What?" he said, his face reddening. "I told you—You could've been shot."

"Sorry," Quinn said, trembling in every part of her body. "I couldn't wait another second."

Schmidt holstered his sidearm and glowered at Quinn, an expression she remembered all too well. He considered her impulsive, she knew, and maybe he was right. Her heart still pounded, but she stepped inside the majestic entry hall with Schmidt. Morning sunlight poured through the clerestory windows, creating a cheerful atmosphere and offering ample view of the ornately framed oil paintings decorating the walls. Apparently, Mrs. Oliver loved the visual arts, as well as literature.

"The house is clear. Nobody around, no evidence of a crime, but you know this woman. Maybe you'll see something significant. Try not to touch anything." Schmidt's admonishment and the silence of the house cloaked Quinn with trepidation. They would find no welfare in this welfare check.

Not even a clock's ticking disrupted the quiet. "Let's go," he said, motioning Quinn to follow. Through the living room and dining room, the house was tidy and clean, undisturbed by a Christmas tree or other display of the season.

The kitchen and breakfast room held a faint bacon smell, borne out by a frying pan, plate, and silverware soaking in the sink, greasy paper towels in the garbage. Someone had eaten breakfast here, not too long ago. A newspaper, folded open to the Dear Abby column, rested on the table next to a colorful placemat depicting Monet's house in Giverny. Quinn realized with a shiver that she knew of Monet because of Mrs. Oliver.

Schmidt leaned over the table and pulled a pen from his pocket. He swiped at the newspaper to expose the top of the page. "Yesterday's paper," he said, grunting as he snapped photos of the table, the paper, and the date.

Schmidt led the way up the stairs to the bedrooms sand down the hall to the primary bedroom. "Nobody's here, but this is interesting," he said, "and I ask you to stay here at the door in case there's evidence." He pointed to the unmade bed, a purple bathrobe, and an open suitcase on a rack at the foot of the bed. A tag on the suitcase said in huge letters, "Elizabeth Lavender, 50 West Street, New York."

"Looks like the victim's been staying here, sleeping in Mrs. Oliver's bed." Schmidt took out his cellphone to snap a photo of the luggage tag.

Quinn looked around. From her vantage point nothing appeared to be out of the ordinary—no sign of struggle or violence of any kind. An unopened art deco jewelry box sat on the bedroom dresser, and bookshelves loaded with hardback books of various vintages decorated three of the four walls. The nightstand next to the unmade bed held eye drops, reading glasses, and three novels, their spines facing the doorway. Quinn had never read any of them: *Beach Music, Lady Chatterley's Lover, and Bonfire of the Vanities.* The unwashed dishes and the unmade bed stood out as being not Mrs. Oliver-ish. If not for the body found in the Gulf, the only real mystery would have been like Goldilocks—who's been sleeping in Mrs. Oliver's bed, and why? Quinn had a feeling there would be much more mystery to come.

Chapter Three
TRISH

I bite my tongue to keep from saying something too caustic. "No, Winslow, I don't want you to come over with rocky road ice cream after you finish rehearsals. I have other plans." I hang up the receiver of the wall phone in my sister's tiny kitchen. Oh, puleeze, I can't believe my sister actually has a relationship with this loser.

Certainly, this will be my last holiday "visit" to Liz's apartment in this God-forsaken neighborhood. To think that some people consider life on Broadway to be glamorous! A week in New York is certainly not the "breath of fresh air" of days gone by. New York's gone down in the past four years, since my husband Marvin died, when my dear sister and I first conceived of switching places at Christmas time.

I should have listened to Marvin when he warned me against being too close to my twin sister. Now my husband's gone, and I'm faced with proof that he was right. Liz has become a lunatic.

Since we're past sixty, Liz hasn't been getting the acting parts anymore. Not that she was ever a Tony award winner, or even a lead in a show that lasted more than a few months. This year she's moved to this tenement. She's crammed five rooms of furniture, mostly inherited from our parents' six-bedroom mansion, into three roach-infested, linoleum-floored, cubbyholes. She calls it her own private paradise. I call it a rathole.

Winslow calls back. He wants to know what time I'll be home from my other plans. I can't very well avoid him. He lives next door, and the tissue-paper walls betray my every move. He's not the brightest, and he doesn't have enough money to keep himself in toilet paper, but I'll admit he's gorgeous and fit, and still young enough to get my juices going—and Liz's, too, I'm sure.

What the hell? One more trip to Nirvana with that babe can't hurt anything. He thinks we're hot. At our age, I call that a plus. Good thing he's never noticed our wrist tattoos are different. He probably doesn't know the first thing about the Greek alphabet, anyway.

The people back home'll be scandalized if they ever find out that prim and proper Trish Oliver has a wild side, but, hey, an old girl should be entitled to a little fun sometime, and how will they ever know?

"Okay, Winslow. You've talked me into it. Come on over after your rehearsal. You can leave the ice cream in your freezer."

Chapter Four

Quinn returned to work in the embalming room after eleven, where she still had several bodies. She donned her plastic outfit, flipped on the overhead exhaust blowers, and rolled out the first. While she treated the gentleman of the hour to his last pampering, her thoughts returned to Mrs. Oliver.

On the way back to the funeral home, Sergeant Schmidt had peppered her with questions, most of which she couldn't answer. She and Mrs. Oliver hadn't been in communication in years, except for chance meetings in the grocery store or movie theater, and the wedding gift. She didn't know anything about the people the woman hung out with.

When Schmidt asked if she knew of any bad blood between Mrs. Oliver and her sister, fingers of ice kneaded Quinn's spine. She could tell he was already thinking that Elizabeth Lavender's death had been a homicide, even though the medical examiner hadn't ruled yet.

Her first reaction was to defend her teacher. She couldn't imagine the stunning and elegant woman she knew in the classroom as a suspect in a murder investigation. No way. She'd said as much, but as to the question about bad blood between the sisters, Quinn didn't really know.

Last year, Quinn herself, had been a suspect when her former BFF, Ana Renfroe, had turned up dead from a head wound. That experience had taught her how vulnerable anyone could be when someone dies from unnatural causes. Anyone connected to a victim can be examined for motive, and the normal ups and downs of relationships can put the survivor in an unpleasant spotlight. She hoped Mrs. Oliver would be alive and safe, and far away from town, so she could be eliminated as a suspect.

The one hope Quinn clung to was based on the fact that Elizabeth Lavender had apparently been staying in Mrs. Oliver's bedroom, sleeping in her bed. If Mrs. Oliver had been around, surely Elizabeth would have slept in the guest room. The dishes in the sink, the racy book in the powder room, yesterday's newspaper—those struck Quinn as *off*.

While she completed the embalming process and prepared to start the cosmetics, the sudden whoosh of a door opening caused Quinn to jump back from the table. "You startled me," she said.

Her father strode to her side and gave her a brief hug. "Sorry. How are things going down here?"

Quinn's parents lived upstairs in a four-bedroom home with polished wood floors, carved moldings, high ceilings, claw-footed bathtubs, and a wrap-around porch. She and her brother Jack had grown up there, never thinking much about the historic grandeur upstairs or the grim reality downstairs.

"Almost finished with this one. Might have time to do two more before I go home."

"Your mother's made a delicious spaghetti casserole. Want to take a break?" His once-broad shoulders sagged a little.

"Nah. I'm not hungry. I want to keep going so I can get Calvin fed and walked before Josh gets home from the hospital."

"Okay, honey. We appreciate everything. Mom will pack up to-go plates for you to take home. Really glad you're here." With a little wave, her dad backed out of the room and closed the door. A softer whoosh punctuated his exit.

Quinn's father had always appreciated her, even though his attention had sometimes felt more like smothering. Still, Quinn held tender feelings for him, and, perhaps because of their family business, she dreaded the time when she would lose him. She hoped that time would be a long way off, and she'd be working elsewhere by then.

Grabbing a minute to text Josh, "I miss you," with seven exclamation points and six heart emojis, she turned back to her patient. She imagined telling Josh about her interesting day. Quinn hummed with the music coming from her iPod, Taylor Swift's "Treacherous." She couldn't help feeling that whatever had happened to Mrs. Oliver's twin, her teacher was in for a treacherous ride, and she didn't like it.

Chapter Five

When Josh's car swept into the driveway and pulled to a stop, Quinn flung open the front door, and she and Calvin ran out into the mild air to meet him. At almost seven-thirty, the sky was dark, but the porch light illuminated Josh's slim frame, his jaunty walk, the golden glints in his hair and stubble on his face. Everything about him attracted Quinn, like a magnet seeking its opposite.

She threw her arms around the middle of his lab coat and lifted her face for a long, warm kiss, while Calvin pirouetted around the two of them, clamoring for affection. As Quinn regained her equilibrium, Josh picked up the westie and allowed the dog to lick his face.

"C'mon, let's go inside," Josh said. "So happy to be home." He ruffled the fur between Calvin's eyes and behind his ears before setting him down.

"Me, too. Mom sent dinner home with me. Hungry?"

Josh's eyes met Quinn's and held them. "Yes," he said. And she knew he meant he was hungry for more than food.

Before she could assess which appetite would be satisfied first, someone's stomach rumbled like a garbage truck. "Yours or mine?" Quinn asked, laughing.

"Mine, I think. Maybe we should eat."

Quinn heated the spaghetti casserole in the microwave and opened a bottle of chianti, while Josh washed up. The aromas of garlic and oregano filled the room. By the time Josh returned to the dining table, she'd lit a candle and turned off the overhead lights. "It's not Jamaica," she said, batting her eyelashes, "but it's still romantic."

"Mmmm, I agree. And after the day I've had in the OR, I couldn't be happier."

"Want to play the adjective game?" Quinn asked, as she spooled a fork with spaghetti and popped it into her mouth. "I've had a crazy day, too."

They'd invented the chord game while lying on the beach in Ocho Rios, giggling as each one tried to outdo the other in describing everything from the setting to the accommodations to the food and drinks they'd consumed.

"Okay, I'll start," Josh said. "My day was frenetic, complicated, and often perplexing. I spent part of it in the ER, where patients were miserable, bloody, infirm, and critical." He took a slug of wine. "One, in particular, really got to me, but I'll tell you about him later. Now you."

Quinn set down her fork. She hardly knew where to begin, with the medical examiner, Mrs. Oliver's house, or the funeral home. "Well, let's say I've dealt with four people today that were silent, pale, smelly, and lifeless. And one of them might have met with an unexpected, unfortunate, and brutal end."

"Oh, no. Nobody you know, I hope." Josh teased Quinn that she was tight with everyone in town, having lived on the small island all her life, but the truth was, she had been an introvert after high school. She had a million acquaintances, people she called, "beach peeps," but few friends.

Quinn gave a loud sigh. "Actually, I do, and that's the hard part. Remember the generous check we received as a wedding gift from my teacher, Mrs. Oliver?"

Josh tilted his head in a perfect imitation of Calvin. "You don't mean she—"

"No, not exactly." Quinn explained the misidentification of the body and her own role in naming the victim as Mrs. Oliver's twin. She rushed on to explain how she and Sergeant Schmidt had visited Mrs. Oliver's house but not found the teacher. "I'm sorry about her sister, but I'm really concerned about Mrs. O."

Narrowing his eyes, Josh drained his wineglass. "How did you get to be a part of this whole thing with the police? Was she murdered?"

"Not clear. Her body was found on the beach. Schmidt knew about my connection to Mrs. Oliver, and he asked to take me to the medical examiner's office to ID her. Mrs. Oliver was a very important person in my life. I couldn't say no."

Josh raised an eyebrow. "But then, after you discovered the tattoo, you still went to Mrs. Oliver's house?"

"Yes, because then I wanted to find Mrs. Oliver. I still do." Quinn sipped her wine, hoping to head off a lecture from her husband. "Look, I know I promised you, and I intend to keep that promise. But I can't turn my back on Mrs. Oliver. She's the one bright spot in my memories of high school. She deserves my help if I can give it."

Reading the look of doubt on her husband's face, she decided the best course was to change the subject. She took another bite of the now-cooling spaghetti. "That's all. Now tell me about the patient who got to you."

Josh scrubbed his face with his napkin. "Okay, but no names, no details. I was in clinic and got a call to come to ER. A guy on the island was busted for raising and selling cockfighters. You know what those are?"

"Roosters, right?"

Josh nodded. "Trained to kill from birth. Mean as hell, and when blades are attached to their legs, they're deadly." He refilled his wineglass and took a drink. "The guy in the ER was an owner. He was getting his rooster ready for a fight and equipped him with a seven-centimeter blade. The bird got antsy and tried to run away. So the owner grabbed him and the knife cut him in the groin."

"Omigod. Sounds horrible."

"Exactly. Cockfights are nasty events. The man was bleeding out, practically gone by the time I arrived. I told him I would repair his wound as best as possible, and he actually spit at me."

"Ugh, totally disgusting. I hope you were wearing a mask." Quinn couldn't imagine the rudeness. Maybe working on the dead wasn't so bad after all.

"Some people are just evil. Any guy who'd profit from cockfighting I'd put in that category."

"Was it vascular surgery?" Quinn loved hearing about Josh's surgical skills. He had assisted in the kidney transplant on her brother last year.

"Yeah, he needed vascular to repair his femoral vein and then I stitched up his adductor longus and sartorius muscles before closing him up He's got a big incision in the inguinal fold, but I think he's going to make it."

"What about the rooster?" Quinn couldn't fathom allowing the guy to go back to abusing animals.

Josh looked up with a twinkle in his eye. "The rooster'll be fine. Seriously, the police shut that down. Turns out he had more than fifty hens and roosters on site. Filthy conditions. Animal control cleaned them out and took them to a shelter. When the guy heals, he'll face serious charges."

Josh stood and gathered the dishes to carry to the sink. "How about if I take Calvin for a quick walk, and you can get ready for bed?"

Quinn's insides melted at the prospect of spending the night with the man of her dreams tonight and every night for the rest of her life. "I think that's a delightful, exciting, delicious, and almost-perfect idea."

Josh clipped on Calvin's leash. "*Almost* perfect?"

"Absolutely. Perfect would include doing the dishes, as well."

Chapter Six

The next morning, a rare cold front blew into the coastal town, so Quinn bundled up to take Calvin for a walk before she headed for work. She was almost home when she received a call from Sergeant Schmidt.

"One mystery's solved. Your teacher's alive and well." Background noise indicated he was driving.

A cloak of dread lifted from Quinn's shoulders. She hadn't realized how much seeing Mrs. Oliver's twin's body had affected her. "What's the story?"

"She can tell you herself. She wants to see you today, if possible. In a nutshell, the twins changed places for the holidays. Mrs. Oliver was in New York at her sister's place." Schmidt's booming voice could probably be heard throughout the neighborhood.

"See me? Why? To make funeral arrangements?"

"Beats me. Maybe the lady doesn't have many friends. Sees you as sympathetic." Schmidt's own emotional intelligence probably hovered near zero.

Images of the interior of Mrs. Oliver's home danced before Quinn. "She didn't go back to her house, did she?" Considering that her twin might have been killed, the house might not be safe.

"Hunh-uh. She arrived there last night. I'd plastered a "do not enter" sign to the glass on the front door, asking her to call the station. She took a room at the Galvez."

Thoughts raced in her mind, as she unlocked the door and turned off the alarm. She needed to change clothes and hustle to work. "What made her ask for me?"

"I told her you were the one who identified the body as the twin sister. That you recognized the tattoo and knew the story." The road sounds from Schmidt's car had come to a stop. "I'm interviewing her in one of the meeting rooms at the Galvez in five minutes. If you can stop by, I know she'd be glad to see you. Poor lady's fit to be tied."

Glad she had caught up on the backlog at work, Quinn decided she could squeeze in a visit with Mrs. Oliver on the way to the funeral home. "I'll try to come by in a few minutes. Text me the location of the room."

She disconnected and called her dad. "Okay if I come in an hour later this morning?"

"Sure, kitten. Thanks to you, the only body we have is Mrs. Oliver's sister. No decisions from her family yet, so no rush. If you need the whole day, take it, and I'll call Jack to come in."

"Not necessary." Quinn hesitated but decided not to tell her father that she was going to meet with Mrs. Oliver. In the old days, she might have felt compelled to explain her every move, but now she was a grown-up, a married woman. She didn't need to raise her hand to ask for the bathroom pass anymore.

The Galvez Hotel was only a five-minute drive from Quinn's house, barely enough time to heat up the car. On the way, Quinn wondered how Mrs. Oliver would look. Surely, she would be shaken by her sister's death. Quinn rehearsed different expressions of sympathy, leaning on her experience in death services. She finally decided a simple, "I'm so sorry for your loss," would be best.

A text from Sergeant Schmidt instructed Quinn to come to the room behind the Monarch Restaurant on the first floor. She entered the lavishly decorated lobby, marveling at the sheen of the black and white marble floor, the gold-trimmed columns, the crimson draperies, and the sparkling chandeliers. The art deco vibe probably meant more to Mrs. Oliver than to Quinn, but she sashayed down the hallway anyway, swinging her shoulder bag, wondering whether Trish Oliver had done the same.

When she stepped into the small room at the end of the hall, Quinn gazed at Mrs. Oliver, who stood by the window, still attractive and fit. The outside light bathed her face in a peachy glow. Her sapphire eyes were red-rimmed. Quinn held out her arms, remembering a time in the past when *she* needed the hug. This time Quinn did the comforting.

She murmured condolences and sat next to her teacher, while Schmidt returned to his questioning.

"Mrs. Oliver has been telling me about the arrangement she's had with her sister over the past few years. The two women spend the Christmas holidays living in each other's homes, enjoying the change of pace, pretending to be the other."

"Far better than spending time together in one place or the other. Really an extension of the tricks we played on people when we were children." *The same raspy voice, the same precise articulation of syllables.*

"You see, we are—were—identical twins. No one could ever tell us apart, unless we wanted them to. You know, sometimes Liz would cut her bangs, or I would wear a dark red lipstick. But we pulled off a lot of switches—even went to social events." She patted Quinn's hand. "One time, before Marvin and I married, I think you dinged her car with your cart in the grocery store parking lot, and Liz called you out. You thought it was me, and you kept apologizing to me. Do you remember that?"

Quinn didn't remember, but many of her high school experiences had been buried after the trauma that Ana and Brad had put her through.

"Anyway," Mrs. Oliver said, "I've just come back from a delightful time in New York, quite possibly my last, now that my sister is gone." She twisted a handkerchief into a tight snake and then knotted it. "I can't believe it."

In a routine manner, Schmidt elicited information about how long Mrs. Oliver had been in New York, who might vouch for her being there, and what her travel arrangements coming home were. The merging of Mrs. Oliver's eyebrows indicated her understanding of why he wanted to know, although she answered each question with her typical aplomb.

Sergeant Schmidt interjected with the gentlest voice Quinn had ever heard him use. "I'm sure it comes as a great shock to you, Mrs. Oliver." He made eye contact with Quinn and said, "And the medical examiner has ruled Ms. Lavender's death undetermined preliminarily, but there was plankton and fluid in her lungs. So, she wasn't dead when she was taken to the Gulf."

A soft wail escaped Mrs. Oliver's lips, even though Quinn guessed Schmidt had intimated the possibility of foul play before Quinn's arrival. Something was a little off about her former teacher. "I can't help wishing I had come home earlier. Or hadn't switched places at all. How foolish for the two of us to play these games, really. I'd wanted to stop, but Liz begged me to continue. Claimed she needed an occasional break from 'chaos.'"

"Blaming yourself isn't productive," Sergeant Schmidt said. "Toxicology will help narrow down the circumstances of her death, but that will take a while. There's always the chance the medical examiner will change his ruling."

An abrupt raising of the eyebrows and patting of a pocket cut into the questioning. Schmidt pulled out his cell phone and murmured something about having to be excused for a moment.

As he left the room, Mrs. Oliver scooted her chair closer and threw an arm over the back of Quinn's chair. Uncomfortable with the curious gesture, Quinn leaned forward and examined her teacher's face for a clue, but Mrs. Oliver's eyes were closed, the long lashes sitting like curlicues, as if she were concentrating on something totally different.

"Mrs. Oliver?" Quinn tried to think of something to snap the woman back to reality. "What can I do to help you through this trying time?"

The woman released a sigh, and her rosebud lips curled into a smile. "Sweet of you." She moved her chair back to its original position. "You've already helped tremendously—just by being here."

Sergeant Schmidt returned, apologizing for the interruption. "Let's see, where were we? I wanted to know whether your sister was a competent swimmer?"

"Oh, yes," Mrs. Oliver said, not missing a beat. "Our parents made sure we both could swim at an early age. In fact, Liz was on the swim team when she was in high school. She was the more athletic of the two of us."

Quinn tried not to show the nausea that crept up her gullet at the thought of a drowning. She slid a glance at the policeman's face, wondering whether his sympathetic tone was fake. The Schmidt she knew considered everyone a suspect until proven otherwise. He was probably mentally building a case against Mrs. Oliver, saving up the details for a time when she would least expect an accusation.

The Mrs. Oliver that Quinn remembered would never kill anyone, much less her twin sister. Quinn tamped down her own distress. She leaned forward and turned toward her teacher. "I'm sure you'll be a valuable resource to the police in learning the truth. If I can help you in any way, please let me know." Quinn marveled at her own ability to give platitudes. In truth, she wanted nothing to do with another murder brought to her doorstep.

Mrs. Oliver wrapped an errant strand of hair around an ear. "Thank you, my dear. You don't know how much help you already are. I feel your support, and I want your family to take good care of my sister."

"Of course. We'll do everything we can to make the arrangements as smooth as possible." Quinn was already thinking of some of the options she could offer, depending on whether the funeral would be here or in New York.

Mrs. Oliver sat straighter and attempted a smile. "That will be wonderful. One less thing to worry about. Of course, there's something I can't get out of my mind, Sergeant Schmidt."

"What's that?"

"Who might've killed my sister. And did they think they were killing me?"

Chapter Seven
TRISH

I must admit, I enjoy meeting with Sergeant Schmidt. I can tell he's doing his best to treat the little ol' schoolteacher with kid gloves. That gentle voice, and those sympathetic eyes. Not that I'm bamboozled by his demeanor. He's probably watching my reactions behind that gummy smile of his, and he wouldn't hesitate to slap handcuffs on me if he could think of a reason.

I find myself flirting a tiny little bit with him. Not so much that he will think me strange, just enough to show my sincere blue eyes and perfect smile to advantage. He might be fifteen years younger, but no man is impervious to an alluring woman, no matter what her age. Mostly, I'd like him to let me back into my house. There are things there I need to do.

Schmidt doesn't pick up on my batting eyelashes. I hope I'm not losing my touch. On the other hand, right now, he treats me with respect.

And why not? I've taught in that boring high school for more years than anyone. I've seen faculty come and go, and I've put up with this initiative and that, never complaining. I've graded enough ungrammatical, illogical, sloppily written papers to heap the landfills to overflowing.

And Quinn McFarland—such a goody-two-shoes. Despite my best efforts to lift her up after her best friend and her boyfriend dragged her through the gutter, Quinn remains quite trusting in her outlook.

I wonder what she'd think of her precious role model of an English teacher if she knew the truth about me. That I've never cared for teaching, the perfect profession for ladylike women, according to my overbearing parents. That sweet Mrs. Oliver never does anything for anybody that she doesn't think through to its logical conclusion. Whatever's best for me, myself, and I is my mantra—always has been and always will be.

Chapter Eight

The next day Quinn prepared for Mrs. Oliver's three p.m. appointment at the funeral home. McFarland's had held off on embalming, but Quinn wanted to clean up the body in case Mrs. Oliver wanted to view it.

Quinn regarded washing as a sacred duty, one of purification. The use of water for religious occasions had given her the idea. When her time came, she hoped someone would bathe her body with the same tenderness that she used on all her clients.

Before she poured the cool water on Ms. Lavender's face and neck and torso, Quinn peered at the woman's skin. Tiny petechiae had surfaced around the neck and under the eyes that hadn't been there before, when she seen the body at the medical examiner's. Post-mortem spots like these, capillary hemorrhages, were not unusual, but in this case, the marks made Quinn nauseated and slightly dizzy. Perhaps the resemblance of the corpse to her teacher affected her.

The medical examiner had preliminarily ruled the death undetermined, despite the location of the body in the Gulf and the plankton in the lungs. The fact that the body was found face-up was perplexing. Drowning victims usually sank into the water until later, when they would float to the surface, face-down. Drowning could be accidental or suicidal, so Paul had been reluctant to make a determination until investigators sorted things out.

But the petechiae might tell a different story. Quinn held off on pouring the water. She took photos of the marks and texted them to Sergeant Schmidt. Within seconds, he called her. "Stop whatever you're doing with the Lavender woman. I'm coming over to check her out, and I might bring Paul with me."

The medical examiner didn't typically make house calls. His workload was heavy, and once he sent the body off, that was the end of his involvement. But the morgue was only four minutes away from McFarland's, and the petechiae might be a game changer.

Quinn remained in the room while Schmidt and the medical examiner examined the body. Nausea had become indigestion, and her thoughts dwelled on how Mrs. Oliver would be affected if the medical examiner revised the cause of death to homicide.

"I'm not surprised," Paul Honey said, as he peered at the victim through a lighted magnifier. "Petechiae and ecchymoses often take up to seventy-two hours to appear. The marks are suspicious, but we can't jump to conclusions, especially since the eyes aren't severely bruised or bloodshot. These discolorations could be self-inflicted, or caused by activities such as martial arts or sexual stimulation."

Quinn couldn't imagine an older woman engaging in self-strangulation of any sort, or even martial arts for that matter. Even a woman like Elizabeth Lavender, whose lifestyle as an actress may have been unconventional by societal norms. She wondered how much Mrs. Oliver would have known about her sister's tastes and habits and whether she would have been critical or amused.

The medical examiner continued in a monotone. "Lethal strangulation, no matter how it occurs, is hard to establish. This lady has no damage to the larynx or discoid bruises."

Sergeant Schmidt stood near the exit to the parking lot, peering through the tiny square window. "You wouldn't mind if I swabbed the neck, would you? Who knows, maybe I can turn up DNA from the hands of another party."

"You can do whatever you see fit, Sergeant," Honey said, "but remember, this woman was lying in the Gulf. If there was DNA on her neck, it's probably washed away now. I've released the body, and I'm sticking with my ruling—death by indeterminate cause. If you find something else, and, of course, when toxicology comes in, maybe I'll revise my opinion." The medical examiner tipped his imaginary hat to Quinn and the policeman. "And now, I must get back to the job. A new one coming in on top of the two I left on ice to come over here."

After the medical examiner left, Sergeant Schmidt stood opposite the body and stared at the floor. His jaw worked double-time.

"Would the medical examiner have checked under the toenails?" Quinn remembered her own abduction last year and the way she'd dragged her feet in the gravel, hoping to leave clues for someone to find her.

"That's a great idea. Maybe not, because of the immersion in the Gulf," he said, perking up. "Let me get my kit from the car." After a few passes, he stepped backwards from the corpse. "I don't know how you do this every day. The odor is making my eyes water."

Quinn pulled a pack of spearmint gum from her apron and handed it over. "Take a few sticks. The mint masks the smell." She turned the overhead blower up to high, as well. The air pollution improved immediately, although replaced by the motor's noise pollution. She wished she could insert her earbuds, but, under the circumstances, that would be rude.

While Schmidt took his samples, Quinn straightened the area surrounding the metal table. She watched, as he bagged his swabs and the solutions that comprised the collection kit. He motioned to turn off the blower. "The toenails may be a dead end, but thanks for noticing the marks on the body, kid. That was a good call."

"What do I tell Mrs. Oliver when she comes here this afternoon? She may want to cremate the body or ship it to New York."

"She's the next of kin, and we can't stop her, but I sure would like to have another twenty-four to forty-eight hours. See if you can stall her. At least until I can finish talking to her neighbors."

Quinn followed Schmidt to the door and ushered him out. She popped two new sticks of gum into her mouth and got back to work on the Broadway actress. "Okay, Ms. Lavender. Not quite the green room, but we do have costumes and makeup. Let's see if we can make you presentable for showtime with your sister."

Chapter Nine

Trish Oliver arrived at the lobby of McFarland's on the dot of three to view her sister's body. Quinn greeted her with a hug. The older woman wore a knit skirt, top, and jacket in shades of black and gray. A strand of pinkish pearls adorned her neck, and two large pearls set in gold gleamed in her ears.

Self-conscious about the "company" uniform, kept in the back closet for meeting with the public—navy pants and a maroon and navy blouse—Quinn escorted her teacher to the upholstered sofa and chairs, where a bowl of fresh flowers and a box of tissues sat within easy reach. Quinn's mother usually met with the bereaved during this initial visit, but at a quick family meeting an hour earlier, Joy McFarland had relinquished the role to her daughter.

"You're the one closest to Trish Oliver. She'll be the most comfortable talking to you," Quinn's mother said.

Her father walked around behind Quinn and placed his hands on her shoulders. "Besides, this will be good practice for you. Someday you and Jack will run this business without your mom and me."

The words, probably meant to flatter, stung Quinn's ears, and heat rushed to her face. He couldn't know yet that she had no intention of remaining in the business. She hadn't shared her ambitions with anyone but Josh. The guilty secret curdled inside of her.

Now, sitting across from Mrs. Oliver, Quinn crossed her legs at the ankle and leaned forward as she had seen her mother do many times. "My parents and my brother and I extend our deepest condolences to you. We appreciate your confidence in us, and we will do everything we can to make this difficult time less so." The words rang oddly in Quinn's ears, and she wished she'd spoken from her heart and not from the script.

Mrs. Oliver must have sensed what she was feeling, because she nodded, smiled, and grasped Quinn's hand. "Thank you, my dear. I'm sure I'll be satisfied with your services. It's just—"

The woman's voice broke, and she reached for a tissue. "When my parents died, and then my husband, I wasn't entirely unprepared. They had been ill, and in each case, we had discussed their wishes. Also, my sister—well, my sister, as different as we were, was around to support me all three times. This time I have no one." She dabbed her eyes. "My sister has people in New York. No husband or children, but friends—theater people, her agent, a young woman she was mentoring. I have no idea whether she even has a will. We never discussed these things. Foolish, but I guess we always thought we'd have time for that later."

"Do her friends know?" Quinn asked.

"Probably not. And they will be shocked, since they think they've been with her over the holidays. Of course, they were really with me. I suppose I will have to notify them. I'm not looking forward to that. They won't like hearing they've been deceived, some of them year after year."

Quinn didn't mind listening to her teacher's ruminations. Her mother always said the point of this meeting was relationship, and the McFarland role was to listen. Still, she needed to steer the meeting toward what was in the realm of business. "Are you thinking the services for your sister should be here or in New York?"

"Oh, my dear. I suppose you need to know that, don't you? It's so hard for me to fathom what Liz would have wanted. She was a 'live life to the fullest' kind of person, and she didn't care a flip about funerals, even those of our parents." She scrunched her eyes and blew her nose. "In fact, she partied hard both times. More than a few eyebrows were raised, I can tell you.

"But listen to me, going on about the past. Before we go any further, tell me about you, Quinn. How's married life? I'm so delighted that you've grown into such a beautiful and accomplished young woman. You've always had so much potential."

Quinn squirmed at the word, "accomplished." Surely Mrs. Oliver didn't think working in the family funeral home or marrying a surgeon qualified as accomplishments. "I owe a lot to you. You have no idea how much you helped me sophomore year. I'll never forget your kindness."

Mrs. Oliver beamed at the compliment— the wide smile Quinn remembered from the past—so she went on. "I don't consider myself 'accomplished' yet, but whatever I am, you deserve the credit."

"Nonsense on both counts. You are young, healthy, and strong. You may not remember, but I do, the tremendous sadness you carried around for a while. You almost let the actions of others crush you, but you stood tough and forged ahead, and here you are a happily married woman with a responsible job, consoling your old teacher instead of the other way around. You did this yourself, Quinn."

The words—or the gleam in Mrs. Oliver's eyes as she issued them—gave Quinn the urge to open up to her teacher again. "I know you will keep this secret," she said, and she whispered her plans to return to school to become a PA. "My parents don't know yet, so please—"

Mrs. Oliver reduced her voice to a murmur, and she touched Quinn's hand. "Don't worry. I won't tell a soul, but I know you will be top-notch at whatever you do. And now, let's get back to business."

Mrs. Oliver squirmed in her chair. "Do you mind if I wait a few days to decide how to handle Liz's arrangements? I'm too distraught to make those decisions now."

"That would be okay. The police want to wait until toxicology comes back, anyway."

Mrs. Oliver stared at her hands. "I have many questions about Liz's death, myself. But I would like to see her now, if I may."

As hard as she'd worked to make the face presentable, Quinn's stomach churned with the prospect of this viewing. She warned Mrs. Oliver of what to expect, and extended her arm.

Mrs. Oliver looped her arm through Quinn's and squeezed, an elbow hug. She kept pace with Quinn as they strolled into the back room. No words needed to be exchanged.

Quinn led her teacher to the less distorted side of the face of her sister and held onto the woman's arm with both hands. The little bit of cosmetology hadn't improved the sister's appearance much.

Mrs. Oliver took one look and stepped back, as if singed. "I've seen enough. My beautiful sister—" She choked back a sob and turned to go. "Whoever did this to my sister, I hope he rots in hell."

Quinn walked out with Mrs. Oliver, turning off the light and shutting the door. Despite the medical examiner's undetermined ruling, Mrs. Oliver apparently believed her sister had been murdered. And Quinn had to agree.

Chapter Ten
TRISH

Jeez! Let me roll down my car window, or I might choke on all the sentiment crowding in on me from that funeral home. Viewing the body is only half of it.

Quinn must really trust me to let me in on her job news. As if I care whether she stagnates in her family's business or flies the coop and breaks her parents' hearts. In a way, I have to admire her, though. Like Liz, she's a bit of a rebel.

I've generally felt envious of Liz for following her dream. Her life has been less stable than mine, but way more interesting. Of course, now that her fun has come to an end, there's nothing to be jealous of.

Those marks on her face, the tangles in her hair—why, she is to be pitied. I hope my grief comes off as sincere. Truthfully, I *am* sad to lose my sister. Two peas in a pod, we've been called all our lives, although many, including my husband Marvin, have thought of me as the quiet twin, and Liz as the wild one. I've heard that comparison so many times, even I believe it. Except when I'm honest with myself, because I know, deep down inside, it's the other way around.

Chapter Eleven

That night, Quinn and Josh had a date at one of their favorite seafood restaurants, Gaido's. The Christmas decorations were still up, and the scents of pine mixed with fresh fish and lemon created a hard-to-beat post-holiday atmosphere.

Josh had reserved a table that overlooked the Gulf. Despite the darkness outside, the front row seats offered a spectacular view of the moon, pouring its magic into the wavy ocean. The waiter filled their water glasses and placed a metal breadbasket full of hot pepper-and-cheese bread on the white tablecloth, before taking their drink orders.

"Let's have champagne," Josh said. He pointed to one of the choices on the menu and shut the folder with a gleam in his grayish eyes. "We're celebrating tonight."

Quinn couldn't imagine the occasion that would merit champagne in the middle of the week—neither birthdays nor anniversary. She didn't ask, however. She loved surprises, and giddy bubbles had already begun rising in her stomach.

The waiter returned with a frosty ice bucket on a stand, a bottle of *Veuve Clicquot,* and two glasses. He made a show of popping the cork, and puffy white smoke billowed out. Quinn did the tasting, eager to add more bubbles to her evening. She nodded, giving a thumbs-up. Still, she waited.

"A toast to us," Josh said, slipping in a tiny wink across the table. "May our honeymoon never end."

"You're in a good mood," Quinn said, licking her lips.

Josh gave a lop-sided grin and covered her hand with his. "Aren't you going to ask me why?"

Quinn dipped her head and gazed at him through her eyelashes. "I'm, you know, prolonging the pleasure."

"Okay. Since you asked, I'll tell you what we're celebrating. Three things."

Quinn put down her champagne glass and tapped the tablecloth in a pretend drum roll. "Celebration number one."

Josh lowered his voice as if revealing a deep secret. "The guy with the rooster wound has survived."

"The one who ran a cockfighting racket?"

"Yeah. He's under arrest and out on bail, but that's not my business. My job was to keep him alive, and I did that."

Quinn held up her glass. "From that standpoint, good news. You said it was a tricky surgery."

Josh clinked his glass against his wife's and took another swallow. "On to the next bit of good news—I think you'll agree. The mother of one of the med students has a litter of West Highland terrier pups. He heard me talking about Calvin and asked if we'd be interested."

Quinn pictured herself and Josh on the couch, a westie on each lap. "It might be good for Calvin to have company when we're not home." She was thrilled that Josh had bonded with Calvin, but uncertain whether Calvin would love the company or hate the competition for their attention.

"I thought so," Josh said. "If we act quickly, we can have the pick of the litter. Would you want a female or a male?"

"Hmmm, I'm thinking a female, but I'd want to take Calvin with us to select his playmate. There needs to be chemistry."

"Like with us?" Josh grinned. "Seriously, if we got a girl, we'd have to neuter Calvin—or her. Unless you want puppies."

"That's too much to think about right now," Quinn said, reaching for a rectangle of still-warm bread. "What's number three?"

Josh adopted the singsong voice that Quinn had come to know as a teaser. "Number three? What do you mean?"

Quinn set the bread on her plate. "Come on, Josh. If I know you, you've saved the best for last."

"Three weeks married, and you already know me too well. Okay, this is why I ordered champagne. I bumped into one of the professors at the medical school, and he asked me about you. He'd heard about your application for PA school."

"Really? Is that normal?"

"I didn't think so. I asked about that, and he told me his wife works in admissions. Then he winked and said, 'Your wife'll be getting an interview very soon.'"

A fiery ball of excitement burst inside of Quinn. "Woohoo! You think it's true?"

"Can't think of any other interpretation. You can't tell anyone yet, of course." He refilled the glasses and made a toast. "To my wife, the smartest and prettiest and most accomplished person on this island, if not the entire planet."

Delicious warmth filled Quinn's neck and face. The long wait to find a loving life partner had been totally worth it. "Thank you, Josh."

The waiter returned, and Quinn ordered their regular favorite, Brooks gumbo, shrimp peques, red snapper, and a salad for them to share. The prospect of an interview, and eventually being accepted to PA school fizzed in Quinn's brain, even more than the champagne, and she doubted she could eat a bite.

She stared out the window at the serenity of the Gulf. In the reflection, the waiter seated an older couple at another table for two behind them. Lost in her happy moment, Quinn paid no attention, until the words, "Thank you, Ambrose. Always good to be back here at Gaido's," broke into her reverie.

Not the words, but the voice caused her head to swivel, and what she saw caused her to gasp. Seated behind them was one of Quinn's favorite men in the world, the very married attorney, David Becker. And across from him, a perfectly dressed and made-up woman, Mrs. Oliver.

Chapter Twelve

Seeing Mrs. Oliver with Dave Becker at Gaido's shocked Quinn to her core. Where was the lovely Mrs. Becker? Also, at almost nine p.m., this was a little late for a business meeting. Gaido's was an upscale place, more for couples or families who wanted to celebrate a special occasion. Quinn leaned closer to her husband and whispered. "The older couple behind us—I think that's my attorney and my favorite teacher."

"You mean the lady whose sister was found dead on the beach? Police beat in the newspaper mentioned it this morning." Josh glanced that way.

"Shhh. I don't want them to know we're talking about them."

"Didn't you say she's a widow? Maybe he's handling her husband's estate. Or maybe she's consulted him about her sister."

"Of course. There could be a perfectly innocent explanation. I'm overdramatizing, I guess."

Quinn and Josh continued to talk about a variety of topics— his mother's newest rescue dog, a surgery scheduled for the next afternoon. The champagne had kicked in, so everything from the moonlight on the water to the flickering candlelight on the table held an aura of romance. Even watching Josh's hands, dipping bread in olive oil, sent thrills through Quinn's body.

When dinner arrived, the gumbo went to Josh, and the shrimp to Quinn. After eating half, they'd switch dishes. Following the whole bottle of champagne and several pieces of bread, that was more than enough food.

While she munched on the shrimp, Quinn strained to hear the animated conversation from the table behind them. Becker's deep drawl was hard to make out, but Mrs. Oliver's raspy lilt cast a few pearls in Quinn's direction. She heard the words, "embarrassed," "lonely," and "couldn't be more different."

"Are you eavesdropping?" Josh asked. The twinkle in his eye said the question was rhetorical. "Let the nice people have their privacy. Would you want them to listen to us?"

"Different situation. We're married—to each other. They're not. Besides, in this town, eavesdropping is an art form." Nevertheless, Quinn attempted to block out the table behind them for the duration of her meal. She attacked the gumbo with a determined gusto. The delicious roux was thick and spicy, and the bowl was filled with seafood. The last spoonful was in her mouth when the memory of *Fifty Shades of Grey,* stuffed in Mrs. Oliver's powder room magazine rack, popped in her brain, almost causing her to choke.

"What's the matter? Too much cayenne?" Josh asked, eyes alert.

"No. I'm fine." Quinn didn't tell him of the fleeting thought that her teacher might have read—or wanted to act out—the racy romance with David Becker in mind.

When Josh had paid the bill, he helped Quinn with her chair, and they left the table arm-in-arm. Quinn stopped at Mrs. Oliver's table to say hello, hoping to pick up a clue about the unlikely duo. "Nice to see you both," she said, "two of my favorite people."

"The honeymooners," Becker said, rising from his seat and giving Quinn a brief hug. "How was Jamaica?" He and his wife Sandy had attended the small wedding and reception, where the honeymoon spot had been mentioned.

"We had a great time," Josh replied, shaking Mr. Becker's hand. "Christmas on the beach, every day."

Mrs. Oliver giggled. "You can do Christmas any year. A honeymoon partner is a lot more fun than Santa Claus, if you know what I mean." Quinn bristled at the suggestive innuendo in her teacher's tone of voice, glancing to see whether alcohol might be involved. Yes, three martini glasses, two empty and one half-empty, graced Mrs. Oliver's side of the table, adding to Quinn's disquiet.

"Wonderful to see you both," Quinn said, eager to leave now. "Enjoy your dinner."

"Bye, Quinn and Josh," Mrs. Oliver said. "You make such a handsome couple."

Strolling out of the restaurant and into the misty night air, Quinn asked, "Did you see those martini glasses by Mrs. Oliver's plate? Do you think the Becker-Oliver dinner party is entirely innocent? Be honest."

Josh laughed out loud. "No comment, after all that champagne we consumed."

"Okay, I've got an overactive imagination. But I wonder if Sandy Becker knows about this dinner." Quinn settled in the car and fastened her seatbelt.

As Josh started the car, he chuckled again. "How about I take you and your imagination home and to bed?"

Quinn couldn't think of anything she wanted more.

Chapter Thirteen

The next morning after Josh left for work, Quinn straightened the house and walked Calvin in the cool, tangy air. The breeze from the Gulf ruffled the palm fronds. Her thoughts were ruffled, too. She couldn't stop dwelling on Mrs. Oliver, her sister, and now, the attorney David Becker. There had to be a connection she was missing, and it bugged her. Even more, she was struck by the irony. She'd done more thinking about Mrs. Oliver in the past few days than she had in all the years since high school. Mrs. Oliver had never seemed so enigmatic before.

When she arrived at the funeral home, Quinn looked over the day's schedule, which was quite open. Of course, everything might change at a moment's notice if a body came in. That was the nature of the business.

Quinn checked on Ms. Lavender, who was resting as comfortably as possible under the circumstances and then went to see what her father or mother was doing. As soon as she stepped out of the embalming room, aka the "beauty parlor," her father accosted her.

"I was just coming to find you. Chief Ramirez is in the coffee room with some of the other usuals, and he wants to talk to you."

"Me? What about?" Quinn had nothing against talking to the police chief, but she had made up her mind to lay low. She'd had enough intrigue and police drama for a lifetime.

"Something about Mrs. Oliver, I think." Quinn's father and Chief Ramirez, along with other dignitaries, had breakfast together every Tuesday, schedules permitting. Long ago, Quinn had asked her father why they met so often and whether it wasn't a waste of business time. Her father had set her straight. "Our business is based on service and trust—and friendship. Chief Ramirez is a good friend to have in this town. He's done more for our business than any ten other people we know. Our coffee hour is time well-spent, and don't you forget it."

Now Quinn entered the coffee room, sniffing the homey aroma of chicory and the powdered sugar of beignets from Gumbo Diner. Four men sat around the table, buzzing like honeybees in the oleanders. Her presence brought an immediate silence, giving her the impression they had been talking about her.

Marty Ramirez stood and hiked up the waistband of his pants. "Hey there, Miss Quinn. Or I should say Mrs. You're looking beautiful as ever. Married life must agree with you." He met Quinn at the doorway and threw a paternal arm around her shoulders. "How about we go somewhere for a little chat?"

Quinn tossed a glance toward her father. "Sure, let's go to the lobby. No one's there right now." She led the chief to the same seating area where she and Mrs. Oliver had talked the day before. He chose the wing chair, and she perched on the edge of the adjacent sofa.

Ramirez pulled a tissue from the box on the coffee table and wiped his forehead, although the room's temperature was quite comfortable. "About your teacher, Mrs. Oliver."

Quinn straightened her posture. Her feelings for Mrs. Oliver appeared to grow more protective by the minute. "I don't know if I can help you. I haven't had much contact with her."

The chief leaned back in his chair, encircling his belly with his arms. If he was attempting to look casual, he'd failed. The rhythmic jouncing of his knee gave him away. "Between you and me, I've got a lot of questions about the lady. Things my officers have turned up."

"Like what?" Her stomach lurched.

"Okay, Mrs. Oliver lives in a nice neighborhood. Houses are set kind of far apart. No security cameras at her place, but she has an alarm system. Evidently the sister didn't see fit to set the alarm." He paused and wiped his forehead again. "This whole thing with the sisters changing places is a mess. Our officers have scoured the neighborhood, asking if anyone saw anything unusual. Lady next door saw men coming to the house at night. Not one man. Men."

Quinn's thoughts flew to the *Fifty Shades of Grey* book in the powder room. Could it be that Elizabeth Lavender, acting as Mrs. Oliver, had men to the house to fulfill some fantasy or need? So far Ramirez hadn't asked any questions, and Quinn was glad.

"An examination of Mrs. Oliver's bed confirms that at least one man spent time there recently." He scooted forward in his chair, his dark eyes meeting Quinn's. "The question is, was this man—or men—invited, and did they think they were visiting Mrs. Oliver, or her sister?"

Still not hearing a question she could answer, Quinn remained on the sofa's edge, gripping her white-knuckled hands together. Surely

Chief Ramirez hadn't brought her out here to ruminate aloud about the perplexing murder.

"You're probably wondering why I brought you out here, so I'll tell you. What I'm about to ask you is highly unorthodox, and perhaps to a degree unprofessional, but I've thought about this long and hard, and I've known you all your life. You've matured into a fine young woman, strong and smart."

Uh-oh, here it comes. Quinn's insides had turned to jelly. She slid down into the sofa, wishing she could disappear from the police radar. Hadn't she done enough to apprehend a criminal last year? And she dreaded the upcoming trial of Lionel French, aka Blackie, in which she would have to testify.

"We need to ask Mrs. Oliver some rather delicate questions surrounding the men who may have frequented her house. Sergeant Schmidt isn't the person to handle such things. Nor am I or any of our officers. We all have the training—we lack the relationship to talk to an older lady about these things."

"What about Mary Hallom?" Quinn's brother's fiancée, a young officer, had the chops.

"Mary's out of town with this cockfighting ring. I can't take her off that, even though this is a murder. I know you have a connection with Mrs. Oliver, and I'm sure she would open up to you. This wouldn't be an official interview, just a private conversation. I'll supply you with the information."

Knots in Quinn's neck and shoulders multiplied, while she pondered the request. "You're asking me to deceive my former English teacher, a woman who has always been kind to me. And, what good would it do for me to question her. Anything she told me wouldn't be admissible."

Ramirez' expression softened. "We're aware of that. If you feel the need, tell Mrs. Oliver the truth—that one of your father's friends is in the police department. That the police are curious about male visitors. As tactful as you are, I'll bet she'll cooperate."

The prospect of talking to Mrs. Oliver about sex in general, and *her* sex life in particular, left a bad taste in Quinn's mouth, but she understood the chief's reluctance to have someone like Sergeant Schmidt to do it. Before she could agree, she had to know one thing. "Am I to assume that Mrs. Oliver is not a suspect in her sister's murder?"

Ramirez looked away before meeting Quinn's eyes. "You may assume that is the case, for the time being. We have a few other persons of interest. Think of it this way. Your chat might go a long way toward keeping her off the list. You might be doing her a huge favor."

Quinn didn't buy all the hype, but she also didn't doubt the chief's sincerity. Not only was he her father's friend, but he also had played a part in her own rescue last year. Maybe she could help him and Mrs. Oliver at the same time.

"Okay, I'll do it," she said. She was already regretting that promise.

Chapter Fourteen

That same afternoon, Quinn looked up Mrs. Oliver's phone number from the funeral home papers. She might as well get this over with. She tapped it into her phone and hesitated before hitting *send*. What she was about to do would cross a line in the relationship with her former teacher, and once she made this call, she could never go back.

A dry, throaty laugh escaped her lips. Everything she'd done in the past year had seemed to cross one line or another. Maybe risk-taking was an inevitable part of adulthood. At any rate, Quinn had wasted enough years living on the fringes of life. Last year's drama with the police had given her a bravado she never thought she'd have. Summoning that spark, she'd do what she could to help Mrs. Oliver, and the police investigation. She pushed the green button.

Mrs. Oliver answered on the first ring. "What a nice surprise, Quinn."

"Good morning, Mrs. Oliver. How are you doing today?" Despite her self-talk, Quinn squirmed from the awkwardness.

"Why not call me Trish? It's been a long time since you were my student, and now you're married, we can talk like friends."

"Thanks." Quinn couldn't ask for a better opening for what she needed to do. "I *would* like to talk like friends. I mean, I would like to get together to talk. Do you have some time today?"

"For you, of course. Would you like to come here, to my house? I gave the police free rein to search it, and now I'm back in. Sergeant Schmidt instructed me to use the security system day and night, even when I'm home, and he promised to have a patrol car drive by often."

Remembering her last visit to Mrs. Oliver's house, Quinn suppressed a desire to meet elsewhere. Nowhere else would afford the privacy Quinn would need to ask Mrs. Oliver—Trish—about her sex life. "That would be great."

A half hour later, Mrs. Oliver ushered Quinn into her marble-and-crystal foyer and set the alarm behind her. "Come on into the kitchen, and let's have coffee. I can't tell you how grateful I am that you called. Gets my mind off Liz a bit."

Maybe the dinner with Mr. Becker helped get your mind off Liz, too. Quinn inhaled the aroma of fresh-from-the-oven chocolate chip cookies as she ambled toward the back of the house. With the spatula, cookie sheets, and yummy little spheres lined up on waxed paper, the kitchen had a homier vibe than last time.

"I couldn't sleep, so I started baking around six a.m. This is my last batch." Trish motioned for Quinn to step around the large island counter, where dozens of cookies cooled on racks, and dozens more filled open metal tins. "I like to take cookies to the support staff at school. Despite being retired now, I consider them family. Take a tin home with you when you leave—if you like them, that is. What would you like to drink? I have coffee, tea, or milk."

"Milk, please." Quinn strolled around the counter, touching the creamy marble top and stopping by the dining table, where the Monet placemat had been replaced by a sunny tablecloth and napkins. A vase of fresh flowers lent a celebratory atmosphere, but, still, Quinn was apprehensive. "I love Gerbera daisies," Quinn said. "Hard to find them this time of year."

"I grow them, but, you're right. It's a challenge to keep the plants alive during the winter months. These are brought in from South America. I ordered them before I left for New York, and they were delivered yesterday. Have a seat, and I'll be right with you."

"Let me help." Quinn carried a plate of cookies to the table, while Mrs. Oliver filled a glass with milk.

When they both were seated, and Quinn bit into a soft, warm cookie that oozed with chocolate, the visit felt more like a party than an interrogation. The two women chatted about cookies and recipes for a while, and then a silence overtook the table.

"Quinn, I love having you here, but I'm not so naïve as to think you came over just to chat. So, what can I do for you?"

Quinn's stomach flipped, despite the sweetness of the cookie inside. She took a deep breath and sighed. "You may not know about my experiences last year with the police."

"You mean after Ana died? I heard plenty of rumors. You know there are no secrets in this town." Mrs. Oliver sipped her coffee, squinting at Quinn from beneath crinkled brows.

"I got to know the police. They seem to think I'm trustworthy or something. That's why they took me to the morgue to ID your sister's body."

Mrs. Oliver nodded. "You were the one who recognized the tattoo on her wrist."

"Yes. I'm so sorry about what happened to her, but I must admit I'm relieved it wasn't you. So, I agreed to help the police by talking to you about your sister. They thought you might be more comfortable talking to me as a friend."

Reaching across the table to pat Quinn's hand, Mrs. Oliver sniffed. Her lips pressed together into a straight line. "Seems I am in need of a friend right now." She sipped her coffee. "I've answered the police questions. I showed them proof that I was in New York when Liz—"

"No, that's not what they asked me to discuss with you. They need information about your sister's habits—and yours, I guess—when it comes to, well, I guess I'd better spit it out—sex."

"Sex?" Mrs. Oliver's eyes widened into cerulean globes, and her lips curled into a smirk. "Well, it's for damn sure I wouldn't discuss sex with Sergeant Schmidt—or any of the police officers. Some were my students, back in the day." Patches of bright pink emerged in her cheeks and neck. "I know. You were my student, too, but you're a woman, and that's different. What does sex have to do with anything?"

"Evidently they found semen on the sheets of your bed." Quinn picked up a half-eaten cookie and put it down again. She tried to form a question around this fact, but no words reached her tongue.

Pink splotches turned to red on Mrs. Oliver's face. "Oh, my Lord. That's why they took the sheets with them. And they probably want to know who was having sex in Mrs. Oliver's bed. Well, it wasn't Mrs. Oliver."

"Was your sister sleeping in your bed during her stay?" Quinn thought she knew the answer to this question, but confirmation would be good.

"Yes, of course. And I slept in her bed in New York. It was part of the experience of switching places. We called it, 'total immersion.'"

"Does it surprise you that your sister most likely had a man in her—your—bed?" The question sounded strange to Quinn's own ears.

Mrs. Oliver didn't answer right away. She fiddled with the flowers, the tablecloth, and the cookies on the platter. "Not really. I suppose this will have to come out, now that Liz has been murdered. My sister was diagnosed with borderline personality disorder."

Quinn startled. She recalled having studied borderlines in a psych class. The disorder could be serious.

Mrs. Oliver explained in a voice that, to Quinn, seemed dispassionate. "Throughout Liz's life she struggled with intense, unstable relationships. When she was a teenager, we laughed it off, called her oversexed, but as she grew older, patterns emerged. On the positive side, she used these traits with success in acting. She was notorious for capturing the essence of deep emotion on stage. When she auditioned for parts, especially in her youth, she usually got them.

"The downside was personal. She had trouble forming and sustaining relationships. Sex was her best conversation starter, but she never managed to take the relationship from the bedroom to the altar, and she came to hate any man with whom she slept. Probably hated herself, too."

Quinn mulled over how different the two sisters were—or at least how they seemed. "Must have made for awkward moments when you switched places." *Reckless, even.*

The hint of a smile flitted across Mrs. Oliver's still-unlined face. "Yes, indeed. Here I was, a widow, with limited experience in such things, and I was inundated with men who expected me to succumb to casual flirtations and propositions. I was both entertained and horrified. And I expect Liz found my quiet, chaste life a bit of a bore."

Quinn flashed on the three martini glasses on the table at Gaido's. Not sure if she bought the "quiet, chaste" bit, she continued. "Did you ever suspect your sister was having sex during your holiday switches before?"

Mrs. Oliver twisted and untwisted her napkin. "Maybe. We only pulled the switch for the past four years. We started after Marvin passed away. I never saw messed up sheets—she always washed the linens before going home. But I did notice certain men looking at me differently from time to time. We never talked about this."

Quinn tried to imagine living in this small town, not knowing which men might think they've slept with her. "Given what happened to your sister, you can understand why the police are interested in whose semen is on the sheets. Can you venture any guesses?"

"Not a single one. It's not as if I had gentleman friends lined up, waiting to take me to bed. I'm thinking Liz had a flirtation with someone, and it got out of hand. When she rejected him, he killed her. If the man who was in Liz's bed is the one who killed her, he's probably headed for the hills by now." She drained the coffee mug and set it down hard.

Quinn cleared her throat. "You're assuming that the murderer intended to kill Liz. What if he thought he was killing *you*, and he learns you're still alive?" *He might come back to finish the job.*

Mrs. Oliver gripped her necklace at her throat. "Omigod, Quinn. You're frightening me. I never realized how complicated this game of switching places could become. Or how dangerous. I can't think of a reason anyone would want to kill me, though."

"Obviously, if you see or hear anything that might be a clue as to the man's identity, you need to let the police know right away." Quinn stood and picked up her dishes. "Let me help you clean up."

"No, leave everything. I have nothing else to do and nowhere to go. I appreciate your coming to talk to me." Mrs. Oliver moved the cookie platter to the island counter.

"Before I leave, may I use the restroom?" Quinn's motivation was two-fold.

When she came out of the powder room, she carried the copy of *Fifty Shades of Grey* in her hand. "Are you reading this book?" she asked, knowing full well how the English teacher who preferred Hawthorne, Poe, Twain, and Wharton would respond.

"Oh, my gracious no! Did you find that in the powder room?"

Quinn nodded, and the two women said in unison, "Must have been put there by Liz."

Chapter Fifteen
TRISH

What fun I'm having with my former student, Quinn! Does she really buy the image of me as a cookie-baking, prim-and-proper educator, scandalized by the behavior of my erratic sister? My "quiet, chaste life"?

I think she does, and, more importantly, I think she'll tell that busybody, Sergeant Schmidt, that I'm a veritable Snow White.

Oh, I've been very careful in my dealings with people, especially men. Not that it's been easy, because practically every man I've ever met has flirted with me shamelessly, regardless of my marriage or my position in the school community.

But I've been discriminating. Nobody breaks through Trish's barriers, unless Trish wants them to. And Trish doesn't want them to, unless they can do something special for her—something she can't do for herself. Marvin, included.

Come to think of it, Liz has had nothing over me in the acting department. I've lived in this nosy little town all these years, and nobody thinks of me as anything other than a nice little old lady schoolteacher.

Oh, Marvin may have had his suspicions over the years, but whenever I saw him raise an eyebrow, I put on my goody-goody face. I remember that saying about picking up rocks and finding crawly things under them. Well, in Marvin's case and others', I've always made sure there are no rocks to pick up.

Now that Marvin is gone, and Liz is gone, I've got practically everything I need. Marvin's money and freedom and nobody dragging me into their problems. In a few months, interest in Liz will evaporate, and I'll be able to blow this pop stand.

Maybe I'll buy a villa in Tuscany, a chalet in Switzerland—or both. I'll brush up on my Italian and French. I might invent a backstory, something like Ophelia's, dramatic and full of tragedy. Fifty years of grading papers will disappear, and I'll make up for lost time.

If I can keep Quinn and those nosy police away from my attorney, Dave Becker, I just might be able to start a whole new life. I'm crossing my fingers that Quinn and her hunky husband will forget they saw us at Gaido's. I can't afford any more mistakes.

Chapter Sixteen

The evening after the interview with Mrs. Oliver, Quinn's brother Jack invited Josh and her to bring Calvin and have dinner at his house.

Quinn sat on the sofa with Calvin in her lap, enjoying the scents of garlic and lemon-butter coming from the kitchen. Josh had donned an apron and insisted on helping Jack with the dinner, saying, "The bros have this under control."

Happy that her husband and her brother had a strong camaraderie, she laughed and said, "Come on, Calvin. We know when we're not needed." She hoped Jack's fiancée and neighbor, Mary, who was purportedly on her way, appreciated having a guy who knew his way around the kitchen.

Calvin yipped and jumped from Quinn's lap, running to the screen door. A moment later, Mary rapped on the door frame and let herself in. She'd changed out of her police uniform and into soft blue pants and matching hoodie. "Hi, y'all," she said, sweeping into the room. Her eyes gleamed as she petted Calvin and rushed over to hug Quinn. "Welcome home, honeymooner."

She moved on to the kitchen, where she hugged Josh and planted a big kiss on Jack's lips. "Mmm, everything smells and looks delicious. When do we eat?" She pushed her thick curls behind her ears, where they stayed for approximately five seconds. "This shift lasted so long. I can't remember when I ate anything."

Quinn admired Mary's tall, fit physique. Like her brother, DeJuan, she'd played basketball in high school, and neither of them had an ounce of fat.

"Just in time," Jack said. "Go ahead and take your seats at the table. Josh and I will serve you."

The table was set with pottery dishes, brown cloth placemats and napkins, and glasses filled with ice. A pitcher of iced tea and a bottle of Pellegrino stood ready on a rolling cart next to the table. Quinn poured everyone's drink of choice into the glasses. Josh set a bowl of green beans and tomatoes on the table.

"The *piece de resistance*," Jack said, brandishing a large platter of fluffy rice and shrimp scampi. "No applause necessary, but feel free to compliment the chef." The men took their seats, and Quinn began serving herself and passing the dishes.

"You have no idea how much I appreciate a meal like this after the day I've had," Mary said. She inhaled the aroma of the steaming shrimp on her fork before depositing it into her mouth.

Quinn placed her hand on Josh's knee under the table. He, too, had had a long day at work. "I've heard through the grapevine that you're working on the cockfighting case." She squeezed Josh's knee, since he also had a part in that case. "Can you talk about it?"

Mary took her time chewing. "All I can say is this is not a simple case. I think we'll be investigating for quite some time."

Without revealing anything about Josh's part in treating the owner of the roosters, Quinn kept the conversation going. "Wasn't the owner arrested?"

Mary made eye contact with Josh. "Somehow I think everyone in this room knows the answer to that question."

Everyone laughed, and Mary sighed. "It's complicated. An operation like this is bigger than that one guy." She lifted her glass of iced tea and toasted Jack. "You, baby, are one heck of a chef."

"How was *your* day at work, Josh?" Quinn asked. She found it harder than she thought to get back into a normal routine after spending their honeymoon together in Jamaica.

"Nothing too exciting. Not like Mary, or the two of you in the funeral business." Josh winked. He stabbed a shrimp with his fork, but before putting it in his mouth, he said, "Quinn has had occasion to reconnect with her high school English teacher."

Mary put down her fork and made eye contact with Quinn. "You don't mean Old Lady Oliver."

Surprised by the nickname, Quinn set her own fork down. "Yes, that's the one. Mrs. Oliver was a big help to me in high school, and she's a friend now."

"Hmm, maybe to you, but DeJuan and I have a different memory. That lady was downright ugly to us."

Quinn almost choked on her sparkling water. She wondered whether Mary was implying that Mrs. Oliver was racist, snobbish, or mean-spirited in general. DeJuan had been in the same honors class with Quinn, and she didn't remember Mrs. Oliver's having treated the Black kids differently. "I'm shocked. What did she do?"

"She blackballed us from the National Honor Society. Not just the two of us, but several of our friends from church, as well."

Quinn couldn't believe that of Mrs. Oliver, who'd always seemed fair and pleasant to everyone in class. "How do you know that? Aren't NHS proceedings secretive?"

"We had our ways of finding out. One of the fathers tried taking her to the school board, but nothing ever happened. Anyway, that's all water under the bridge. Didn't stop DeJuan from being a successful attorney, and I'm happy right here, right now." She winked at Jack and continued eating.

"I'm sure you know Mrs. Oliver's sister was killed, and the police are handling the investigation," Josh said.

Mary looked from Quinn to Josh and back to Quinn. "Don't tell me you've gotten yourself involved with another police investigation."

Quinn gulped. The muscles in her neck tightened. She'd never live down the criticism she'd had from her family for her role in solving a few murders last year. "Not really. I helped ID the body."

Three pairs of eyes bored into Quinn's. She scooted her chair back and set her napkin on the table. "I'll be back in a minute." A visit to the bathroom gave Quinn the opportunity to catch her breath. She hoped when she returned to the table, the subject would have changed.

Calvin trotted next to her as she retook her seat. Jack mentioned that he and Mary were close to setting a date for their wedding. "We don't want to wait too long," he said. "Not that it's a race, but I'd like to be the first one to give Mom and Dad a grandbaby."

Josh's eyes met Quinn's. Having babies wasn't on their radar yet. He had another year to go before he could set up practice, and she was focused on PA school. "No problem," he said. "When are you thinking?"

"Maybe this spring? Mary thinks that would be the best time of year for her extended family to come to town."

Quinn relaxed. "That is so exciting. I'll be happy to help you plan the wedding, and I'll give you a shower, too."

Mary smiled with her whole face, and she covered Quinn's hand with her own. But then her eyebrows crinkled, and she squeezed Quinn's hand hard. "Do me a favor, though. Stay away from Mrs. Oliver. I can't have my maid of honor involved in another dangerous situation."

Chapter Seventeen

Another slow day at work gave Quinn the chance to sit in the office with a cup of hot cocoa and the computer open to Canva. One of her favorite tasks was designing ads for the funeral home. She loved putting photos and words together in tasteful arrangements. Her mother, father, and Jack had no aptitude for such things.

While she pulled previous projects from a folder, Quinn rehashed the conversation from last night's dinner at Jack's. Mary's comments about Mrs. Oliver swarmed in Quinn's mind like flies around a picnic lunch. She tried but couldn't recall a single example of racism in Mrs. Oliver's teaching. Could Quinn have been blind to such things because she wasn't Black? Admittedly, Mrs. Oliver had shown favoritism to certain students, Quinn's being one of them, but the story of preventing Black students from being accepted into the National Honor Society—that was outrageous and hard to believe.

Were there Black students in NHS? Quinn couldn't remember any, so maybe Mary's assessment was accurate. But if Mrs. Oliver had been instrumental in excluding students based on their race, Quinn couldn't look at her in quite the same way again.

While she typed copy for a quarter page in *Galveston Monthly* magazine, Quinn turned on the small television in the office. One of the morning news programs was interviewing a well-known psychologist, a mature woman wearing a navy suit, speaking with a New York accent. A panel on the bottom of the screen said, *Dr. Pamela Stallings, Johns Hopkins.*

Alicia Cartwright, the beautiful co-host, asked Dr. Stallings, "What makes the study of twins so fascinating?"

When Quinn heard the word, "twins," she turned up the volume and set down her pen.

"Identical twins offer psychologists perfect subjects for studying genetic and environmental influences on personality and behavior. We are interested in similarities and differences, as well as how twins adapt to separation and individuation."

Cartwright leaned forward, gesturing with a pointed index finger. "I know the interconnection between twins is something you've given a lot of attention. Can you tell us how the twin relationship is more powerful than other sibling relationships, and what that might mean for twins as they age together?"

Dr. Stallings nodded, and the screen switched to a PowerPoint slide with statistics. "The odds of having twins is 33 in 1000, while the odds of having identical twins is three in 1000." Dr. Stallings referred to a paper on her lap. "The rarity of identicals makes for compelling research. We used to think that identical twins had identical DNA, but recent studies have shown that there can be as many as 100 points of genome mismatch. From this we can conclude that even subtle differences in environment can lead to differences in disease and human development."

Quinn enjoyed topics related to research and medicine, which was partly why she wanted to enroll in PA school. This conversation popped off the screen at her, though, because of Mrs. Oliver. Was the universe conspiring to surround her with thoughts about twins?

Alicia kept the interview going. "Are you saying that genome mismatch can explain why one twin might become an artist or an alcoholic, while the other twin may follow a completely different path?"

A broad smile spread across the expert's face. "Not exactly. Except for identical twins, human beings have significant variations in genomic DNA sequences. The genomic mismatches found in identical twins are miniscule, compared to the matches. Differences that emerge as twins mature, individuate, and separate into adulthood can be largely attributed to environment, but the similarities in biological and chemical makeup remain. So, in your example, if one twin becomes a visual artist, the other may become a musician, not wanting to compete. But the innate talent, aptitude, propensities for art may reside in both."

Dr. Stallings went on to plug her new book, *The Crack'd Mirror: The Separation of Identical Twins*. Quinn clicked off the television and finished writing the copy for her new advertisement.

Mrs. Oliver and her sister remained in her thoughts long afterward. If one twin was borderline and hypersexual, must the other be also? The actress and the teacher appeared to have settled into different lives, one single and one married, one big-city and one small town. If maturation meant separating and forming individual lives, why did the now-elderly sisters perpetuate a switching places game?

The past eighteen hours had Quinn doubting her own judgment about Mrs. Oliver. Maybe her teenage impression of her teacher had been clouded by Quinn's own problems. And something else stuck out in her mind about the twins. Quinn had always heard of twins who were so close, they intuited each other's thoughts and feelings, felt each other's pains. Mrs. Oliver didn't seem to have this strong connection with her sister.

Before she got too deeply involved with the murder investigation, maybe she'd better step back and stick to things she knew—like providing quality services for the dead and those who mourned them.

She forwarded her new ad to the magazine and shut down the computer. As she turned off the light and locked the office door, she almost collided with her father.

"Oh, that's where you were, kitten. I've been looking for you." He fell into step with Quinn as she walked through the parlor toward the embalming room. "Chief Ramirez called a few minutes ago. He said we can proceed with whatever Mrs. Oliver plans to do with her sister, now that the toxicology report is back."

"She hasn't decided yet. We'll have to contact her." Despite her resolution to back away from the case, Quinn had to ask. "Did he say what the report revealed?"

"Yes, he did. There was poison in her system. The medical examiner and police now think Elizabeth Lavender's death was quite complicated. She may have been poisoned, strangled, *and* drowned. Somebody really wanted her dead."

Chapter Eighteen
TRISH

Whew! I'm finally finished delivering all the chocolate chip cookies. I can't stop thinking about the surprised smiles on the faces of the administrators and custodians, as well as the ogling looks from three of the men. I guess they think good-looking women who bake cookies are coming onto them. Ha!

Of course, seeing Henry in the storage closet is practically the whole motivation for taking cookies to the school. I love it when he expresses his gratitude to me. My little habit of giving him books to read and slipping him a few dollars to pay his tuition at the local college has paid dividends. Henry's a wonderful, inventive lover, even wedged between the shelves and the floor polishing machine.

Taking the two extra tins to the neighbors on either side of me is sheer genius. Never hurts to butter up the neighbors. Never know when I might need them to be on my side if and when the police come asking questions.

As for the police, the patrol car swings past my house often. I appreciate the protection, but I'm not afraid of bogeymen. I refuse to live my life cowering inside with the security system powered on. Maybe Liz would, but not me.

I'm much more forward-thinking than Liz has ever been. I couldn't have succeeded in my job as a teacher otherwise. For example, I know how to handle young Turks like that Winslow in her apartment building—use 'em and lose 'em, I say.

Liz, on the other hand, gets into trouble every time she gets involved with my acquaintances. How can I feel sorry for her, when she has created her own problems? I've told her a million times to stay away from men who are smarter than she is. That includes the highly educated and the uneducated. I've learned not to confuse brain power with savvy. There are smart—and sneaky—people with and without college degrees.

Case in point—Marvin. My husband's estate exceeds all expectations, despite Marvin's limited education. I credit myself with giving him lots of vicarious experiences through good literature. I find self-made men to be the biggest turn-ons. They're high performance, low ego.

I certainly miss Marvin, and I'm starting to miss Liz, too, even though Liz can only be characterized as high performance, high ego. And, she's always been a scaredy-cat.

Chapter Nineteen

The next morning's mail brought Quinn's long-hoped-for interview invitation for PA school. The letter said she would be notified of the specific date and time shortly. Eyes brimming, Quinn skimmed over the details. Everyone said getting the interview was the hardest part.

Quinn shoved aside the discomfort of needing to tell her parents. She'd think about that later. Right now, she wanted to celebrate. Josh was already in clinic, so she sent him a text. *Guess what came in today's mail? Here's a hint: I'm buying an interview outfit!*

Giddy from the excitement, she scooped up Calvin and hooked his leash onto his collar. A quick run around the neighborhood before work would help organize her thoughts. Calvin's trot, jauntier than usual, kept pace with Quinn's heartbeat, as if her elation had transmitted to the westie through the leash. The air was crisp and cool, and a whiff of dried leaves scented the air, perfect for a bright winter day on the island.

Calvin tugged toward a pair of squirrels chasing each other around the base of a tree, but Quinn kept him focused on the sidewalk. As she jogged, she marveled at her good fortune. Her grades and test scores had been stellar, but PA school applications far outnumbered seats in classes. She'd also counted on recommendations from her high school principal and college dean. Evidently these had done the trick.

The neighborhood circuit completed, Quinn filled Calvin's water dish and dressed for work, humming a tune. She made a spontaneous decision to stop by the college and high school on her way to the funeral home. Since her potted orchids had re-bloomed, she chose two jade dendrobiums to give away as thank yous for the recommendations.

Her first stop was at the office of the dean. The college administration building stood on the corner of campus and offered several visitor parking spots in front. Quinn grabbed her potted orchid and dashed into the office, hoping to have a moment with the dean without an appointment.

Dr. Roeper happened to be leaving through the outer glass door as Quinn entered. After an initial gasp at the near collision, they greeted each other, and Quinn showed the orchid to her mentor.

"Thanks so much for the recommendation. I want you to have this token of my gratitude. May I set it in your office for you?"

"Does this mean you got into PA school?" Dr. Roeper's face split into a wide, toothy grin. "Congratulations."

"Not yet. But I did snag an interview." Quinn realized she would have to tell her parents soon. Everyone in town knew everyone else, and even good news would travel fast. "Couldn't have done that without your help."

"Well, thank you for the beautiful plant. Not necessary, but it will go perfectly on my window ledge." She set down her briefcase and hugged Quinn with her free arm. "I'll just put it in my office and be on to my meeting. Best of luck."

Quinn stopped next at the front of the high school building. She, her brother Jack, and her father had received their diplomas from there, a point of pride in the McFarland family. Dr. Greenwood's long tenure as principal had seen the school through many changes. Quinn credited her leadership.

On her way to the principal's office, she passed a custodian who was cleaning the glass display cabinets in front of the auditorium. "Good morning," he said, a lilt in his voice, as if she were a guest, entering his private residence.

The school staff prided itself on being friendly, but Quinn chuckled inside. She didn't remember any of the custodians being that good-looking when she was in school. She caught the name patch on his shirt. "Good morning, Henry."

She waltzed into the principal's office and set the dendrobium on the green marble ledge. Ms. Fraley, the principal's assistant, hung up the telephone and hurried to the counter to greet Quinn. In her haste, she knocked a large, sealed cookie tin onto the carpet.

"Clumsy me," the woman said, lifting the container and setting it on the counter with a clatter. "How can I help you, Quinn?"

"Looks like someone's brought a treat. Hope nothing broke." Quinn touched the familiar-looking tin. "Is Dr. Greenwood in?"

"At district office. Can I give her a message?" She eyed the green orchid before meeting Quinn's eyes.

"Sure. Give her this plant and tell her thanks for the letter of rec. She'll know what I mean." In a way, Quinn was glad to leave the message rather than elaborate about her interview. The mission to tell her parents now burned with urgency. She didn't want them to hear the news from someone else first.

As she turned to leave, Quinn remembered where she'd seen a similar cookie tin—in Mrs. Oliver's kitchen. "Did these cookies come from Mrs. Oliver, by any chance?" she asked.

The assistant touched her hand to her chest. "Why, yes, they did. Why, do you want some?"

"Oh, no," Quinn said. "I thought I recognized the tin. I happened to be at her house when she was baking them."

Ms. Fraley scrunched her face, so forehead and eyebrows met the bridge of her nose. "Somehow that surprises me. I didn't know you were friends."

Taken aback by the words and icy tone, Quinn backpedaled. "We aren't friends, exactly. She was my teacher, and I went there on an errand." Quinn needed to leave before she'd blurt out too much. It was nobody's business that she'd done a favor for Sergeant Schmidt.

"Well, in my humble opinion, you should keep it that way. Just between you and me, that lady can be trouble with a capital "T.""

Chapter Twenty

On the five-minute drive to work, Quinn reviewed the bits of information she'd recently gleaned. Doubts about Mrs. Oliver buzzed in her thoughts. Had the teacher's kindness during her high school years blinded Quinn to the woman's faults?

Seeing her at Gaido's with three empty martini glasses at a table with a married man, had opened Quinn's eyes. Mary's story of how Mrs. Oliver had blocked Black students from National Honor Society and now the secretary's use of the word, "trouble," continued to paint a worrisome picture. The words from the television spot on identical twins haunted Quinn, too. Something didn't line up right with the death of Mrs. Oliver's twin. Quinn was glad she was going to be a PA, and not a police officer.

She checked the time as she parked in the back of the funeral parlor. She wanted to catch her parents before the day's activities stole them away. The back door opened into the embalming room. Quinn locked the door behind her and sped through the room to the first floor living room and offices. Her mother sat at the front desk, posture perfect, wearing a charcoal and white tweed skirt and jacket with gold buttons. A bowl of potpourri lent a Christmasy aroma.

"Hi, Mom, got a minute?" Quinn plastered a smile on her face that she hoped disguised the shakiness in her voice.

"Of course, sweetheart." She set her pen down on the paper and folded her hands. "How are you and Josh doing?"

Ever since she and Josh had become a couple, her mother treated them as a unit, as if Quinn, by herself, wasn't important enough to ask about. Quinn pushed back her annoyance. "Actually, where's Dad? I'd like him to be here for this conversation."

Joy McFarland raised an eyebrow. "Really? I think he's having another cup of coffee. Let me call him."

Before she could punch in the number, John McFarland appeared at the door to the office. "Hello, kitten." He hugged Quinn and stood beside her. "Everything okay?"

"Quinn has something to tell us. Why don't you sit?" Joy patted the side chair next to her at the desk. While he took the seat, she said, "I hope it's good news. Honestly, Quinn, we're so happy that you've finally settled down, and we couldn't be happier with our new son-in-law."

What? Can't we have a conversation anymore that isn't about Josh? Quinn's hands clutched her elbows, fingers splayed and squeezing. She inhaled, praying for calmness, but before she could phrase her next words, a geyser of resentment burst forth inside of her. She'd played second fiddle to Jack her whole life, and now, apparently, she would have to stand in line behind Josh, as well. And maybe Mary, who had a profession more important than being just an embalmer.

"You know what? I don't really have anything to share right now. I'd better turn around and get to work." Embarrassed by the heat in her face and the tremor in her hands, she pivoted and darted toward her office.

From behind her mother's voice whined. "What on earth? Was it something I said?"

Chapter Twenty-one

Furious with her mother's attitude, and even more with her response to it, Quinn returned to the embalming room. Rory and Zeke, long-time employees who drove and delivered for McFarland's, had texted they were en route with a body, coming from the hospital. She donned her protective garb, turned on the blowers, set up the table with tools and equipment, and met them at the back door.

"Who've we got today?" she asked, as they wheeled in the covered body. Rory and Zeke were almost like family. They'd been working at the mortuary, mainly transporting bodies, since high school, and, like Jack, they treated Quinn protectively.

"A guy from mid-island, Julio Martinez. He was having trouble breathing. EMT took him to the hospital. Doctor swabbed him, and he died within minutes. COD—pulmonary infection." Zeke wheeled the gurney up to the embalming table. "Sister chose McFarland's. You want him here or on ice?"

"Table, please." Quinn lifted the cover on the man's face. "He looks young. Glad I got my flu shot. I hope you did, too." She opened the cabinet where the personal protective equipment was stored. Always careful when working with dead bodies, she took extra precautions when she knew death had come from disease. In this case, she would wear both an N95 mask and headgear with a plastic panel over her face.

"Yep," Rory replied. "Your dad requires us to get all them vaccines. Covid, too." He grabbed the top end of the bedding, while Zeke took the lower. They slid the body onto the stainless-steel table and rolled it expertly to free it from the sheets beneath. They left the top sheet on, a courtesy to Quinn, who could do the honors whenever ready.

Quinn's cellphone rang, and Zeke waved the paperwork at her, signaling that he was taking it to the front office. Rory folded the stretcher and carried it outside to the vehicle. *Business as usual.* Sergeant Schmidt's name on her caller ID sent her stomach into a lurch. "Hello, this is Quinn."

"Hey, I just wanted to tell you that was a good call you made about checking the toenails on that Lavender lady's body. We hit paydirt." He guffawed a bit too long. "Sorry for the bad pun. The vic had soil in the toenails on both feet, more in the right."

Quinn didn't bother correcting the police officer about Liz's name. His use of nicknames served as a kind of trademark. The deceased probably wouldn't mind. "Wouldn't the soil have washed away when the body was in the Gulf?"

"Yeah, you'd think so. That's what makes it even more newsworthy. The lady must've dug her toes into the soil hard. It was wedged in there good. Just like you said. Maybe she was trying to resist being taken, wanted to leave a trail."

"Hard to imagine somebody barefooted in the winter. You think it was dirt from the bottom of the ocean?" Quinn pictured Mrs. Oliver's sister, struggling in the surf.

"Nope. This here's gardening soil. The lab found bits of compost, fertilizer, and peralite in there. Just like those turf builder brands. And something else—we found bits of that same stuff in the sheets from Mrs. Oliver's bed."

"So, you think she dug her feet in a garden and then went to bed?" The conversation verged on the preposterous.

"Not exactly. The traces of soil in the bed were on the sheets below the semen stains. I'm thinking the guy who bopped Ms. Lavender had his feet in the same dirt as she did."

Quinn disconnected the call but continued to think about Mrs. Oliver's sister. When Rory and Zeke scooted back through the exit door, she checked with her mother to make sure the Martinez family had requested embalming and a funeral.

After the confirmation, she donned her mask and headgear before placing the deceased's head on a plastic head block and wedging body supports on both sides of his trunk. Nothing to worry about with the police in this one, since his death came from natural causes. Still, she removed the man's jeans and hoodie, decorated with a palm tree and saying, "Island Life." She bagged the clothes in case the family would want them. Then she examined the body, just for the heck of it, paying particular attention to the toenails.

Before washing him with a germicidal soap, Quinn gloved up and pulled out an instrument similar to the kind found in manicure kits. She scraped under the toenails and tapped the matter onto a sterile paper circle. She folded the paper and inserted the end into a small paper bag, one of many she kept on the shelf for such purposes.

Maybe the phone call had predisposed her thinking, but the toenail detritus from Mr. Martinez certainly resembled soil.

She sealed the bag and washed the instrument before repeating the process with the man's fingernails. These, too, yielded a black dirt that reminded Quinn of potting soil she used with her orchids. In an abundance of caution, she placed the fingernail dirt in another bag and labeled them both.

Fretting over her inability to stay away from police business, she took off her gloves and picked up her cellphone. Speed dialing Sergeant Schmidt's number, she considered hanging up. Anybody could have dirt in their fingernails and toenails. Why stir up something with this unfortunate corpse, who'd died from natural causes?

When Schmidt answered, she glanced at the sealed bags and mumbled. "You probably won't be at all interested in this, but you started me thinking about toenails."

"Are you kidding?" Schmidt said. "Don't ever hesitate to tell me about *anything*. I mean that. After all we've been through together, I trust your instincts to the max."

"Okay then," Quinn said. "You might want to take a look at the body I've got on the table right now. Julio Martinez. Died on the way to the hospital, maybe flu. I pulled black soil from his nails—finger and toe. Bagged it for you."

"I'm about five minutes away. Don't move a muscle till I get there. And, Quinn?"

"Yes?" Already beginning to regret having called him, she sighed.

"Thank you." The click in her ear meant no turning back.

Chapter Twenty-two

After Sergeant Schmidt left with the matter found under the nails of Mr. Martinez, Quinn put everything out of her mind, except for preparing the body for his funeral. There was no need to wait, based on possible police investigation, even if the toenails contained incriminating dirt, since the death had been attended by a doctor.

Quinn liked to think of herself as treating each body to a respectful and heartfelt "spa day," one meant to last for all time. Everyone deserved this aftercare, no matter what his or her station in life had been. Life could be tough at times, but death should be as calm and soothing as possible. As much as Quinn wanted to be a PA, she would miss performing this act of reverence.

Such a young man. As she prepared to wash and shampoo, she ran her gloved fingers over the muscled planes and angles, imagining the kind of life he had, the relationships left behind. No scars or blemishes marred his round face, but she did find something curious. On the neck, behind the right earlobe, sat the tattoo of a crowing tri-color rooster. Quinn shrugged the symbol off. Many of the bodies she worked on were inked, especially if they were under forty.

The afternoon was waning, and something told Quinn she should wait until tomorrow to work on this one. Maybe it was the dirt or the rooster on his neck. Her instincts told her not to rush. Gently, she covered the body and tucked him away in the cooler for the night. She cleaned up and changed clothes, grateful for a few extra daylight hours.

Josh had texted her the name and contact information of the woman with the westie litter, Eunice Reid. *Don't wait for me. I'm working late. Much more important to take Calvin with you.*

Quinn called Mrs. Reid to set up the viewing and swung by home to pick up Calvin. "We're going to meet some puppies, Callie," she said, as she leashed her fur baby. "You don't have to like any of them. We'll be perfectly fine as a family of three. But if there's a little one you like, we can bring her home to live with us and be your friend. Got that, buddy?"

Calvin tilted his head as if he understood completely, and he leaped into the passenger seat of the car. The Reids lived in the same affluent neighborhood as Mrs. Oliver, about a ten-minute drive from

Quinn's. In fact, Quinn spotted Mrs. Oliver's greenish Cadillac in her driveway as she turned the corner toward her destination.

She pulled into the circular driveway of a sprawling white ranch house with pink columns and shutters. Built up on a small hill, and perfectly landscaped, the yard featured geraniums, bougainvillea, and patches of impatiens. Quinn clutched Calvin in one hand and pushed the doorbell with the other.

An auburn-haired lady with a smooth complexion answered the door, wearing a turquoise silk tunic with matching pants and flats. A pair of West Highland terriers woofed, one on either side of her. Calvin squirmed in Quinn's arms, but held his bark, as if realizing he was a mere visitor.

"You must be Quinn," the woman said, opening the glass storm door. "Don't mind the barking. Come on in."

The gray slate floor of the foyer opened into five interior doorways. The fabric-covered walls in a light gray provided backdrop for several museum-sized paintings. The aroma of Italian seasonings—garlic and oregano—wafted into the room. Presumably, dinner was being prepared. A cacophony of yips came from beyond one of the doorways.

Mrs. Reid smiled, revealing pearly veneers and a dimple in one cheek. "There's our litter. Why don't we take all the dogs into the back yard, so your guy can meet them?" She opened the gate to a play yard confining the nine pups, and she herded them and the two parents out through a sliding glass door.

Quinn followed, still holding Calvin like a football. The thought of having her dog mark territory in the posh Reid home set off embarrassing flashes in her brain. The back yard was fenced and neatly manicured like the front. The dogs congregated in the central portion. Each of the puppies wore a different colored collar. Together they made a rainbow. No bigger than the size of Quinn's hand, the white fluffballs romped in circles around their parents and then Calvin.

The twelve dogs made for an adorable scene in the crisp afternoon air, and Quinn relaxed a little, as she made conversation with Mrs. Reid about her son, the medical student.

"Martin has such good things to say about your husband. I think Josh has inspired my son to specialize in surgery."

Quinn kept her eye on Calvin, who held his own with this bunch. The father extricated himself from the fray and curled up under the covered porch. The mother remained watchful, but calm, while her babies circled about Calvin in a frenzy.

"Are you thinking about a male or female?" Mrs. Reid asked.

"A female. We don't want competition between two males." Quinn couldn't tell the pups' genders, but Calvin had definitely taken notice of a particular little one, probably the quietest of the bunch.

"Let me segregate the puppies for you, then." She lifted a large wicker basket from a table on the porch and proceeded to fill it with boy pups. "Let's see—green, purple, orange, and yellow. These are the boys." She whistled for Roxie and Whitney, the adult dogs, and led them back into the house, clutching the basket to her chest and circling her arms around the rim to keep the pups from leaping out.

Amused, Quinn concentrated on the five remaining puppies, including the quiet one with the pink collar, who had captured Calvin's complete attention. "Is that your new girlfriend?" Quinn's heart tugged as her dog nudged the pink-collared pup with his nose, and she licked him in response. "Looks like the answer is yes."

As if an unspoken rule of etiquette had been established, the other pups moved away from Calvin and his chosen one. They clustered around each other and fell into a puppy pile. The scene was charming, and Quinn closed her eyes, trying to etch the moment in her memory.

Returning through the patio door, Mrs. Reid said, "Looks like the match has been made. All without human intervention." She motioned Quinn to a wooden rocking chair on the porch. "Why don't we sit here and let them play, while we talk about the details?"

Quinn took the seat and gazed out over the expansive yard and beyond. Because the house was elevated, she could see beyond the fence into other beautiful homes and yards. This was a neighborhood she rarely visited, although she knew many of the wealthy residents had passed through McFarland's en route to their final resting places.

Quinn nodded, while Mrs. Reid enumerated the various steps she had taken to start the puppy with a healthy life. Pink-girl had been vaccinated and microchipped. She'd been fed the highest quality puppy food and filtered water, and house training had begun.

"They're not perfect, of course, but the pups know the difference between inside and outside, and if they want a treat, they need to pee and poop outside to get it. I try to take them out at least once every couple of hours." Mrs. Reid flicked her hair back. "And one other thing—Pink-girl likes to chew. Give her lots of chew toys. Also, I'll loan you this bottle of bitter apple spray to keep her from ruining your furniture and draperies. Whenever you don't need it, just bring it back."

Quinn would have to take breaks from work to keep up that schedule, but her house was only five minutes from the funeral home. *Better to train her now, so when I start school in the fall, I won't have to worry.* Quinn went to get her checkbook, which she had locked in the car. She texted Josh, too. *Calvin's picked out a puppy. Bringing her home.*

He replied immediately. *Two boys, two girls. We're a perfect family.*

Having no doubt that she was doing the right thing, Quinn returned to the back yard to pay and collect her doggies. The novelty of having two dogs brought a surge of pleasure. Double the fun.

Standing on the porch before she collected her fur babies, Quinn realized that the back yard adjacent to the Reids' looked a lot like Mrs. Oliver's. "Does that house belong to Mrs. Oliver, by any chance?"

Mrs. Reid pulled her chin back and inhaled with a wheeze. "Yes, it is. How do you know Mrs. Oliver?"

Quinn thought before replying. Lately it seemed she didn't know Mrs. Oliver at all. "She was my English teacher."

"Well," Mrs. Reid said with a new, strident tone of voice. "Perhaps she was a better teacher than she is a neighbor. That's all I'll say."

Quinn left with her puppies and a bevy of misgivings swirling around her. The halo she'd placed around Mrs. Oliver's head had been chipped away so many times now—there was hardly a piece of it left.

Chapter Twenty-three
TRISH

By golly, if my eyes aren't deceiving me, that's Quinn McFarland, or whatever her married name is, standing in Stan Reid's back yard, talking to that bitch, Eunice. What on earth do those two have in common?

Wait. Let me get my binoculars. Oh, looks like what these two have in common is those pesky little white dogs. I can't imagine why Stan puts up with those yappers, Eunice included.

When we were all in school together, Eunice was the biggest socialite snob of the bunch. I never would've pegged Stan as a person who'd fall for that kind of girl, with that high-pitched whine, even though Eunice's family owned the largest clothing store downtown.

Kids don't think about things like that with high school crushes. I know that from my own experience and from watching my students. High school boys go for the girls with the largest boobs, the longest legs, the roundest butt. That's why Liz and I have counted all of the most popular boys—men now—among our former suitors. Fine men, rich men, like Stan Reid, Dave Becker, and, yes, Marvin Oliver.

Sometimes I see Stan in his back yard, practicing his golf swing, and, maybe it's my imagination, but I think he stares at my back yard. Perhaps he's missing his golf buddy, Marvin. Or perhaps he's thinking about Marvin's still-fine-looking widow, just a few yards away.

Personally, I've never found Stan all that exciting, even when he left his date at the senior prom to make out with me behind the gym in the backseat of his car. Liz is another story, though. Liz has always carried the torch for Stan Reid.

Wouldn't it be fascinating to discover that Liz and Stan hooked up last week, while she was pretending to be me? Maybe, disgusted with all the barking and puppy mess, he crossed through the gate at the back of his yard after Eunice went to sleep. He might've believed he was romancing me, a woman with as much money as his wife.

That's got me thinking. There's a bunch of dirt tracked in through the garage entrance, caked on the carpet mat, too. I'm ready to blame Julio, and I have reason to think he's the culprit, but I haven't seen him since he pruned the rose bushes before I left for New York.

Like mine, Liz's taste in men has always been eclectic. Cultured Stan Reid, the gardener, that neighbor of hers in New York. Julio, in my opinion, has a good body, although he also has a big mouth. And he's ambitious—he won't be a landscaper for much longer.

Anyway, maybe Stan sneaked over here and wiped his muddy shoes on that mat. Or maybe his bare feet. He wouldn't have wanted to leave tracks.

Hmmph. Quinn's pointing at my house now. I'll bet she's asking Eunice about me right this minute. And I'll bet Eunice is giving Quinn an earful.

Chapter Twenty-four

Excited about the new addition to the family, Quinn took a photo of the tiny Westie and texted it to Josh. *Can't wait for you to meet our new baby.* She sent a second text to Josh's mother, who rescued dogs and currently owned seven. As an afterthought, she texted her own father and her brother Jack.

Within seconds her phone started to beep, but the messages could wait till she got home. She secured the little one in a zippered carrier and seat belted it into the back seat of her car, next to where Calvin sat.

Quinn pulled into the garage and let Calvin out into the fenced back yard. She carried the new puppy in one hand until she could set her down on the grass. "Watch what Calvin does, little one." She'd always heard it was easier to housebreak a second dog, because the younger one would mimic what the older one did. Calvin raised a leg and peed on the magnolia tree, and within seconds, the new puppy squatted nearby.

Quinn checked her phone. Josh had sent a text. *Let's celebrate. Be home by 7. Pick up dinner?*

She quickly thumbed back. *No, I'll cook.* She had all the ingredients for stir fry shrimp, a quick and easy recipe. The thought of the tangy oyster sauce made her salivate.

A second text had come in from her brother. *Can't wait to meet my new dog-niece. How 'bout if Mary and I swing by after dinner? Mary wants to talk to you.*

Before responding, Quinn brought the dogs into the house and set about feeding them. So far, so good.

When Josh came home, Calvin met him at the door, leaping into his arms. Quinn followed, holding the puppy next to her cheek. Josh kissed Quinn and then the puppy, and the puppy licked him.

Quinn transferred the puppy to Josh. "We need to wash our hands and eat. Jack and Mary are coming over afterwards."

"Okay. Shall I take the pups out in the back for a quick potty break?" The chuckle in Josh's voice was contagious.

Quinn could only imagine how excited Josh would be as a father to a real baby. But that was a long way off. She set the fragrant shrimp dish on a trivet and poured glasses of chardonnay.

"Success," Josh said, opening the screen door. "A double header from both dogs." He washed his hands and took his seat, beaming.

The couple clinked their wine glasses. "To potty success. If she keeps this up, I won't have to come home every hour to walk her. We need to think of a name," Quinn said. Piquant aromas burst forth from the steaming dish—teriyaki, garlic, onion, and soy. "She's starting to answer to puppy already."

"I always thought a cute name to go with Calvin was Hobbes, like in the comic strip." Josh dug into his dinner.

"Isn't Hobbes a masculine name?" Quinn had been thinking of girly names while cooking. She didn't want to leave Josh out of the decision, though. Naming rights were among the most fun aspects of getting a new dog, and this was their first dog *together*.

"Yeah, I guess. And she doesn't look much like a tall tiger. How about Minnie, as in Minnie Mouse?" Josh shoveled a large bite into his mouth and chewed. "This is so delicious, by the way."

"She doesn't look much like a mouse either. How about Misty? Wendy? Lily? I like dog names ending with a 'y.'"

"Okay, how about Fluffy, Happy, Joey? I still like Hobbes."

"I've got it," Quinn said, slurping her wine. "A compromise— how about Holly? Her name will always remind us of the season when we got married and when she came into our lives."

Josh high-fived his wife and grinned. "Perfect." He finished his meal and pushed away from the table. Scooping up the little puppy and bringing her to his face, he said, "Hello, Holly. Welcome to the family." He carried her in one hand as he cleared the table with the other. "What time are Jack and Mary coming?"

A screech in the driveway caused Calvin to bark and Holly to yip. "I think they're here now," Quinn said, rushing to put away as much from their dinner as possible. Josh rinsed and stacked the dishes, accompanied by the canine choir.

Quinn picked up Holly and opened the door. Calvin rushed out to welcome his uncle and aunt-to-be. He had lived with Jack last year for several days, while Quinn was away. "Meet our new baby, Holly."

"Oh, she's beautiful," Mary said, giggling from the licks Holly gave her. "When did you get her?"

"This afternoon. Isn't she sweet?" Quinn cuddled Holly against her chest before holding her out to greet Jack. "Calvin needed a playmate. At least that's what we told ourselves."

"Are you going to have puppies?" Mary looked in Jack's direction.

"Not sure. Would you want one if we did?" Quinn had a vision of a westie fest whenever the McFarland-Brady family got together. "Come on and sit down. Anybody want a drink?"

"Nah, we just had dinner." Mary said. "If I'd known about little Holly earlier, I would've brought a chew toy or something."

"Jack said you wanted to talk. Is it about the wedding?" Quinn waved Josh over to the loveseat next to her, while Jack and Mary sat on the sofa opposite. Calvin sat at Jack's feet, being petted, while Holly curled up in Quinn's lap.

"No, it's actually about the guy you have at the funeral home, Julio Martinez."

A shiver climbed up Quinn's spine. She'd given Sergeant Schmidt the dirt from the man's finger and toenails, but she hadn't thought much about him since. A victim of the flu, she thought. "What about him?"

"I can't say too much, but he's the brother of Francisco Martinez, the leader of the cockfighting ring we're investigating."

The image of the tri-color rooster inked on the decedent's neck floated before Quinn's eyes, and she swallowed hard. "Oh, that's why—"

Josh leaned forward, interrupting. "The guy I operated on. That is one nasty dude."

"You don't know the half of it," Mary said. "Cockfighting is bad enough, but it's part of the seedy narc underworld. Francisco claims it's a legitimate entertainment business, part of his culture. Meanwhile, he's suspected of having toes in a narc cartel with ties to South America. We've shut down the roosters, rehomed them with the help of the humane society, but the guy's out on bond. Cockfighting's only a misdemeanor here.

"Anyway, the brother's the legit one. Works around town as a landscaper. Squeaky clean, no record, no arrests. Turns up dead right after the raid on the roosters."

"You don't think he was murdered, do you? I thought he died of flu." Quinn stood and handed Holly to Josh. "Anybody else need a glass of water?"

Jack nodded and raised two fingers. "Death services is the end of the line. We are the last to know anything."

"I know you're trying to be funny, but I'm not laughing." Quinn brought back two glasses with ice and water and handed one to

Jack. "I started to say earlier, Julio's got a tatt of a rooster on his neck. Maybe that's a connection. Do you suspect foul play, Mary?"

"Let's just say I don't believe in coincidences. Interesting about the tattoo. We've been watching the brother for some time. He lived modestly, got up and went to work, came home at a decent hour, paid his bills. If we didn't know he was Francisco's brother, we never would've believed they came from the same parents."

Josh shifted Holly from his lap to his chest and leaned back. "Not too many young guys die from flu these days."

"Exactly," Mary said. "As my police officer granddaddy used to say, 'When gooseflesh starts rising, it's time to dig deeper.'"

Quinn's own antennae relayed disturbing thoughts. "I removed detritus from Julio's nails and gave it to Sergeant Schmidt. Since he worked as a landscaper, that makes some sense." The fact that soil was also found under Elizabeth Lavender's nails and in her sheets gave Quinn another jolt. What if the two dead bodies were somehow connected? "The body hasn't been processed yet. I planned to do that in the morning."

Mary stared into Quinn's eyes, as if she could read her mind. "I don't mean to scare you, Quinn, but you need to hold off on Julio Martinez. We're working on a warrant, so we can send him for autopsy. I'd bet my last dollar he didn't die from the flu."

Quinn's eyes landed on Holly, sleeping peacefully on Josh's chest, and she thought of the healthy-looking young man resting in the cooler at the mortuary, and a sharp chill caused gooseflesh to rise on her forearms. At that moment, she couldn't wait to pass her interview, so she could start PA school.

Chapter Twenty-five

After Jack and Mary left, Quinn asked Josh to join her in the back yard. She hoped Calvin wouldn't mind foregoing his neighborhood runs at night. Holly was too little for those, and, after hearing about the cockfighting ring and narc cartel, Quinn wasn't eager to hit the pavement in the dark. Maybe tomorrow morning she'd run with Calvin before work.

"Was Calvin ever this tiny?" Josh asked, as he set Holly down on the grass. "I've seen powder puffs bigger than her."

"Really? When's the last time you saw a powder puff?" Quinn asked. She loved to call him on things like that. As brilliant as he was, Josh had very little experience with girly stuff. He had no sisters and claimed not to have had any serious relationships before Quinn.

"Okay, I've seen cotton gauze bandages bigger than her." He draped his arm around Quinn's shoulders and leaned in for a kiss.

"Look, Holly is following Calvin around." Quinn would have liked nothing more than to keep kissing, but she couldn't take her eyes off Holly. "And now look—Good girl, Holly."

"Where is Holly going to sleep?" A frown crested Josh's gray eyes. Maybe he was rethinking this puppy thing.

"I pulled out Calvin's crate from the attic. We can set her up in the bathroom, so she can hear and smell us, but she can have her own sleep-space."

"Let's hope she doesn't cry all night." Josh scooped her up and patted her head, as Calvin bounded ahead of them. "Before we go to bed, I want to chat about this rooster business."

Quinn ushered everyone into the house. "Okay. Want another glass of wine?" Josh wasn't usually this moody. What was it about the cockfighting that had his dander up?

"No, I'm too tired. Let's just sit for a few minutes." He eased into his chair at the dining table and toyed with the edge of his placemat.

Quinn gave Calvin his bedtime treat and broke another one into two, giving half to Holly. "Okay," she said, sitting next to Josh. "I'm all ears, babe."

"You remember my telling you about this Martinez guy who spit in my face before I operated on him? No one's ever treated me that way before. After the surgery, I did some research on him. Trust me, spitting in someone's face is the least of his offensive habits."

"I'm sure, between what you've said and what Mary just said. He sounds like a scumbag." Quinn had an idea where this was leading.

"That gives scumbags reason to revolt. Quinn, he's been on the police radar for years. He's been suspected of a wide range of violent acts, including drugs, gambling, domestic abuse, and rape, but they've never been able to pin anything on him until now.

"I know Mary's wrapped up in assisting with this case. It's probably the first time she's ever been involved in anything this ugly. But I don't want you drawn into any part of it. Please, keep away from anything and anybody related to Martinez."

Quinn exhaled. This wasn't the first time Josh had been concerned about her involvement with police matters. "You don't have to worry. I have no association with that guy. Tomorrow his brother will go to the medical examiner, and I'll have no responsibility for him, either."

"I heard you say you sent dirt from the guy's nails to Sergeant Schmidt. That means he'll have you smack-dab in the middle of something before the sun rises in the east."

Quinn attempted a reassuring smile. "Mrs. Oliver's twin had soil under her toenails, and on the bedsheets in the room where she was sleeping. Schmidt is looking for a match. I doubt anything will come of it. Martinez is much younger, and what would he be doing in Elizabeth Lavender's bed?"

As soon as the words came out of her mouth, Quinn remembered the sex talk she'd had with Trish Oliver. Maybe her sister *would* have taken a younger man to bed, but she wouldn't relay that to Josh right now.

Josh took her hand in his and rubbed it with his thumb. "All I'm saying, Q, is I don't want you to take any risks with these Martinez dudes, dead or alive. When the body comes back, let Jack work on it—or your mother. And I'm really worried about the funeral."

"I appreciate your concern, Josh, really I do. But I don't see how embalming a dead body would put me in any danger. We don't even know whether Julio and his brother were close."

"One thing I can tell you for sure. Francisco Martinez had the same rooster tattoo on the right side of his neck."

Chapter Twenty-six
TRISH

I've made a discovery that gives me a clue about Liz's time here. The book, *Lady Chatterley's Lover* is sitting on my nightstand. I'm sure it hasn't leaped from its place on the bookshelf with the other L's on its own, and I am certainly not the one who moved it.

The only reason I can think of that Liz would be interested in D.H. Lawrence's tale of a woman's affair with her gardener is a fling with Julio. Not that I am judging her. Julio is a bright, friendly, reliable, and good-looking young man, with the emphasis on young. I doubt he's even celebrated his thirtieth birthday.

Now I have two suspects for having wiped muddy feet on the door mat: Julio and Stan Reid. I wouldn't put it past Liz to have slept with either one or both. I should have warned her about the men around here.

Why am I worried about the people Liz may have slept with, when there are much larger issues to think about? Like murder, money, and that annoying gnat, Quinn, snooping around in my business. Ordinarily, I wouldn't let someone that inconsequential get under my skin. I've actually felt sorry for Quinn, and even cared about her, in the past. I remember thinking if I'd had a daughter, I would have wanted her to be like Quinn. So pretty, with her green eyes and curly black hair. And she loves to read, just like me. It gave me pleasure to buoy her up when her best friend and boyfriend betrayed her.

But that was before she brought down my friend and partner, Lionel. That cost me big-time and forced me to work with unsavory characters like Julio's brother. Now I have to watch Quinn with all the cunning of a spider, protecting its web. If she gets any closer to that Sergeant Schmidt again, I might have to take action to stop her. That girl is ten times smarter than any of the cops. I know, because I taught almost all of them.

Meanwhile, I wish Julio would show up. If he doesn't come tomorrow, I'll have to track him down. The rose bushes need pruning, but, more importantly, I need an accounting from him. I haven't given him twenty thousand dollars without strings attached.

He's promised me a proper return on investment, starting in January, and, hello, here we are!

Maybe I need to question him more about Liz, but Julio has never let me down in financial matters, and I keep thinking of Marvin's favorite line, "It takes money to make money." I would rather invest my money with people I know, like Julio. And Lionel, although the adult entertainment business hasn't turned out to be such a great investment, especially without Lionel to oversee it.

Meanwhile, I need to find a good excuse to lay eyes on Quinn. Play up the kind and loving English teacher. She'll never suspect an ulterior motive. She's so wrapped up in her doctor husband and her little dogs. She has no idea how vulnerable she really is.

Chapter Twenty-seven

Holly spent her first night in the Brady household whimpering and yapping from her crate in the bathroom. Bleary-eyed the next morning, Josh asked Quinn if she could handle the puppy, since he had an eight a.m. meeting at the medical center.

"Sure," Quinn said, as she poured herself a mug of tea and filled a thermos of coffee for him. One benefit of working with the dead—and something her family often joked about—was "no deadlines." Of course, there *were* deadlines. Wakes and funerals couldn't be fudged timewise, but Quinn's patients never complained if she came in to work a few minutes late. She would miss this benefit when she left the business.

She kissed Josh goodbye and threw on a pair of sweats and a hoodie. Still wearing her fuzzy house slippers, she opened the back door and followed Calvin and Holly outside. Quinn forgot about the sleep disruption, watching Holly frolic with wild abandon in the back yard. Calvin modeled a more dignified romp, already a good big brother.

Thinking of all the times her brother Jack paved the way for her—at school, in the business, and in life—Quinn decided Holly was a lucky little pup. Now, if she would only sleep through the night.

Back in the house, Quinn put breakfast in both bowls and segregated them by gating Holly in the kitchen. While they ate, she showered and dressed for work, feeling guilty for cheating herself and Calvin out of a proper walk. *I'll make up for it later.*

By the time she arrived at McFarland's, a current model Cadillac, olive green, was parked in the visitor lot. Quinn pulled into her usual spot in the back and hustled into the work room. As tranquil as ever, the work area stood clean and quiet, just as she'd left it. Julio remained in his cooler, and no new bodies threatened to disrupt the serenity.

Recognizing the Cadillac from Mrs. Oliver's driveway, Quinn tiptoed into the living room area, where her mother held court, smiling and chatting. "—delighted to have your business, although we're so sorry for the circumstances."

"Yes, of course. I finally came to a decision about what my sister would have wanted."

The raspy voice confirmed the identity. *Mrs. Oliver.* Quinn's gut clenched—an odd reaction, not entirely unpleasant. Memories of the comforting teacher roiled with recent warnings. Quinn remained behind a Corinthian column, hidden from view. Hadn't her mother proposed that *she* meet with Mrs. Oliver?

"Your sister is lucky to have you to act on her behalf. I'm sure she would have done the same for you." Quinn's mother's platitudes rolled off her tongue, so familiar that Quinn tuned the words out, much more interested in Mrs. Oliver's. But Joy McFarland continued. "And I must say, we were all so grateful to you for taking Quinn under your wing when she was in high school. Kindness we'll never forget."

Quinn's cheeks burned. Not that she hadn't benefitted from Mrs. Oliver's kindness, but to be reminded of it fifteen years later, as if she had been a helpless object of pity—*will I ever live this down?*

"That was a long time ago. Quinn has become a strong and independent young woman now. You must be very proud of her."

Quinn stared at her mother, who merely nodded. "Of course."

"Speaking of Quinn, I hoped I might see her while I'm here." Mrs. Oliver turned her head from one side to the other, as if Quinn might appear at any moment.

"I can see if she's come in. She said she'd be a little late." Her mother showed her teeth in what Quinn and Jack called her fake smile. "She has a lot of adjustments to make, you know—husband, house, meals, dog—actually two dogs. She just got a new puppy. If you'd like to wait a minute, I'll go look for her."

Quinn tiptoed backwards into the embalming room, not wanting to out herself. She had no particular desire to see Mrs. Oliver, but the teacher's complimentary remarks had touched her heart, and it wouldn't hurt to say hello.

Quinn donned an apron and quickly began wiping down the stainless-steel table. When her mother burst into the room, she opened her eyes in what she hoped was a surprised expression.

"'Mornin', Mom."

"Good morning, dear. I'm glad you're here. Our client, Mrs. Oliver, is in the living room. She would like to speak with you." Quinn's mother referred to *clients* as people with money or social position. Everyone else, she called *customers*.

"Of course," Quinn said, removing the apron and turning to wash her hands in the large sink. "Is this about her sister?"

"I doubt it. She's decided to cremate, signed the docs and paid. I've been chatting with her for the better part of an hour already. I think her interest in you is more personal."

That same gut-clenching filled Quinn with hesitation, and she chastised herself for being wimpy. She pasted a smile on her face and hurried to the sofa where Mrs. Oliver stood, perhaps for a hug.

"I'll leave you two to chat," Joy said. "I'll be in the office if you need me for anything."

Quinn passed on the hug and sat on the opposite sofa where her mother had warmed the upholstery. "Nice to see you," she said.

"Likewise." Mrs. Oliver removed a handkerchief from her handbag and dabbed her nose, seemingly unfazed by the slight. "Your mother tells me you have a new dog. So much to keep you busy, and soon back to school."

Quinn shrugged, wondering whether it was wise to have told Mrs. Oliver—or anyone, really—so much of her business. "I guess I have been pretty busy lately. I'm looking forward to getting back to reading. That's one habit I learned from you."

"Lovely to hear. Listen, I won't keep you from your work. I wondered if we could meet for lunch one day this week. To celebrate your aspirations. I'd take you to dinner, but I doubt you'd want to leave your new hubby."

Whatever the motive, Mrs. Oliver's sudden interest in reconnecting with her caused Quinn's radar to beep. "I—uh, I don't usually eat lunch on workdays. I appreciate the invitation, though."

"Well, how about Saturday?" We can go to Rudy and Paco's, or I'll fix something elegant at my house. I have some news of my own to share." The woman's smile spread like a thick molasses, slow and too-sweet.

Quinn saw no way out. Mrs. Oliver had supported her in her most difficult high school days, and now the woman had lost her sister. Maybe it was time to repay the favor. "Okay," she said. "Rudy and Paco's at noon?"

"That'll be wonderful. I'll make a reservation. See you then." Mrs. Oliver air-kissed Quinn and slung the strap of her handbag over her shoulder. "Thank you, my dear."

As she breezed out of the living room, all-too-jauntily for someone who had just made arrangements to cremate her murdered sister's body, Quinn shivered. *What have I gotten myself into?*

Chapter Twenty-eight

When she returned to the back room, Quinn began processing the latest client, a woman who died in a fire the previous night. Of all the causes of death that Quinn had dealt with, death by fire upset her the most. As a teenager, Quinn had volunteered at the Shriner's Burns Hospital, so the ravages of fire had left their imprint on her.

Before she could open the body bag, someone pounded on the back door. A whoosh of cool air announced Sergeant Schmidt, who greeted Quinn with a two-finger salute and a flash of his pink gums. "Having a good morning? Hope so. I've got a warrant for Julio Martinez, dead or alive—well, in this case, dead. I hope you haven't embalmed him yet."

Schmidt's attempt at levity fell flatter than his flat-top haircut, but Quinn was glad she hadn't started on the Martinez job yet. She glanced at the warrant and set it aside for her mother in the office. "No embalming. You can take him now, if you'd like." She peered around the officer to see if EMS or any other transport was behind him.

"Can I come in?" he asked, stepping into the room and crinkling his nose. He closed the door behind him and opened the snaps on his jacket. "We'll arrange for transporting Martinez to the medical examiner, but I also want to talk to you about the toenails. The dirt you collected from Martinez matched the stuff from the Lavender lady and on the sheets. Guess they stomped in a flower bed or something first."

"Unusual to be barefooted in the winter." Quinn shifted her weight from one foot to the other. Apparently, the warrant wasn't the only reason for this visit.

"Weather's not the issue. What would bring two people together in a place where they'd get dirt under their toenails—a playground, a burial, a ritual? And these two in particular. Not the same gender, nationality, age, occupation. Martinez was a landscaper." He removed his jacket and folded it over his arm. "It's baffling, but we'll get to the bottom of it, eventually."

The policeman stared at Quinn, as if he expected a response.

A few seconds of silence caused Quinn discomfort. She finally said, "I guess you'll need to find out if Martinez was the landscaper for Mrs. Oliver to start with."

"Yes, and whether she had a personal relationship with him inside the house, if you know what I mean. I'd like you to broach that subject, if you don't mind."

"Look," Quinn said. "I helped you out the other day. I didn't like it, but I did it that once. I'm no police informant. I don't have the training, the inclination, or, frankly, the stomach for it."

"That might be true," Schmidt said, "but you have the access. You have the relationship. If we send out a patrolman, even a woman, the Oliver lady's going to see the interview as adversarial. With you, it's just two women coffee-klatching over their personal lives."

Quinn sighed. "Not that you're being a little sexist or anything. I'm sorry, Schmidt. I promised my husband I wouldn't get involved anymore, and he's already upset that I went with you to Mrs. Oliver's house and went back a second time."

"So, you're telling me no?" Schmidt asked, his face squinting into a shar-pei imitation.

Quinn nodded. She didn't expect the policeman to give up easily. Her assistance in the past had spoiled him and brought him back to ask for more.

"Maybe this will change your mind," he said, pulling a small retangular device out of his pocket and holding it out in his palm.

"What's that?" Quinn asked, the familiar electrical shocks creeping up her spine.

"Oh, just a tracker I pulled from behind the right back fender of your car just before I came inside. I saw Mrs. Oliver jump into her Cadillac and drive off right after she placed it there."

Chapter Twenty-nine

Stunned by Sergeant Schmidt's statement about the tracker on her car, Quinn gasped and sunk into a desk chair on rollers. Her mind clogged with thought fragments—Mrs. Oliver's kindness, Mrs. Oliver's wedding gift, Mrs. Oliver's house, Mary's warning, Mrs. Reid's warning, Mrs. Oliver's "date" with Dave Becker at Gaido's, Mrs. Oliver's invitation to have lunch at Rudy & Paco's. Why would Mrs. Oliver do something so sinister as to track Quinn's whereabouts? Surely Schmidt wouldn't make up a story to get Quinn to cooperate with him.

The police officer stood near the outside door, tossing the tracker from hand to hand, his eyebrows drawn into a single line. "You're probably wondering whether I've made this whole thing up," he said, "but I assure you I have better things to do than to invent stories. There are enough real ones to keep me busy forever."

Quinn's relationship with Schmidt had vacillated, just as the one with Mrs. Oliver had, but, when she had literally put her life in his hands last year, the police officer had not let her down. Her inclination was to trust him. "What reason would Mrs. Oliver have for tracking my whereabouts? I basically don't go anywhere but work and home. And, other than her sister's murder, why would a retired schoolteacher be following people?"

"She obviously considers you important or dangerous enough to watch." Schmidt set the tracker on the desk and walked away from it.

Quinn crossed her arms, grasping her elbows, and suppressing a shiver. "I agreed to meet her for lunch on Saturday. Maybe I should cancel."

"On the contrary, what better way to find out what she wants with you? We could put a wire on you and---"

"What part of, 'I don't want to be involved,' don't you understand?" Quinn's voice came out as a hoarse whisper. Quinn reviewed all the positive changes in her life in the past year—her marriage, her application to PA school, her pups—she had so much to look forward to. She couldn't let Mrs. Oliver pull her into God-knows-what trouble. On the other hand, she had the feeling she was already *in medias res*, the concept Mrs. Oliver has taught her about with reference to the play, *Oedipus the King*.

"Look at it this way, Quinn." Schmidt flashed his gums in a twisted expression, probably meant to be a smile. "You can run from Mrs. Oliver, but you can't hide. In a town like this, you're bound to cross paths with her. Maybe this isn't the only tracker. Maybe she's bugged this room, or your bedroom at home."

Quinn thought about the wedding card. The tin of cookies. Any gift from Mrs. Oliver could be bugged. "I wish I knew what she thinks I know. I barely knew her sister, and I'm starting to think I've never really known *her*, either." Quinn began pacing around the stainless steel table, where the covered body of the fire victim lay. A reminder of how fragile life could be, even her own.

"Can Mrs. Oliver tell that you've discovered the tracker?" A plan was beginning to form in Quinn's mind.

"Not at the moment. The device's location shows up on her cell phone, but this desk is close enough to the exit where the car is parked. When I was throwing it around a few minutes ago, she could have seen movement. That's why I stopped and set it down." Schmidt's eyes burned into Quinn's. "I'm not pushing you into anything. Whatever you do has to be your choice."

"Stop staring, and don't get too excited. I'm thinking we should put the tracker back on my car."

One of Schmidt's eyebrows lifted. "O-kay—"

"As you said before, what better way to figure out what Mrs. Oliver's up to than to stay in close touch. While she's tracking me, I can flip the plan. She's given me the ability to lead her around wherever I want."

Chapter Thirty

The sun drew its blue and yellow petticoats across the sky, while Quinn drove to PetSmart for doggie treats and a pink leash for Holly on her way home from work. Conscious of the tracker on her car, she considered various stops that might surprise Mrs. Oliver—a liquor store, a smoke shop, a gay bar, a strip club.

The latter hovered over her mind like a smothering fog. Quinn had frequented several adult entertainment venues last year, hoping to find answers to questions from her past. She learned the hard way that digging up answers only led to more questions.

Just before leaving McFarland's today, she'd received a phone call from Bryce Ryder, the assistant criminal district attorney in charge of the Lionel French case. Charged with two counts of murder, but rumored also to be involved in drug and prostitution rings, French, otherwise known as Blackie, had been in custody, awaiting trial.

Ryder called to remind her of the trial date, one month away. Quinn dreaded having to face Blackie in court, but her testimony was key. "I need you to come to the office tomorrow for a brief meeting to review the discovery material. How about eight a.m.?"

Quinn had given a statement months ago. She assumed Ryder meant documents from the defense attorneys. The County Criminal Courts building wasn't far from McFarland's, so Quinn agreed to meet early the next morning before work. She wondered how Mrs. Oliver would react to that destination. When she arrived at home with her items from PetSmart, Quinn turned off her security system, intending to put the dogs out in the back yard. Calvin met her at the front door, however, barking like an attack dog, and running to the back door. There he stood at attention, tail pointed skyward, and continued his diatribe.

"What's the matter, Cal?" Quinn asked. He hadn't acted this way when she'd come home to walk Holly at mid-day. She looked through the small pane of glass into the back yard, cloaked in shadows now that the sun had set. She turned on the porch light and opened the door. No birds, squirrels, or other critters—other than the whistle of a wind picking up, everything seemed normal.

By now, both dogs were scratching at the screen door, needing to go out, but Calvin kept barking. "You're never like this, buddy,"

Quinn said, opening the outer door. "I wish you could tell me in words."

Quinn followed the two pups into the shadowed yard, peering past the garage and over the fence, then over her shoulders. Holly peed immediately, but Calvin dashed to the farthest corner, continuing the furious yapping.

Quinn jogged to the fence line and bent at the place the dog pointed to. There, nestled in the overgrown grass, sat a regular-sized hot dog. Quinn grabbed the fleshy meat and sniffed it, unable to discern any odors beyond the ordinary salt and fat. Thankful that the dogs hadn't taken any bites, she stuffed the hot dog in her jacket pocket. She pulled her cell phone from the pocket on the other side and turned on the flashlight.

In the chill of the night, she shone the light on the perimeter of her yard, and then the center, searching for other items. No wonder Calvin barked so much. Someone must have thrown the hot dog over the fence.

Quinn's yard had the only fence on the block. Behind her garage, an alley separated her lot from that of her neighbor's. Anyone could have come through the alley and tossed the frankfurter over the fence without being seen, especially on this dark January evening.

But why? Quinn didn't want to jump to conclusions, but fear that the hot dog was poisoned and intended for her dogs caused perspiration to gather at her scalp, despite the shivering that had started in her midriff.

"Come on, Calvin. Come on, Holly. Let's go inside and get you some healthy dinner."

Quinn placed the suspicious hot dog in a brown paper lunch bag and sealed it with tape. She stuck the package in the back of the refrigerator, not sure whether to tell Josh about it or not when he got home.

Concerns over Mrs. Oliver's tracking her whereabouts faded into the background as this evening's situation took center stage. Quinn had handled being in danger before, but this was worse. She couldn't let anything bad happen to her puppies.

Chapter Thirty-one
TRISH

I've succumbed to distractions ever since I got back from New York—mainly having to do with that spoiled brat, Quinn McFarland. Quinn has no idea how badly she's wrecked my life, and, indeed, my financial returns on investment, since she ratted out Lionel. But that's another story, and I can put Quinn aside until Saturday when I meet her for lunch.

What I really need to concentrate on between now and Saturday, is figuring out where the police are in determining who killed Liz. I can't wait around for Sergeant Schmidt to take me, Liz's next of kin, into his confidence. The newspaper makes it seem like Liz is low priority, even though a murder should rank higher on the criminal justice scale than a chicken fight, in my opinion.

At the moment, I'm sure the police are as confused as anyone else in this town, not only because Liz and I are identical twins, but also because she has spent the holidays pretending to be me.

If the roles were reversed, and I were killed in New York, I'm sure there'd be an equal amount of perplexity concerning who the victim really is, who has a motive to want her dead, who's been sleeping in whose bed, and so forth.

I'm also certain that the surviving twin must come under scrutiny, regardless of whether it's Liz or me. After all, the un-killed twin is mainly responsible for agreeing to switch places in a crazy pretense, and she has quite the convenient alibi, being more than fifteen hundred miles away at the time of death.

So here I am—a bereaved sister, a likely suspect, a supposedly rich widow with major concerns about money, and a person with friends in low places. And that reminds me, I still haven't seen hide nor hair of Julio. This is the longest he's been absent from my garden and my bedroom since I've known him. The garden can go a little longer—it's winter, after all—but cold beds aren't my thing, and they aren't his thing either.

Back to Quinn. That little trouble-maker lives such a boring existence. She drives to work and back home without any adventurous detours, unless you count a stop at PetSmart or the grocery store as having fun. One day's tracking does not a story tell, but I can't resist hoping she does something a little naughty soon. Otherwise, I may take to watching paint dry.

Little does she know that everything revolves around her. That's why I'm going to such great lengths for our little luncheon on Saturday. Hopefully my plan will draw the queen bee out of her hive.

Chapter Thirty-two

When Josh arrived home from work, Quinn stormed around the kitchen, slamming cabinet doors, slapping placemats and dishes onto the table, and clanging the lid on a soup pot. A large lump occupied her throat, and acid bathed her insides. She couldn't remember a time she'd felt so out of control except when chained to a bed, half naked.

"What's wrong?" Josh asked. Usually, Quinn greeted him at the door with hugs and kisses. He tossed his laptop onto the sofa and sidled up to his wife, arms open.

The spoon Quinn used to stir the soup clattered onto the stove top, as she wrapped her arms around her husband's waist. A pang of guilt washed over her. It wasn't Josh's fault that she'd had such a bad day, and she hadn't made up her mind whether to tell him about it or not.

"I'm tired. That's all. A long day, and I'm trying to cook and take care of the dogs. Laundry, too." She buried her face in the warmth of his chest, and didn't want to let go.

"You should have told me. I could have picked up dinner." He pulled back to examine her face. "You don't have to do everything by yourself, you know." Josh ran his fingers through her black curls, as if each one contained strands of pure gold.

Quinn had waited a long time for someone to treat her with such tenderness, and this simple action brought a wellspring of emotion. She broke away from his embrace and plopped on the sofa, covering her face with her hands.

Calvin leaped onto the sofa next to her and began licking her neck. Josh picked up Holly, who was whimpering and wagging her tail. Sitting on the couch next to Quinn, he stretched his arms to encircle the whole family. "Q, talk to me. This isn't like you. And I don't think it's dinner and the dogs. Please tell me what's going on."

"I'm sorry," Quinn said, reaching over the dogs to hug her husband around the neck. "I'm not being fair to you." She leaned closer for a long kiss, while she thought about how much she wanted to explain. "Let's have dinner first, and then we'll talk. Okay?"

Josh seemed satisfied, and they sat down to a meal of soup, garlic bread, and wine. Afterwards, as he swirled the merlot in his wineglass, Josh reached for Quinn's hand. "Ready to talk?"

Quinn had been debating with herself, but, remembering her resolution to come clean with her husband after evasiveness had caused problems in the past, she squeezed his hand and took a long swig of her wine. "Mrs. Oliver came to the funeral home today. Making plans for cremating her sister. She also asked me to have lunch with her on Saturday, and I accepted. Then I had a visit from Sergeant Schmidt."

A pink flush took over Josh's face. "Oh, no. Not again. What did he want?"

"He didn't say outright, but he hinted about my talking more with Mrs. Oliver. At first, I didn't want to tell him I was having lunch with her. I made it clear I was not interested in any more involvement. But he stopped me in mid-sentence. He saw Mrs. Oliver, sticking a tracker on the back fender of my car."

"You've gotta be kidding me. Did she really? Or was he trying to manipulate you?" Josh began pacing around the table, his hands curled into fists.

"I don't think so. He showed me the tracker. And Mrs. Oliver had just left when he showed up."

"Quinn, this is terrible. Do you really think you should meet her for lunch?"

Quinn started clearing the table, mainly to avoid meeting Josh's eyes. "I accepted. That was before I knew about the tracker."

"Well, make up an excuse. I don't think you should associate with that woman, especially if she's tracking your movements." He joined Quinn at the sink to help with the dishes. "Did you destroy the tracker?"

"You'll probably disagree with my logic, but I insisted on keeping the tracker on my car. I'm going to meet her for lunch, too. The best way I can keep from being manipulated is to become the manipulator. I know what I'm doing."

"But you're so upset. You could hardly talk when I came in the house."

"That wasn't why I was upset. At least, that wasn't all of it." Quinn explained about the call from Bryce Ryder's office, the pressure of having to testify in the upcoming trial. "I've lived with this cloud hanging over my head, but now the storm is close, and I don't want to relive everything."

Josh wrapped his arms around her again. "I know, babe. That whole Blackie thing was a nightmare. Not just for you, but for all of us."

"And don't forget, I killed a man. Even though it was self-defense, my conscience won't let me off." She dried her hands on a dish towel and ran them through her hair. "I'll be okay once this is over with."

Quinn pulled away from Josh. "Will you set the left-over soup in the refrigerator?" For some reason she dreaded telling him about the possible poisoning attempt on their dogs. She knew how outraged he would be, and she thought it would be better to wait until the police could test the hot dog for toxicity.

Josh carried the soup pot to the refrigerator and moved things around to make room for it. When he shut the door and returned to the sink to help with the rest of the dishes, he was opening the paper bag from the back of the shelf. "Hey, babe. What's up with this?" He drew the contents out and held it up, as if to eat it. "Who put a wiener in the back of our refrigerator?"

Chapter Thirty-three

Early the next morning, Quinn drove through a chilly rainstorm to the criminal district attorney's office. Bleary-eyed, and nursing a thermos full of hot tea, she took her time on the slick road. Even at 7:45, the parking lot at the criminal courts building was almost full, and she had to park in one of the back rows. Her McFarland's umbrella kept her fairly dry, but couldn't protect her spirits from being dampened.

Bryce Ryder, the most seasoned prosecutor in the office, met Quinn with a warm, but too-firm handshake. "Come on in. Can I get you some coffee?"

"No, thanks. I've just had breakfast." Not quite the truth, but she hadn't sworn to tell the whole truth at this point. She sat in the chair Bryce pointed to, not wanting to get too comfortable. She had a lot on her plate this morning.

"I won't keep you long." Ryder opened a thick binder to the first of many pages marked with bright pink sticky notes. "These docs came from the defense. This'll be the first trial, charges from the Dawn Chrysler murder. I've marked sections you may have knowledge of. I'd like you to look them over and confirm whether you can provide information to the court."

Quinn glanced at each of the sections, fifteen in all, before commenting. She wished she could confer with her attorney, Dave Becker, before replying, but she didn't want to tie up proceedings. It wasn't as if she were a defendant, or even a suspect. She had only been a witness.

"I'm probably not the best person to testify to most of this," she said. "Ana's parents could tell you more about their relationship with the defendant, the location of their house, etc. The only thing I can speak to is what I saw from the fig tree across the alley." She pointed to one of the earmarked pages.

"Everything else I know stems from the events of last year, and those aren't really pertinent to this case." Anxiety roiled inside, as Quinn remembered the deep involvement she had in bringing the defendant to trial for two more recent murders.

"That's fine, Quinn, but you realize we're going to need you for both trials." His eyes met hers in a deep stare. "I know you don't want this guy to get off."

Quinn tamped down her desire to flee the office and never come back. That would be selfish and irresponsible. She'd come this far. She wouldn't go back. "You're right. Let me know when you need me again."

Ryder shook her hand once more, and she scooted out of the prosecutor's office. As soon as she could, she would make an appointment with Dave Becker. His advice about testifying might save her a lot of problems.

Her next stop was to take the suspicious frankfurter to the police station. The fact that Josh had almost put the hot dog in his mouth the night before had shaken her, so much that sleep had eluded her.

Fortunately, the outdoor temperatures were in the upper fifties, so she didn't have to worry about spoilage in the trunk of her car.

If the meat turned out to be free of poison, she could calm her husband's nerves and her own. If not—well, she didn't want to think about how ramped up their anxiety might be.

Either way, she drove with the heightened tension of knowing Mrs. Oliver was likely following her movements to the police station. And what would that indicate to her teacher-turned-spy?

The windshield wipers slashed against the rain with a rhythm that matched Quinn's thoughts, hard and fast. Quinn couldn't picture Mrs. Oliver as entirely evil, despite the mounting evidence that the kindly old schoolteacher was not what she appeared to be. Perhaps the death of her sister had thrown her off-kilter, and she had become obsessed with solving the murder. That might have motivated her to take atypical action.

The lunch date tomorrow would offer an opportunity to find out more. Quinn intended to ask more questions and give fewer answers. If nothing else, lunch at Rudy & Paco's would make for a rare treat, and Quinn had a plan of her own.

The rain had slowed to a drizzle in the short time it took for Quinn to pull into the parking lot at the police station. The earthy smell that Quinn associated with grass and trees, but which really came from ozone chemicals, filled her with thoughts of barbecues and picnics and sporting events in the months to come. January had never been her favorite month.

A whoosh of heated air enveloped her as she opened the door. The station hummed with activity, no matter what time of the day or night, and today was no exception. Crime apparently took no days off.

"May I help you?" the dispatcher asked. Her eyes appeared to be drawn to the damp paper bag in Quinn's hand.

Quinn used her other hand to run fingers through the dark curls on the top and sides of her head. Nothing like a cold, humid day to bring out the ringlets. Quinn introduced herself and asked for Sergeant Schmidt.

"Out in the field. Something I can help with?" Her blunted fingernails played with the telephone cord. Two buttons flashed on the phone, calls waiting for attention.

Before Quinn could respond, the door leading to the secure part of the station opened, offering a glimpse into the chatter and activity beyond.

"Hey, Quinn, is that you?" Mary, her brother's fiancée, rushed out toward the front door, opening her arms. A quick hug almost caused her to drop the bag with the wiener inside.

Slim and fit in her officer's uniform, Mary winked at the dispatcher as she locked arms with Quinn. "Come on, girlfriend. Let's find a place to talk for a minute." She led the way to an unoccupied room with a table and a scattering of chairs. "Sit and tell me why you're here."

Quinn set the paper bag on the table and explained about her dogs' howling and finding the hot dog in the yard by the fence. "Can someone test it? I don't know why anyone would want to poison my little doggies, but I have to find out."

"No problem. We can check it out in-house, but you'll have to complete some paperwork. Can't promise you the fastest turnaround. Depends on what's there ahead of you." Mary placed a hand on Quinn's forearm. "Meanwhile, we can't let anything happen to Calvin or Holly. I know you'll be vigilant, especially at night."

"Yeah," Quinn said, rubbing her itchy eye. "I've lost too much sleep over this already."

"Speaking of sleeping, I'm coming off duty now. I'm headed home to get some shut-eye." Mary yawned. "I'll be glad when we get this case wrapped up."

Assuming she meant the cockfighting case, Quinn perked up. "How's that going? Any word on the Martinez autopsy?" With all the excitement over the car tracker and the hot dog, Quinn had almost forgotten about Julio Martinez.

"Nobody told you, I guess, and you didn't hear this from me. We heard from the medical examiner late yesterday. The Martinez brother did not die a natural death. He was poisoned." Quinn shivered. Another poisoning, on the heels of Mrs. Oliver's sister.

When Quinn left the police station, the sun was shining, and the air felt more like March than January. Seagulls chattered over her head, and landscapers were planting petunias in beds around the courthouse. That's how things went on this Gulf Coast island. She wished everything else in her life could make such a quick turnaround.

Chapter Thirty-four

After leaving the police station, Quinn helped her parents and Jack with the fire victim's funeral, but otherwise the mortuary was dead, unusual for a Friday. Unless a new body with special circumstances arrived soon, Quinn would be free on Saturday to keep her lunch date with Mrs. Oliver.

While she cleaned and sanitized her work area, wondering who might replace her in this job a few months from now, she thought about Mrs. Oliver and the lunch at Rudy & Paco's. One thing was for sure. Since the travails of the previous year, Quinn had vowed never to be a victim again. If Mrs. Oliver wanted to track her whereabouts, that was one thing, but Quinn would not let her teacher control her. She would make that very clear.

Quinn told her parents she was leaving early to run errands. Her first stop was Galveston Bookshop. She loved the paper-and-ink smell of the two-story building where rows and rows of old and new books waited to be discovered. A book would be the perfect hostess gift for Mrs. Oliver, a thank you for taking Quinn to lunch.

Mrs. Oliver wouldn't expect such a thing. She would ooh and ahh over Quinn's thoughtfulness, and then Quinn would pop the question, "Why did you put a tracker on my car?" She couldn't wait to see her teacher squirm.

As quiet as the mortuary had been on this Friday afternoon, the bookshop was buzzing with customers. Some rolled suitcases, most likely shopping for reading material before boarding the cruise ships docked at the port, a few blocks away.

A girl Quinn knew from high school worked at the desk and usually welcomed everyone who entered the store, but today a line of customers occupied her attention, and Quinn slipped past her.

Selecting a book for a former English teacher was no simple task. The most well-read woman Quinn had ever known also owned an extensive library. Quinn recalled the books she had seen at Mrs. Oliver's house when she had walked through with Sergeant Schmidt and afterwards by herself.

A leather-bound copy of *David Copperfield* tempted Quinn, but maybe that was too English-teacherish. She glanced at the biographies, briefly, before returning to the fiction shelves. *Fifty*

Shades of Grey peeked at her from a corner, and heat rushed to her face, thinking about the book in Mrs. Oliver's powder room.

Finally, she picked up a short story anthology, *Short Story Masterpieces by American Women*. She carried the book to a table and sank into the wooden chair. The first story, "Heat," by Joyce Carol Oates, grabbed her attention. Identical twins, Rhea and Rhoda. Quinn twirled a curl over and over as she began reading the story. She couldn't help thinking of Mrs. Oliver and her twin.

"Rhea and Rhoda were the same girl; they'd wanted it that way. Only looking from one to the other could you see they were two." Quinn read on, unable to stop until she'd squeezed all the truths from the story. Maybe Mrs. Oliver would cringe to discover both twins died, but Quinn didn't care. This and the other stories in the collection would make a charming literary gift.

She waited in line to pay for her purchase, smiling and chit-chatting with the clerk, but not revealing that the book was a gift for their former teacher. Some things were none of anybody's business.

After leaving the bookshop, Quinn drove to Walmart. Another discreet purchase gave her a twinge of—what? Secrecy, independence, sneakiness? She'd never make a good spy.

As soon as she started her car, her cell phone rang. "Sgt Schmidt" flashed on the caller ID. Quinn held her breath against the hammering of her heart.

"Hey, Quinn. Your lunch date still on for tomorrow at Paco's?" Traffic sounds told her he was driving.

"Yeah." She wished she hadn't told him about Mrs. Oliver's invitation to begin with.

"You want me to hang around—just in case?"

Quinn couldn't tell whether his offer came from a desire to assuage her fears or his own. "Nah, I'll be all right. Thanks for offering, though."

"Okay," he said, his voice a little crestfallen. "I'll be here if you need me, whenever."

"I know that," Quinn said, the tension leaking slowly from her chest, like air from a balloon. She shifted the call to Bluetooth and headed for home.

"Oh, I almost forgot—" the policeman said. His tone had hardened. Icy fingers tickled Quinn's neck. "What?"

"That hot dog you brought to the station? It was toxic. Would have made whoever ate it sick or worse."

Chapter Thirty-five

Saturday morning arrived with cerulean blue skies and a soft breeze. A perfect day for golf, but Josh couldn't get out of his hospital shift, and Quinn couldn't get out of lunch with Mrs. Oliver.

Not that anything to do with Mrs. Oliver went down easy with Josh, and after Quinn told him about the poisoned hot dog, his level of concern had gone off the charts. Quinn had calmed him by reminding him that the dogs never went outside without one of them to supervise, and they would need to be extra-vigilant. "I can take the dogs with me to work, if that would help. My mother would enjoy spoiling Holly, I'm sure."

"That's a Band-aid, when what we need is a surgery." Josh still hadn't come to terms with all the trouble that had surrounded Quinn and her home when they were dating. "Maybe we need to move. After this year I could set up practice anywhere."

"Are you forgetting about PA school?" Quinn had no intention of leaving town just as all her dreams were about to come to fruition.

"I'm sorry. You're right," Josh had said, hugging her in a close embrace. "I worry about you and us and our little family. I know you're taking precautions, but I don't trust that Mrs. Oliver."

Now, as she drove to the restaurant with the gift-wrapped anthology on the seat next to her, the beginnings of a headache throbbed in her temples. Maybe she was foolhardy to think she could outsmart her teacher.

Rudy & Paco's smelled of fine wine, mango salsa, and starched linens that draped the tables in a black-and-white motif. Well-known for its Columbian cuisine and elegant service, even at lunch, the restaurant was a haven for the discriminating diner. Quinn wore her newest funeral outfit—a charcoal-gray zip sheath dress with leather pockets from Calvin Klein and high-heeled black patent shoes from Nordstrom's Rack. Her shoulder bag completed the look. Despite the gathering headache, Quinn imagined herself as a celebrity.

Quinn nodded at her good friend, Jan, who was the restaurant's comptroller and public relations person. Normally they would have hugged, but today Quinn concentrated on the lunch with her teacher. Mrs. Oliver was seated in the rear of the restaurant, wearing a red ruffly blouse, her back against the large mirrored wall. Quinn couldn't help thinking of the scene in *The Godfather*. A gift bag with tissue paper and curly ribbons sat at the place opposite her teacher.

"Hello, Quinn. So good of you to come." She pointed to the chair adjacent. "Sit here, so we can talk more privately."

Thinking of the fly being lured into the spider's web, Quinn set her gift on the table at the place next to her. "Of course."

The waitress delivered menus and a platter of plantain chips flanked by bowls of two different types of salsa. "May I take your drink orders?" she asked.

"A martini," Mrs. Oliver said, almost too quickly. "With an olive *and* a twist. As usual."

"I'll have a cup of hot tea," Quinn said, thinking the caffeine might calm her headache.

"Come on, Quinn. Tea? You're a married woman now. How about a glass of wine?"

"Just tea," Quinn said to the waitress. "I thought you might like this." She handed the package to Mrs. Oliver.

"A book? I'm sure I will. Never met a book I didn't like." Mrs. Oliver pushed the plantain plate away from her and unwrapped the gift. "Oh, you're too kind." She opened the anthology to the table of contents and read. "Ha! The story, 'Heat,' by Joyce Carol Oates. My sister and I used to talk about it all the time. A twin story."

Suddenly Mrs. Oliver snapped the book closed and frowned. "The twins both die. They're killed." Frown lines framed the teacher's red-lipsticked mouth, and Quinn wondered whether the woman might cry.

"I didn't mean—" Perhaps Quinn should have selected something light or humorous. Her gift had landed like a torpedo.

"No worries. I'm sure you didn't realize, or you wouldn't have." She sniffed and flicked her gift bag, pushing it toward Quinn, as the waitress returned with the drinks.

"Here's to all the good things in life—health, wealth, and safety," Mrs. Oliver said, holding her martini glass aloft, and then clinking it against Quinn's teacup.

The word, "safety," raised hairs on the back of Quinn's neck. *What an odd toast!* "I'm sure you have something to talk to me about." She stared at Mrs. Oliver as she sipped her tea.

"Yes, we'll get to that. Open your gift first."

"Just a minute." Taking a long sip of her tea, Quinn picked up a plantain, spooned sauce over it, and took a large bite.

Immediately, Quinn spit the unchewed plantain into her napkin, gulped a mouthful of water, and jumped out of her seat, murmuring. She grabbed the platter and her shoulder bag, scooted past the other tables to the front of the restaurant, turned left at the bar, and confronted Jan.

A few minutes later she returned to the table, apologizing profusely. "Do you want more plantains?" She put her napkin in her lap and took a deep breath. "Something nasty in that sauce. Very unusual. Anyway, I gave the chef a piece of my mind. He offered to bring us a different appetizer, but I said no. Hope you don't mind."

Shrugging, Mrs. Oliver said, "I don't care about the plantains. I want you to open my gift already."

Quinn removed the triangles of colored tissue paper from the top of the bag and peered inside, half-expecting a hissing rattlesnake. Instead, she found another layer of tissue paper. Beneath that, an oblong jewelry box, wrapped in shiny paper with curling ribbon, sat on a third layer. "Beautifully wrapped," she said, as she removed the box from the gift bag and set it on the tablecloth.

"Are we ready to order?" the waitress asked, gazing at the pile of wrapping paper cluttering the table.

Mrs. Oliver swung her arm across the table, picking up most of the trash with one swipe. She balled it up and stuffed it in the gift bag. "I'm ready if you are," she said to Quinn.

Mrs. Oliver ordered the fish tacos, and Quinn did the same. Quinn used her knife to cut the ribbon, and she opened the wrapping without tearing it. The weight and shape of the box hinted at jewelry—maybe a watch or bracelet. But why would Mrs. Oliver give her something like that?

When she lifted the lid, she couldn't believe her eyes. She gasped a thank you and grabbed the shiny silver bracelet from its velvet nest. Two hearts, interlocked, decorated the band. Quinn flipped it over. Tiny engraved letters said, "Love, QM."

"Where did you get this?" Quinn asked, her voice quivering and low. She had given this bracelet to her BFF, Ana French, shortly after they had performed the blood sister ritual in sixth grade. She'd forgotten all about it.

"Part of the valuables Ana stashed in a closet at work. One of Lionel's employees found the metal box and asked me to give it to Ana's parents. They thought you might like to have the bracelet as a memento."

"Wait a minute. I'm confused," Quinn said, turning the bracelet over and over in her palm.

Mrs. Oliver chuckled. "You're wondering how I'm connected to all this, I'm sure." She took a long swig of martini and dabbed her lips with her napkin. "Lionel—or Blackie, as you probably know him—is what you might call a friend. Our relationship is quite complicated, but suffice it to say that the people who work for him know me and know I taught Ana—"

Quinn had stopped listening after the first mention of Lionel. If Mrs. Oliver had a connection to Blackie, that sealed everything. Quinn wanted to grab the bracelet and run from the restaurant.

But Rudy & Paco's wasn't the kind of place people ditched before their food came. Quinn didn't want to create a scene that would reflect on her family business, either. She sucked in sweet air and forced herself to focus.

"—of course, I wasn't as close to Ana as I was to you. I couldn't abide the way she and Brad had treated you."

Gathering random thoughts into what she thought was a coherent theory, Quinn interrupted. "So, you're friends with Blackie, and you're upset that I'm due to testify in his upcoming trial. Is that it? So that's why you put a tracker on my car?"

Mrs. Oliver reared her head and shoved her hand out like a traffic cop. "Stop right there. You've got this all wrong."

Quinn crossed her arms and scooted her chair back a few inches. "You thought I didn't know about the tracker, but I do. If you want to explain, I'll listen, but I'm more than a little ticked off."

"Listen, Quinn." Mrs. Oliver had lowered her voice to a whisper. "I admit, I did put a tracker on your car. But you've got to believe me—I'm not the enemy. That's why I invited you to lunch. I want to help you."

"Help me? How?" All the bad things she'd heard about Mrs. Oliver were pounding in Quinn's forehead in a full-fledged migraine.

"I swear, I would never do anything to hurt you. I put the tracker on your car so I could *protect* you. You don't realize how vulnerable you are."

Chapter Thirty-six
TRISH

After our not-so-pleasant lunch, I must admit I've underestimated Quinn McFarland—or whatever her married name is. That girl is sharper than a surgeon's scalpel, no pun intended, since word has it that handsome husband of hers is the best scalpel-wielder at the medical center. Word has it Francisco owes his life to the guy, even though he won't ever acknowledge it.

Speaking of Francisco, I still haven't heard from Julio. The weather's warming up, and there's yardwork to do around here, not to mention what I lovingly call his indoor work. If he doesn't show up soon, I may have to take drastic action.

Back to Quinn, I don't know how she found the tracker. I can't blame her for thinking of me as the enemy, since she doesn't now and may never know the whole truth. Heck, even I have a hard time sorting out my relationship with Lionel after all these years. He and my sister have had a thing going for each other since they were in kindergarten. I honestly think if he hadn't gone all entrepreneur in the adult entertainment business, they might have gotten married and had a great life together. Two flamboyant personalities, both risk-takers, leading unconventional lives. Unbelievable that one's gone, and one's in jail, facing double homicide charges.

More to the point, without Lionel and his trusted henchmen (and henchwomen), the businesses are in trouble, and that leaves people like little ol' me wondering how or when we'll see our dividends again. Marvin's left me well-fixed, no doubt, but my investments in certain, let's say, unconventional businesses have put me over the top—until now, that is.

I have plenty to worry about, with my sister dead and Julio missing in action. Now I have to worry about Lionel—and Quinn, and maybe myself. Too bad our little luncheon hasn't served its purpose. No worries, though. I'm not one to give up on anything.

I think I'll fix myself a nice hot toddy and curl up in bed with the new book from Quinn. There's nothing in the world that a good piece of literature can't cure.

Chapter Thirty-seven

After the lunch with Mrs. Oliver, Quinn removed the tracker from her car and set it on a shelf in her garage. The teacher's claim of protection didn't make sense, and when Quinn probed to find out exactly who or what threatened her, Mrs. Oliver had muttered nonsense about being friends with people in low places.

Surprised by that admission, Quinn didn't doubt its truth. The more she learned about Mrs. Oliver, the more tarnished the woman's trustworthiness became. The friendship bracelet told a tale, as well. When she'd opened the gift, a certain delight of memory filled her heart, but sadness trailed in its wake, like the funky odor of cut flowers after they've died. If Ana's parents had wanted to gift her with the bracelet, why hadn't they done so, themselves?

Mrs. Oliver's connection to Blackie was even more disturbing. Quinn supposed everyone had a public and private persona, and the two could be very different, but she couldn't imagine her high school English teacher palling around with a porn star/entrepreneur/murderer. Maybe Mrs. Oliver's sister was killed because of some weird connection to Blackie. Except that he'd been incarcerated for many months.

Quinn shook off the need to theorize about criminal acts unrelated to herself. She blamed her empathy for the dead on working at McFarland's from such a young age. Now she needed to concentrate on transitioning to a new career.

First, she had to get past testifying in Blackie's murder trial. After talking it over with Josh, she called Dave Becker, the attorney who had assisted her after Ana's death last year.

"I hate to bother you on a Saturday afternoon." Though he often worked on Saturdays, his assistant, Ethel, had the day off.

"Never a bother. Always glad to hear from you. Everything okay with you and the family—and that great young doctor you married?"

Quinn ignored the flash of irritation. She hated being treated as if her only value in life came from having married a surgeon. Probably a generational thing. Becker was almost old enough to be her grandfather. "Everyone's fine. I need some advice and hope you can fit me into your schedule next week."

"Bah. Next week? Why don't you come over right now? I'm finishing up some work on a case, and it's too early to go home. Sandy's bridge club day."

"Okay. Be there in ten." The drive to Becker's office was uneventful. Fewer tourists and almost no traffic on the seawall boulevard, although restaurants and hotels had turned on neon lights and marquees for the date-night crowd. Still full from Paco's red snapper tacos, Quinn looked forward to a cozy evening at home with Josh and the pups.

When she entered the familiar office, the paper and ink smell of old books reminded her that this had been a haven of security for her at one of the most insecure times of her life. She'd hoped not to have to return so soon.

"C'mon in." Becker's booming voice echoed through the empty office. Quinn sauntered into the back office, her spirits lagging behind.

Dave Becker crossed in front of his desk, arms open wide for a hug. "How's my favorite renegade client?"

The kind attorney was one of the few people Quinn allowed to tease her in this way. While she completely trusted his knowledge and experience with legal matters, she *had* gone rogue on him in the past. The toothy grin on his face said he'd forgiven her.

"Trying to stay out of trouble for a change," Quinn said. "But I need some advice—in confidence, of course."

"Sure." Becker pointed to the client chair and circled the desk to take his own seat. "What's going on?"

Thoughts tumbled in Quinn's brain, vying for priority and tying her tongue. She gripped the arms of the chair and took a deep breath. "Three things worry me. The first two are easier to talk about, but the third—well, you had dinner with Mrs. Oliver the other night, and the third thing involves her."

Becker's eyebrows gathered on his forehead, like drapery pleats drawing closed at night. "I see." He rolled his fancy ballpoint pen between his palms. "I don't believe that should be a concern, but why don't you tell me the first two worries first."

Quinn explained about the poisoned frankfurter. "Maybe we're being paranoid, and there's an innocent explanation for it, but we don't take things like this lightly. Our puppies are too precious to us. I don't expect you to offer a solution. I've filed the appropriate paperwork with the police. I just wanted to put it on the record with you."

She shifted in her chair. "The second thing is Blackie's first murder trial. I've been asked to testify, according to Bryce Ryder. Before I get on the stand, I'd like you to brief me. Ryder plans to do that, but with him, I'm just a pawn in the game to convict Blackie. I trust you to help me protect myself."

Becker closed his eyes and leaned back in his chair. A full minute went by before he spoke. "Quinn, it's true you are a key witness. You're the only remaining eyewitness, and Ryder needs you for that. But there's a heap of evidence against Blackie, and, ultimately, the case does not hinge on you. My advice to you is to tell the truth. Answer every question, but don't answer questions that haven't been asked, if you know what I mean. Be honest, to the point."

Leaning forward and peering into Quinn's eyes, he continued. "Don't give me that puppy-dog look. You are quite capable; however, if you want me to be there in the courtroom when you testify, I'll do that for you."

"I'd really appreciate that," Quinn said. "And I'll pay you for your time."

"No need. You'll just have to tell me the date as soon as you know, so I don't book anything else." He glanced at a leather notebook on his desk, presumably an old-fashioned calendar. "And now," he said with an inscrutable expression, "tell me what your concern is with Mrs. Oliver."

Quinn took another deep breath and fidgeted with the fabric of her windbreaker. Remembering the cozy dinner Mr. Becker and Mrs. Oliver had been having at Gaido's, she needed to proceed delicately. "You know she was my teacher. She helped me a lot back then." She studied Becker's eyes, trying to figure out where his loyalties lay. "We've kept in touch over the years, some times more than others, but more since her sister's death." Quinn summarized how she had identified the body and cooperated with Sergeant Schmidt to talk to Mrs. Oliver. "The day she came to the funeral home to arrange for her sister's cremation, she put a tracker on my car."

Becker's eyebrows shot to his hairline. "How do you know this?"

"Schmidt witnessed her. He showed me the tracker right away." Quinn hugged herself, remembering her own shock. "And she invited me to lunch, too. I left the tracker in place and met her for lunch, figuring I could learn more by playing along."

"That sounds like you," Becker said. "So, what happened then?"

Quinn explained about the bracelet. "Turns out Mrs. Oliver is connected to Blackie. I'm not sure how, but I think it's partly financial. Anyway, I confronted her about the tracker, and she said she did it for my own protection."

The attorney squinted and scrunched his face into something resembling a leaky inner tube. "And you don't trust her. Is that right?"

Quinn nodded. "I guess I've been naïve about her for a long time. Recently I've heard some ugly things about her, and anyone who associates with Blackie can't be all that virtuous." She looked around the tidy office, wondering whether she had gone too far. "I know you're her friend. I hope I haven't put you in a difficult position."

Becker clasped his hands, tenting his index fingers. "I've known Trish McDaniel—Mrs. Oliver—a long, long time. We even dated back before I met Sandy and before she got together with Marvin. And she's a client, so I keep her confidences in the same way as I keep yours." He paused and stared at his hands before nodding and meeting Quinn's eyes. "I will only say this—I've been worried about her, myself, ever since Liz's death. When you have to interact with her, I think you are right to be very careful."

As soon as she returned home, Quinn replaced the tracker on her car. Even though Mrs. Oliver knew she knew about it, she wanted the woman to follow her. She couldn't be too careful now.

Chapter Thirty-eight

The next day, Sunday, posed no funerals and no surgeries, so Quinn and Josh stayed in bed longer than usual. "Hey, we're still honeymooners," Josh said, when Quinn looked at the time in shock. He tugged at the strap of her camisole, and she swung around, rethinking her intention to get up and let the dogs out.

"Hang on a little longer, Holly." Quinn giggled, as Josh pulled the covers over both of their heads.

"I wish we could do this every day," Quinn said, coming up for air a few minutes later.

"We can. We're married, remember?"

"I mean, stay in bed as long as we want. No other commitments." A bit of melancholy flashed through her, as if the word, "commitment," had opened Pandora's box. She brushed her dark curls from her face and stretched her back before climbing out of the bed. "Not that I'm against commitments in general. A certain amount of commitment is good." She padded a few steps to the bathroom. "I'm babbling, aren't I?"

"Not a problem," Josh said, pulling on a pair of sweats and a hoodie. "I'm taking the dogs out in the back. Don't worry. I'll watch them."

Quinn took a quick shower and ceded the bathroom to her husband, who had just returned with the dogs. "What would you like to do the rest of this glorious day?" she asked, peering out the window at the cloudless blue sky.

"Whatever you want. How 'bout straightening up the garage? That's a two-person job, if I ever saw one." He hummed as he cleaned up and brushed his teeth.

Marrying Josh had been one of Quinn's best ideas ever. He was naturally laid back and easy to please. Not that he didn't have certain red-hot buttons, but so did everyone. "Maybe a rainy day job. Today's too nice to spend inside that stinky ol' garage. Actually, I'd love to take Calvin for a run. Since Holly—and since the hot dog—neither one of us has gotten enough exercise."

"It's pretty warm outside. You want to go to the dog park and let the pups run around?"

"Better yet, let's take a picnic to the beach or the state park." Quinn peered into the refrigerator. "I've got cheese and peanut butter and grapes. There's a loaf of French bread in the freezer, and some of Mrs. Oliver's cookies."

Josh grabbed a bottle of wine and a corkscrew. "Sounds like a perfect day."

Getting away from everything with their little family appealed to Quinn, also. As she donned her leggings and running shoes, she suggested they go in Josh's car. Not wanting to spoil the moment, she didn't mention that it was none of Mrs. Oliver's business where they spent their Sunday afternoon.

At the last minute, Josh threw a fishing rod and some lures into the trunk of his car. "Who knows? Maybe I'll drop a line and see what happens."

They took off for Seawolf Park in Josh's Audi, loaded with food, leashes, blankets, water bowls, and giddy enthusiasm. "This is going to be great," Josh said.

Holly wiggled on Quinn's lap, and Calvin looked out the window in the back seat. After crossing the bridge, Josh parked the car at the picnic area. "Let's go for a run first," he said. "Before we unpack all the food and equipment."

"Cool," Quinn said. "The path leading to the submarine and destroyer is good for running. We can set up at the picnic area after." They started off at a slow jog, with Josh holding Calvin's leash, and Quinn holding Holly's.

After a minute or two, Quinn picked up Holly and snapped the dog into her vest, snugly against her chest. Then she picked up the pace. The movement caused the cool, salty air to whip against Quinn's face, blowing the hair away from her eyes. Her leg muscles practically sang with the joy of stretching.

She pulled ahead of Josh, who still paced himself with Calvin. Around a curve and about even with the entrance to the submarine, Quinn slowed and turned, expecting the pair to be a few steps behind her. Instead, she saw nobody. The pavement was empty.

"Josh?" She yelled as she retraced her steps. He couldn't have disappeared in the few seconds—or was it minutes—since she'd picked up Holly.

Back around the curve, heart pounding in fear, she ran along the pavement, calling his name and gazing from side to side.

"I'm over here." A voice came from the right, behind a row of bushes, followed by Calvin's distinctive howl.

Quinn followed the sounds to the grassy spot where Josh sat on a mound of dirt, holding his left ankle across his lap and other thigh. "Oh, no. What happened?" Quinn plopped beside him and put her arm around his upper back.

"Calvin led me off-track toward the bushes, and I tripped on this curb. I don't think it's broken, but it's swelling already."

Quinn raised her head, trying to gauge how far it was to their car. The picnic cooler had plenty of ice inside. "Let me get you some ice." She kissed the top of his head, patted Calvin, and secured Holly inside her vest again. She sprinted back toward the parking lot.

The submarine loomed ahead, a row of visitors climbing the stairs into the exhibit. Quinn rerouted, hoping to save time if a refreshment stand was inside. The last person in line had just bent his head to enter the sub when Quinn approached.

Inside, a grandmotherly woman selling tickets said, "I'm sh-shorry. You can't bring your dog onboard."

"What?" Quinn said. "Oh. I'm not in line for a ticket. My husband hurt his ankle. I hoped you might have some ice."

The woman's face opened into a large smile, showing overlapping teeth. "Of course," she said, pushing against the table to raise herself to a standing position. "Shtuff like this happens all the time out here. Gotta be prepared."

She left Quinn standing there while she hobbled into the interior of the massive ship. When she returned, she carried two sealed plastic bags with ice cubes inside. "Here ya go, Mishy. Hope your honey feels a whole lot better shoon."

Delighted that she hadn't had to run all the way back to the car, Quinn dashed back to where Josh and Calvin waited. When she leaned over to pack the ice around Josh's ankle, Holly wriggled out of her vest and scampered to where Calvin had nestled next to Josh.

"Sorry to put a damper on our Sunday outing," Josh said, wincing a little at the first sensation of cold. "Oh, that feels good."

"After about twenty minutes, we'll see how you feel. I can bring the picnic over here, if you want."

Josh shook his head. "Too much trouble, and I'm not really hungry now."

Calvin climbed into the space created by Quinn's crossed legs, and Holly followed suit. "That's right. Everybody make yourself comfortable." She grabbed Josh's hand and brought it to her lips.

"You're going to be an outstanding PA," he said. "But I advise against kissing the hands of all your patients."

"You must be feeling okay if you're making jokes." Quinn removed an ice cube from one of the packets, so Calvin and Holly could lick it. "This is my way of flirting shamelessly with you when your position is compromised."

"I'll be fine in a few minutes," Josh said, pressing the ice around the circumference of his ankle. "Getting numb already."

At that moment, Quinn's cell phone blared from inside her pants pocket. Startled, she leaped up. She pulled out the phone as it went into the second verse of ringtone, and she glanced at the caller ID. "What? It's Trish Oliver!" She punched the speaker function.

"Hey, Mrs. Oliver. What's going on?" Dread pulsed at Quinn's throat. Whatever this was, it couldn't be good.

"Don't mean to alarm you on this beautiful Sunday afternoon, but I thought I'd ask if you've just been to the wharf and back in your car?"

Quinn stared at Josh, wondering whether he wanted to reply. He shook his head and held a finger to his lips.

"What? No, I'm out with Josh in his car." A dim understanding began to creep into Quinn's mind. "Are you referring to the tracker?"

"Yes, dear. If not you, there's a mystery on your hands. Someone took your car to the docks and back within the last fifteen minutes. I thought you'd better know."

Quinn began to quiver, but she composed herself enough to thank Mrs. Oliver and disconnect the call. She turned to Josh, an apologetic tone in her voice. "I'd better call the police to meet us at the house. Do you think you can walk?"

Josh was already taking off his other shoe and sock and tying the ice packs around his ankle with the two socks. "I can bear some weight on it. Maybe I can lean on you a little bit on the way."

Quinn wrapped her arm around Josh's waist on the side of his good ankle. She began humming a familiar tune, as she carried the leashes and led her wounded warrior toward the car.

Chapter Thirty-nine

Two officers and a German shepherd stood behind Quinn's Toyota in the driveway, next to a police car with flashing lights. A second squad car, parked across the street, had another dog inside.

Quinn parked Josh's car on the street and helped him out, so they could join the group. Quinn recognized the dog's handler, Tom Porter. The two nodded at each other.

"We brought Rufus here right away to check out your car for explosives. Glad to say he didn't react."

Calvin and Holly sniffed around Rufus, and Holly leaped to gain his attention, but Rufus sat erect at his trainer's feet, ignoring her. "What's next?" Quinn asked. She shifted her weight, trying to get comfortable while supporting Josh.

"I'll sit on the porch," Josh said, hobbling to the three steps in front of the door. "C'mon, pups."

"Next, we switch dogs. Brad can explain while I take Rufus to the car." Tom whispered something unintelligible as he led Rufus away.

Brad introduced himself. "I'm new to the department, but I worked on the mainland for three years. I brought Max with me. We've partnered since he was a puppy." He shook Quinn's hand and waved at Josh. "Max is a highly skilled narcotics sniffer. He's got the best nose record of any police dog on the Gulf Coast.

Hearing his name, Max fidgeted behind the window of the squad car, already on alert. Brad hurried to the car door and opened it. Quinn expected Max to jump to the ground and run to her car, but the dog was much more disciplined than that.

Brad opened the car door and gently grabbed Max by the leash. He led the dog to where Quinn was standing, near the sidewalk leading to the porch.

"With your permission, we're going to check out your vehicle now. Can you open the doors or trunk if he cues us?" Quinn nodded. Brad lowered himself to the ground on one knee next to Max. He ruffled the fur on the dog's neck and spoke to him in low tones. "Max, ready to go to work?"

The dog panted, tongue lolling, and his front paws tapped the concrete. He was ready to take off.

At Max's eye level, Brad swung out his hand, palm up. The arc he cut in the air included the area of Quinn's house and yard. With the other hand, he held the leash loosely at his side. "Let's go, Max. Let's see what we can find."

The dog circled his head in the same direction Brad had indicated. Ears standing, he darted toward Quinn's flower bed, nose to the ground and trotted quickly in the direction of the driveway.

By now, several of Quinn's neighbors had noticed the flashing lights and hubbub on her yard. Mrs. Tartt, the elderly lady next door, stood at her front stoop, holding her Scottish terrier, Duffy, in her arms.

Two families from across the street stood at the curb. Officer Porter held them back with sweeping arm motions. Dogs barked from inside their houses, and the afternoon sun shot slanted rays, spotlighting the scene.

None of these affected Max. A dog on a mission, he sprinted from yard to driveway to car, sniffing the pavement, the air, and eventually the car.

Quinn gestured to Josh, an unasked question, and then shrugged. If there were no bomb and no drugs in her car, why would anyone have taken her car to the wharves? For that matter, how did the offending party move her car there and back, parking it exactly as she had left it? And what of Mrs. Oliver? Was her tip-off phone call the work of a friend or foe?

As Max approached the trunk of the car, he began whining and panting hard. He jumped a few inches from the ground and pawed the rear bumper, scratching. Brad rushed to the dog and called to Quinn to open the trunk.

She pulled the key fob from a zipped pocket and punched the trunk button. As the lid lifted, a collective sigh filled the air. The rear of the car contained a brick-shaped package that might be a kilo of cocaine.

"Good boy," Brad said to Max, handing him a treat and patting him on the head. "You've got another success story to add to your resume." The dog gobbled the treat and sat for more. "Okay, buddy. You deserve another one. Now let's go back to the car."

Officer Porter examined the car and took multiple photos. Backup was already on the way to relieve the officers and canine units and to take over the processing of the contraband in the trunk. As the owners of the car, Quinn and Josh needed to be interviewed, and the car needed to be towed for further inspection and investigation.

Whatever the intent, having drugs in the car could only mean trouble. The police shooed away the onlookers. Quinn pulled the picnic basket from the trunk of Josh's car and carried it to the porch. "Shall we have an indoor picnic?" she asked her wounded husband.

"Sorry," Officer Porter said. "Hate to interfere with your picnic, but Sergeant Schmidt is on the way. This isn't a routine operation, and he's gonna want to talk to you right away."

The package in her trunk, the call from Mrs. Oliver, the swelling of Josh's ankle—all caused a perfect storm of exasperation for Quinn. "Don't tell me we're going to be suspected of drug trafficking now. I surely wouldn't have called you to come check my car if I'd had anything to do with this."

Porter took a step back and turned away from Quinn's stare. "I'm sorry, Ms. Quinn. Sergeant Schmidt will explain things better than I can do. I'm sure he wouldn't want you to be upset."

Something about the boyish expression on the policeman's face touched Quinn. "I understand. I'll save my questions for Sergeant Schmidt."

She turned to help Josh unlock the door and turn off the alarm. He limped into the house behind the dogs and ahead of Quinn. He sat at the dinner table and rubbed his ankle. "I forgot all about eating, but I guess I'm hungry."

Quinn began unloading all the food they had packed that morning to take to the park. "Let me get you a painkiller and a fresh ice pack, and I'll sit with you."

"Yeah. Maybe Sergeant Schmidt'll want to share in our picnic."

Quinn filled the dogs' water bowls on the way back to the table. She put her head in her hands and gave a wry laugh. "Whatever. All I can say is today has turned out to be no picnic."

Chapter Forty

"C'mon, Quinn. You know I have to follow certain protocols. I can't let our relationship interfere with investigating a brick of cocaine in the trunk of your car."

While Sergeant Schmidt interviewed Quinn on the back porch, another officer sat with Josh in the living room. After they talked, Schmidt would interview Josh by himself.

All-too familiar with the divide and conquer strategy, Quinn shrugged in annoyance. "You didn't hesitate to trust me to help you with Mrs. Oliver, but now, all of a sudden, you don't trust me? It's obvious I'm being framed."

"I never said I didn't trust you, did I?" Schmidt pulled a notepad from his jacket pocket and flipped through the pages. "I agree, it's a frame, and a clumsy one at that. Still, my job requires me to investigate. If you'll just cooperate and answer a few questions, I'll leave you alone."

"And that's another thing," Quinn said. "Interviewing Josh and me separately, like we're criminals in collusion or something. Josh has nothing to do with this. The drugs were found in *my* car. Mrs. Oliver warned *me* that my car had traveled to the wharves. And most of all, *I'm* the one who called the police station to report the situation." Her throat tightened with the fear that once again she had brought trouble to the doorstep of her marriage.

"Quinn, can you please just answer these few questions?" The irritation in Schmidt's voice was clear. Maybe he'd had a hard day, too.

"Okay, shoot." Quinn held Holly in her lap, while the sun dropped lower into the horizon, and the temperature cooled. "Sooner we start, the sooner we finish."

"Let's start with the easy one. Where was your car when you left the house this morning, and was it locked?"

"I've been thinking about that," Quinn said. "The car was parked in the identical spot on the driveway when we got home as when we left. If it hadn't been for Mrs. Oliver's phone call, I never would have suspected it had been moved."

A dog barking inside made her want to run in, but she stayed put. "As for being locked, I'm a hundred percent sure it was. I'm super careful with locks and alarms these days."

"Who else has a key to your car?" Schmidt asked.

"Only Josh. He probably left it on the dresser in the bedroom, since we were going in his car." Quinn gazed at a squirrel scurrying on the branches of the old pecan tree in the center of the yard. Pretty soon it would disappear from view, leaving the back yard quiet and serene. But tomorrow it would return, and so might whoever had stuffed her trunk with drugs.

"No signs of break-in to the house. Probably key-cloned the car." Schmidt rubbed the side of his face and chin in a single motion. "To the best of your knowledge, what were the contents of the trunk before?"

"Spare tire and a couple of zippered insulated bags for groceries. I don't keep much in my trunk." Quinn wondered if she would ever be able to unsee the kilo of cocaine. "I've never had illegal drugs in my possession. I've never even seen them before."

Shrillness crept into her voice, and she began pacing, carrying Holly in the crook of her arm. "Schmidt, you know me and my family well. We are respectable citizens. I don't use illegal drugs, and I sure as hell wouldn't involve myself with buying, selling, transporting—whatever. The only stuff I'd fill my trunk with is groceries, dog food, or orchids."

Schmidt stood and leaned against a wooden post on the porch. "Relax, Quinn. I'm not trying to pin anything on you. I want you to think hard about this. Who might have gone to all the trouble and expense of setting you up? Someone with a grudge? Someone who wanted to ruin your reputation?"

"I have no idea. Except for Blackie and his crew, I don't think I have any enemies. As soon as Mrs. Oliver told me my car had been moved, I knew something was really wrong. That's why I called the police station immediately. Surely you can exclude me from suspicion, simply based on that."

Schmidt harrumphed and broke eye contact. He stared at his feet, as if contemplating running away.

"Well? What are you thinking?" Quinn asked.

"You might as well know." He paused. "Yours wasn't the only call to the police."

Dread climbed up Quinn's spine and wrapped itself around her neck. "What are you saying?"

"We got an anonymous tip that drugs could be found in your car. That you're dealing drugs out of the funeral home."

Chapter Forty-one
TRISH

I've locked my door and set the alarm tonight, and I'm going to do that all the time from now on. First, my sister gets herself killed. Then Julio disappears. Now someone's hijacked Quinn's car and taken it to the wharves and back. That can only mean one thing—drugs. Hmmm, I can't imagine who's responsible for some or all of that, but a girl can't be too careful in these rough times.

Of course, I'm no expert on illegal drugs in this town. Okay, so I've made a bad investment with my old friend and Liz's former boyfriend, Lionel. His expertise in running a huge drug operation in addition to strip clubs and dirty movies has given me false confidence and false security.

Now, too late, I recall Marvin's advice about trusting the wrong people: "A dog that brings you a bone is gonna take a bone away."

After putting five hundred thousand with dear old Lionel in a "sure-fire" scheme a year ago, I'm having regrets, big-time. The big monthly payments have dried up and stopped. I can't inquire about them, or my "seed money," because Lionel is sitting in jail. I don't know who's running the business, but I suspect Francisco.

I've blamed Quinn, since she's been instrumental in putting Lionel away. On the other hand, is it her fault that Lionel's committed crimes in the first place? Some days I want to wring that girl's neck, and other days I want to protect her.

The tracker on her car is an example. Following her whereabouts might lead me to the people who run Lionel's empire. They have a huge hard-on for her, not only because of her actions last year, but, I assume, because she's testifying in the upcoming trial. Even without knowing who they are, I know how they operate.

My original intent has been to use Quinn to find them. I need my money. But now, since Liz's death, I've seen a different Quinn. She's stronger and smarter, and she doesn't deserve this mess she's in. So, the tracker serves a dual purpose. It gives me an idea about Lionel's people, and it enables me to stay close to Quinn. Like it or not, she's part of my plan.

Today, for instance. On a Sunday afternoon, the main action at the wharves is cruise ship business, a perfect distraction for smuggling at the docks. Not that I know that much. As I say. you can thread a needle with the amount of knowledge I have about such things. Ask me about American literature, and I can talk for hours.

Meanwhile, I've put in a call to my old boyfriend, Dave Becker. His advice from that night at Gaido's isn't cutting it. I need to find out who's in charge of Lionel's operations and how to access my money. Thankfully, my conversations with Becker are protected by attorney-client privilege. I've made sure of that by putting the ol' guy on retainer. I don't need to fool around with drug dealers by myself.

Maybe Becker can advise me on security, too. I'm no safer than my sister. With all these things going on around me, I can't help being paranoid. In fact, the last two nights I've heard noises outside my bedroom window. When I peek through the drapes, shadowy shapes taunt me.

Of course, there have been loads of times when my sister has irritated the hell out of me. Her fiscal irresponsibility, her *laissez faire* attitude, even that raucous laugh. And then those times when she's put on those holier-than-thou airs. I'm not missing those, to be honest.

I need to calm down. I take a Xanax and climb into the cool sheets of my bed. Tomorrow I'll be able to think more clearly. I almost drift off when I open my eyes to a sound downstairs. A beep from the alarm, silence, and footsteps coming from the kitchen.

Oh, help me. What have I done?

Chapter Forty-two

After the police questioned Josh and left, Quinn knelt on the floor to tend to her husband's swollen ankle. "Maybe you should get an X-ray."

"I'll be all right. I didn't hear a pop when it happened, so that's a good sign. I need to stay off it and keep icing. I'll X-ray it in the morning if it's not better." He hugged her from behind. "Meanwhile, why don't we eat something and go to bed early? I'm exhausted."

The picnic food sat on the table, untouched, and nowhere near as appetizing as it had been that morning. "Do you want this, or I can heat up a frozen pizza?"

"Let's just eat the bread and cheese. And grapes. No wine for me, since I've taken pain killers. And I wouldn't touch Mrs. Oliver's cookies with a ten-foot pole."

"You think they're tainted?" Quinn asked. The poisoned hot dog popped into her mind. She hadn't thought of that but was glad they hadn't eaten any cookies. "We aren't the only ones she gave them to."

"Right now, I'm not ready to trust anything associated with that woman. Maybe it's not fair to blame her for any of this, but something's fishy with her and that tracker. For all we know, she's the one who stole your car and put coke in the trunk."

Quinn filled glasses with ice and water and carried them to the coffee table, where Josh had his feet elevated. "Whew. I'm tired, too." She brought the picnic food and plopped next to him. "Here's to a better day tomorrow."

The couple clinked and then drained their glasses. "Did Schmidt tell you about the call to the station?"

"No," Josh said. "What call?"

Quinn had lifted a bit of cheese and bread to her lips, but she set it down on her plate. "Evidently, they received an anonymous phone call reporting the drugs in my car. Whoever it was said I've been dealing from the funeral home."

"See? I wouldn't put it past Mrs. Oliver to have done that, too. I tell you, the woman is crazy."

Quinn's throat constricted at the thought of all the things Mrs. Oliver had told her, all the things the woman knew about her. "You know, she gave us a generous wedding gift. The cookies. The tracker. And I never told you. Yesterday at lunch she gave me a bracelet—the friendship bracelet I gave Ana years ago." She had stashed the trinket in her pocket and forgotten about it, but now she hurried to the closet to fish it out.

"This is beyond weird, Quinn. I don't care how she explained herself. You've put Ana behind you, and with good reason, and here comes your old teacher stirring that old pot?"

Quinn repeated what Mrs. Oliver had said about getting the bracelet from somebody at the strip club. "She offered it to Ana's parents, and they suggested she give it to me."

"That's according to Mrs. Oliver." He turned the bracelet over and stared at the inscription. "You have no way to verify that or anything else she's told you. What's an old lady like that doing at a strip club, anyway?"

Quinn wanted to cover her ears and scream. Not that she didn't appreciate Josh's perspective. The things he was saying were all things she agreed with, and she knew he wasn't implying anything derogatory about her. Still, the catalog of Mrs. Oliver's strange actions had started a buzzing in her head that threatened to put her over the edge.

She took a deep breath and let it out slowly. "You're right. I need to keep my distance from her from now on." She looked at her plate. "I can't eat."

Josh set his plate on the coffee table, as well. "The police don't seriously think you have anything to do with selling drugs, do they?"

"I don't think so. Sergeant Schmidt suggested I put it out of my mind for now." She put away the leftovers and set the dishes in the sink. "Easy for him to say. Not to mention that I don't have a car for however long it takes them to process."

"Well, that's one problem that's easy to solve, my love," Josh said, pointing to his ankle. "You can drive my car for however long it takes my ankle to get better." He reached for her hand and squeezed. "Now let's get the pups out and go to bed. Tomorrow's going to be a very interesting day."

Chapter Forty-three
TRISH

The friggin' Xanax has no sooner slid down my throat than someone's entering my house and disabling the alarm system. My heart pounds in my temples, and I may actually faint. Seconds seem like minutes as I debate whether to lock myself in the bathroom or sneak downstairs with the baseball bat I keep under my bed. Neither seems terribly efficient if the intruder is armed with a gun. I'm a sitting duck on the second floor.

My thoughts fly to Liz and the fact that she's gone. I go cold thinking that perhaps I'm destined for a similar fate. My eyes land on the laundry chute, which goes from my closet into the laundry room, next to the back door. I tighten the sash on my bathrobe and tiptoe to the closet in the dark.

The door to the chute is open from when I tossed my dirty clothes there a few hours ago. There's rustling, as though someone is moving through the kitchen and maybe the pantry. A stream of light rays, like from a flashlight, flits about at the edge of the small section I'm privy to.

The home invasion notwithstanding, I'm encouraged by the fact that no one is thrashing about, clambering up the staircase, or firing shots. Maybe the Xanax has taken effect, and I'm kidding myself.

I prop myself on the baseball bat and lean into the hole, hoping to catch a clue of what's going on. More rustling, and a few minutes later, a whoosh of cool air hits the chute. Another whoosh, and the airflow ceases. The back door has been opened and closed again.

I dash to the bedroom window, which overlooks the back yard. In the triangle of light emanating from the back porch onto the yard, a short, stocky figure, wearing a hoodie, moves quickly—not sprinting, but not strolling, either.

I make a snap decision. I'm going after them. I may be making a godawful mistake, but I must know who this is, a person who can so easily slip in and out of my house. I can't stay up here, fretting. For all I know, a bomb is ticking on my kitchen table.

I run down the stairs, still carrying the baseball bat, but I set it in the corner of the kitchen. It's slowing me down, and time is of the essence. As I pass the table on the way to the door, two objects register my attention, a keyring and a piece of paper.

Shivering, I keep going, hoping the intruder hasn't disappeared. I have questions.

Standing on the back porch, I peer into the dark night. A few lights gleam in the Reids' house across the way. I shade my eyes from my own porch light, then flip the switch, throwing the back yard into obscurity.

When my eyes adjust, a fine line of light shows up in the corner of the yard, about fifty feet from me, into the yard of an unoccupied rental house. I want to go back into the house to get a flashlight—or a lantern—I've read somewhere that candlelight can be seen for up to thirty miles on a dark night, but I don't have the luxury of time.

I gather the hem of my robe in one hand and grab the banister with the other, as I hustle down the stairs and into the grass. I curse myself for wearing flimsy house slippers, so thin that the chill in the grass seeps through.

Stop! Come back. I wish for the winged feet of Mercury. The intruder preserves the fifty-foot lead but may be unaware of the locked gate ahead on the neighbor's property. I speed up, hoping to use that to advantage.

The sliver of moon and sprinkle of stars give just enough light to keep me from veering into trees or bushes, but who knows what I'm stepping into on the ground. My eyes stay on the moving flashlight ahead. Its owner has either not heard me, or has chosen to ignore me, but I can't turn around and go back now.

Suddenly my ankle brushes against something gnarly, and I lose my balance. "Shit, help me!" I'm no longer polite as I squirm in the grass, holding my right wrist with my left. Apparently, I've used my arm to break a hard fall, and now it hurts like a sonofabitch. My head is spinning, and I might throw up, but I still squint, hoping the flashlight rays remain visible.

I can't get up on my own. I need two hands to distribute my weight, and my right hand is useless, throbbing. "Ayyyy." The plaintiveness in my voice surprises and scares me. I've never been a wienie about pain, but I've never been through so much at one time before, either.

I give into the situation for a few moments, scrambling in my now somewhat drugged mind for a solution, glad that the January temperature is mild. On the other hand, I'd love nothing more than something cold to press my wrist into. I curl into a fetal position and close my eyes, mustering a healthy dose of inner strength.

Clomping footsteps increasing in volume pull me out of the self-induced trance. I open my eyes to a chubby face, masked from the eyes down, and framed by a hoodie. A flashlight shines into my eyes.

"Come on. I'll help you," the person says. "Grab onto my ankle, and I'll help you stand." The voice, tinged with a Spanish accent, seems familiar. I try to place it but can't.

I get my feet beneath me and fix my bathrobe, one-handed. Pretty sure this is the same person who knows the combination to my alarm system, I measure my words carefully. "Thanks. I don't know what I'd have done without you." I turn on the sweetness, but I don't trust anyone who breaks into my house. No way.

"*De nada.*" The intruder removes her hoodie, revealing a mass of thick, dark hair. She wraps my right arm gingerly around her shoulder, and I lean into her frame. "Your wrist. Swelling already."

"Yes. Please come into the house with me. I'll get something for my wrist and something for you, as well." I think of what I can do to keep her with me, long enough to pump her for information.

We enter the kitchen through the back door, and I invite her to sit at the table, while I stumble to the freezer for an ice pack. The contents of the frigid compartment bring tears to my eyes for more reasons than one.

I turn to my erstwhile guest and say, "How would you like some chocolate chip cookies?"

Chapter Forty-four

The next morning, Quinn took Josh into the hospital to have his ankle X-rayed. Thanks to his buddy, a fellow in radiology, they didn't have to wait for the results. No fracture. Just a torn ligament, and only grade one. And thanks to another buddy, a fellow in orthopedics, Josh was able to fit himself into a boot and put weight on his ankle.

"I'll be fine now. You can go on to work and pick me up at the end of the day." Josh hobbled toward the exit to the parking lot, his hand nestled in the small of Quinn's back.

"Don't be a hero. When you get tired, take a break. Elevate and ice your ankle." Quinn didn't feel right about leaving her husband, but she didn't want to baby him, either. "I'm only ten minutes away, and I can drop everything to pick you up if need be."

"Thanks, Q. I promise I'll be careful." He winked and held the car door open for her. "You have your own dragons to battle at that so-called drug-dealing job of yours. Of the two of us, I'd say you have to be more vigilant today."

Josh gave her a dizzying kiss that said, aside from his ankle, nothing at all was wrong with him. She drove off to McFarland's with the car windows down, enjoying the cool air, blowing the curls away from her face.

When she arrived at work, her dad was waiting for her in the embalming room. Something was up. She could tell by the way he paced along the length of the room, hands clasped behind him.

"'Morning, Dad." Quinn dropped her key fob on a chair and gave her father a hug. "What's up?"

Not one to beat around the bush, John McFarland sighed. "Nothing, unless you count all the new gray hairs in my head. Let's sit. I have a few things to share with you."

A stomachache took root inside Quinn. Her dad's typical jovial demeanor had all but vanished. "Is it you? Or Mom? Or Jack?"

"No, kitten. Nothing like that." He handed Quinn's fob to her and pushed the only two chairs in the room together into an odd arrangement in a place not designed for conversing. He sat on the rolling chair and clasped his hands.

"A bit of a long story—hear me out. Marty Ramirez called. Even though the police aren't taking seriously the call about selling illegal drugs here, I'm upset to be targeted. Someone is out to ruin our reputation. Do you know why?"

The knot in Quinn's stomach loosened a bit. "No, Dad. I don't. But I've learned that evil people like drug dealers don't need reasons to be evil. Probably isn't personal. Maybe just a way to deflect attention from them, and they pick somebody at random."

Quinn reached out to touch her dad's hands. "Since the police aren't taking this seriously, why should we?"

"You're probably right," her dad said, rubbing his eyes. "Sometimes being the third generation in this business is burdensome. I try not to let the reputation of McFarland's tarnish on my watch. I have a feeling you and Jack may feel the same when you're in charge."

There it was again. The guilt of leaving the funeral home to pursue another career would never leave her. "I can tell something else is bothering you."

"You know me so well, kitten. It's about Mrs. Oliver."

Quinn straightened her posture and leaned forward. "What about her?"

"Well, you know we cremated her sister last week after she met with your mother. We held the ashes, because Mrs. Oliver ordered a customized urn, and that didn't come in until this morning." He stood and walked around the embalming table, talking and making eye contact. "After Marty told me about the anonymous call to the police, he switched topics. He said Mrs. Oliver is at the center of this investigation. He asked about the plans for the sister's remains, and when I told him, he asked a favor."

Quinn smiled. Unlike Sergeant Schmidt, the chief of police didn't ask for many favors, but when he did, her dad usually accommodated him. "And?"

"He wanted you to be the one to give Mrs. Oliver her sister's remains, and he had specific questions he wanted you to ask her. He was going to talk to you directly."

Quinn's sigh came from deep inside and sounded more like a long whine. "Again? I hate to disappoint you—and Chief Ramirez—but I really need to keep a distance from Mrs. Oliver. Besides, my asking questions isn't the same as having an officer ask them."

"I understand and agree, and so does Marty. He had some kind of strategy worked out. He figured Mrs. Oliver would open up to you, and then they could follow up with a more formal interrogation."

"You're talking in past tense, Dad. Has the strategy changed?"

Smiling for the first time in this conversation, her dad sat and took her hand. "Very perceptive. Everything's changed. I called Mrs. Oliver this morning to tell her the urn had come in. I was hoping we could get this over with quickly and get her out of our hair."

"Were you planning to check with me first?" If not, Quinn didn't like the implication.

"Whether you agreed or not, we still had to get the remains to her. Let me finish, Quinn." He took a long breath. "I called right at nine o'clock. You were driving Josh, and I knew you'd be a little late. Anyway, immediately, I got a weird message—something like, 'The person you're trying to reach is unavailable. Please leave a message after the beep.'"

"Nothing strange about that, is there?"

"Except there was no beep. The phone went dead and made a weird sound. I called Marty, who said they'd check it out and get back to me. Evidently the phone company said the phone had been disabled."

"Like she put it on airplane mode?" Quinn couldn't see where this was leading.

"No, like the phone had been damaged or submerged in water— something like that. So, the police went to Mrs. Oliver's house to see what was happening. When they arrived, the garage door was open, and the car was gone. The door to the house was unlocked, too. They entered and found a mess. Drawers open, empty hangers on the closet floor. Like someone had packed and left in a hurry."

"Maybe Mrs. Oliver had to go out of town suddenly. A sick relative or something." The scenario sounded implausible, even to Quinn.

"That's what they thought, too, at first. But then they went into the kitchen. On the counter was a hammer, and next to it, Mrs. Oliver's cellphone—smashed to smithereens.

Chapter Forty-five
TRISH

Here I am, so upset and hurting. My wrist is swollen and red, maybe sprained. I'm having a hard time lifting or carrying anything, and I could sit on the hard floor and cry my eyes out. But who would hear me, and who would care?

I keep playing the words of my intruder in my head. "You are in *mucho* danger." I trust her intentions, but the things she's warned me about have done a number on me. First, she tells me she's Julio's *hermana*, his sister. I think, yes. That's what is so familiar about her face.

Julio is dead, she says, followed by a rush of Spanish words, uttered like a hurricane's torrent. All I can gather is that the whole Martinez family is at risk because of the older brother's nefarious activities.

"You are not safe, either," she says. "That's why I come to your house. To give you your keys and a message from Julio." She's panting and teary-eyed when she says this. "Many months before he dies, Julio tells me, 'You must go to Mrs. Oliver if something happens to me. Her alarm code and keys, you must get them out of here. Warn her about Francisco.'"

I have tears in my eyes, even now. Sweet Julio. Always thinking of me. I miss him already, and the Xanax in my system exacerbates my grief.

The sister—named Maria—insists that I hurry. "You must leave," she says, along with another avalanche of words in Spanish. I catch the word *dinero* repeated several times, and I wonder whose money she refers to—Julio's or mine. Either way, she has an earnestness about her, and I can't help taking her seriously. I thank her and send her on her way, loading her up with several tins of cookies from my freezer.

To be honest, Francisco scares me, even without the warning from Maria. My comfort level with Blackie doesn't exist with Francisco. Julio has been a buffer for me, an insurance policy. I've always believed with Julio in my employ and in my bed, I'm safe.

But things change. After Liz, I can't quite think of Julio in the same way.

And Francisco is a hothead. Blackie's arrest has multiplied Francisco's power and made him lust for more. The cockfighting bust and his little brush with surgery hasn't stopped him a bit.

After Maria leaves, I fix a makeshift sling for my wrist. Not easy to do with only one working hand. An ice pack from the freezer makes a perfect liner. I trudge upstairs and stand in my closet, staring at all the belongings and wondering how I can possibly take them all, and how I can possibly leave them behind.

My eyes land on a couple of handbags inherited from my mother, Melinda McDaniel, a most proper and elegant lady. I've had them since she died, but I've never used them, never even opened them. I pull down a turquoise suede bag with a gold handle, so sixties.

The clasp has tarnished a little, but I can picture my mother carrying this bag at the side of her hip, her posture ramrod straight, and her Jackie Kennedy hair perfectly coiffed. A few treasures lie inside—three yellow tissues, a book of matches, a pair of matching suede gloves, a receipt, and a ticket stub from the movie, *The Spy Who Came in from the Cold.*

I fight against more tears. My mother's gone, and also my father, my sister, my husband, and Julio. Too much loss, no matter the circumstances. I conjure my mother's image again and realize I can't sit and cry all night. I must take matters into my own hands. I must leave—and soon.

I throw clothes and toiletries into a suitcase, literally without a plan or a destination. I pack the suede purse, too, and that book of short stories Quinn gave me, maybe for good luck. I ignore the pain in my arm and the drowsiness that drags me toward the bed.

The last things I do before I leave the house are set my cell phone on the kitchen counter and grab a hammer. The cell phone is a liability I must get rid of.

As I walk out the door, leaving it unlocked, I think of Quinn. I'm a whirling force of energy, stronger than all the impediments in my way.

Except for one. And that one, when it hits, reminds me that I'm not in control at all.

Chapter Forty-Six

Quinn went through the motions at work, while her mind stayed focused on Josh and Mrs. Oliver. The former, apparently, was making it through the day without any problems. They had only texted each other once by noon, and, no, he didn't need to leave early.

Mrs. Oliver was a different matter. Despite having vowed to stay away from her former teacher, Quinn found herself curious, her emotions thawing, knowing they couldn't visit, even if she wanted to. Was Mrs. Oliver's disappearance voluntary or forced? Temporary or permanent? The smashed cell phone gave an ominous impression, but maybe Mrs. Oliver had disabled it herself and left the hammer on purpose.

Surely the police were gathering information from the scene, checking for fingerprints, and inspecting the phone's memory. As much as she disliked being involved with the police, she now had a perverse wish to tag along with whichever officer was investigating at Mrs. Oliver's house.

After taking care of some last-minute details in the embalming room, Quinn relocated to the office, where she proofread obituaries before sending them in to the newspaper. Her parents and Jack were working a funeral, so she had the place all to herself.

Just after noon, the front door chimed. Quinn jumped from the sound and popped her head around the office door.

"Got a minute?" her future sister-in-law asked. Mary's lips were pursed, and her eyebrows furrowed

"For you, anytime." Quinn gave her a hug and ushered her into the small office. "Have a seat."

With limited options, Mary sat on the desk, swinging her long legs over the side. She panned the room, as if to ensure no other ears could eavesdrop on what she was about to say. "Hey, the medical examiner's released the Martinez body back to you, since the family requested McFarland's to begin with. Sad story. Everything we've learned—he was a good guy. Worked hard, stayed clean. Only hinky thing's the relationship with the Oliver woman's sister— maybe both of them. We can put him in the bed with the semen and the dirt for sure."

Quinn's previous conversation with Mrs. Oliver about sex had prepared her to believe that the sister had been promiscuous while switching places, but *both of them*? She couldn't picture her English teacher having an affair with the gardener. "Mrs. Oliver told me about her sister's sex life, and I reported that to Sergeant Schmidt. But not Mrs. Oliver's. She told me hers was a 'quiet life.'"

"I hate to break it to you, girlfriend, but the lady was playin' you. We've asked around, talked to neighbors. She had many a late-night visitor in that fancy house of hers since her husband died, and not when the sister was visiting, either." Mary picked at a cuticle and popped the finger in her mouth. "This Julio drove a truck with a flatbed trailer to transport his equipment. Sometimes at night, the neighbors saw his truck, without the hitch, driving into Mrs. Oliver's garage, and then the garage door closing. Hate to say it, but I think he fertilized more than the lawn over there."

Conflicting memories of Mrs. Oliver battled in Quinn's head. If true, Mary's story meant Mrs. Oliver had out-and-out lied. When she said her sister suffered from a borderline personality, was she also describing herself? Quinn flashed back to the television show she'd watched about twins. Didn't the psychologist say the genomic mismatches found in identical twins are miniscule, compared to the matches?

Maybe *none* of the things Mrs. Oliver had told her were true. "Assuming you're right, how does that affect me? Why are you telling me this?"

"You and Jack and your parents, too, need to be very careful dealing with the Martinez family. You could opt to send the body elsewhere. Tell them you're too busy right now. Whoever they send to make arrangements for Julio, they will also pump you for information. Everyone in town knows you have a relationship with Mrs. Oliver. You even went out to lunch with her recently, right?"

Quinn bristled at the lack of privacy, but this was nothing new. "So what?"

"Let's just say, Mrs. Oliver is not on Francisco Martinez' good list. And if the cockfighting ring is linked to the adult entertainment business, as we suspect, Martinez and Blackie are partners. Unfortunately, that puts you in the same pool as Mrs. Oliver."

The formula, "If A is like B, and B is like C, then A is like C," ran through Quinn's head. She didn't like being one of the letters. "So, what are you suggesting?"

"If you take the funeral on, let Jack, or better yet, your parents deal with the Martinez family. Make yourself scarce whenever they call or come around. If you see or hear anything suspicious, don't wait. Call for help." Mary paused and stared at her hands. "You know, this isn't an official conversation. I could be disciplined for sharing all this. But I'll do anything I can to protect you." Mary jumped up, wrapped her arms around Quinn's shoulders, and squeezed.

When she hugged back, the hard edges of Mary's gun pressed into Quinn's side—a reminder of the perilous position Quinn found herself in, again.

Chapter Forty-seven
TRISH

I've packed some stuff in a few bags and bounced them down the stairs, one at a time, with my good hand. I'm so winded I think I might faint, but I can't stop to catch my breath. I have one more item to stuff into the suitcase before I take off.

While Julio has been an insurance policy, this item has been a total ace-in-the-hole. It's after midnight when I head for the storage shed behind the garage. The three-quarter moon is almost directly overhead, sharing enough light for me to find my way without turning on my flashlight. I grip the key to the shed in my left hand, knowing how awkward unlocking the door will be.

But when I reach the entrance to the shed, the door is unlocked and slightly ajar. My hand shakes, and my mouth goes dry. I hope it's not a setback. Only two people have keys to the shed—Julio and me. And Julio's key, left by Maria, is the one in my hand. I push the door open, not knowing what to expect inside.

An earthy smell greets me first, much stronger than usual. I wave the flashlight straight ahead. The bins and boxes on the far wall rest neatly on their shelves, as always. Bags of fertilizer, mulch, and wood chips are stacked to my left, along with colorful plant pots from Mexico, waiting for spring. I'm not interested in those now.

I turn to the right, intending to lay eyes on the deep horse trough that lines that side of the structure. I've filled the trough to the brim with gardening soil and covered the whole thing with tarps, giving Julio a bogus explanation about volume discounts. Truthfully, I've used the soil to hide a very valuable object, the one I need to take with me.

Illuminated by the flashlight, the trough causes acid to rise in my throat. The tarps lie on the floor amid huge piles of moist, black soil. The trough sits more than half empty, a fortress violated. Gasping with disbelief, I plod through the dirt, easing myself closer and shining the flashlight into the massive container. Topsoil covers my shoes, and I resist the impulse to remove them.

The trough is nearly empty. The item I've come for, so carefully wrapped and craftily hidden, is nowhere to be seen. So much for having an ace-in-the-hole. I remember the urgency in Blackie's voice when he handed me the "hot" pistol. "Here, take this ACP and put it someplace safe. As long as you have it, nobody from Martinez' gang will bother you. They know you're my surrogate."

"Well, Blackie, I've lost your automatic Colt pistol. I've failed you," I say aloud. "And more importantly, I've failed myself." But then I remember Marvin's.

Chapter Forty-eight

After Mary left the funeral home, Quinn emailed the obituaries to the *Daily News*, and she shut down the office computer. Her family hadn't returned from the church and cemetery, so she still had the place to herself. Being alone in the deadly silence usually didn't creep her out, but after Mary's information about the Martinez family and the news about Mrs. Oliver's disappearance, Quinn couldn't wait to pick up Josh and go home to the puppies. The only problem: she was ready to leave work for the day, but Josh wasn't.

The whirr of the vacuum cleaner from one of the chapels startled her as she turned off the light and closed the office door behind her. Grateful for the company, Quinn followed the sound to chat with Marlena Castellanos, the seventeen-year-old daughter of her neighbor, Anise.

"Hey, Marlena. You got your braces off? Your teeth look beautiful." Marlena had been coming in after school to do light cleaning three days a week for more than a year. Quinn appreciated Marlena's sweet smile, boundless energy, and willingness to help with anything. She would miss these when Marlena went away to college a year from now. Although, come to think of it, Quinn, herself, would be gone from McFarland's by that time.

"Hi, Miss Quinn," Marlena said, shutting off the machine. "I haven't seen you since the wedding." Today Marlena wore a dozen or more braided bracelets on each wrist.

"I'm happy to see you, too. How's your mom doing?"

"Fine. She's at home, studying. One more semester, and she'll be finished with her master's degree. She can't wait."

"That's wonderful," Quinn said, throwing an arm around Marlena's shoulders and squeezing. "And soon it will be you graduating and moving on." *And me.*

Anise was at the tail-end of graduate studies in psychology. Her goal was to work with agencies to help those who couldn't afford private psychotherapy.

Quinn said goodbye and left Marlena to finish and lock up, assuming her parents didn't return beforehand. A brainstorm brewed in Quinn's mind. While she waited for Josh's text, she'd see if Anise was up for company.

Quinn's neighborhood was only a few blocks away. The sun's glow bathed the western sky in pinks and oranges as the air cooled in its wake. The aroma of smoked meats and barbecue sauce permeated the air from the nearby mid-island restaurant. Quinn could taste that tang without taking a bite.

A twenty-year-old rusted Chevrolet stood in Anise's driveway. Through the living room window shone a quiet scene of study, including an overhead light, a computer, a stack of books, and a long-haired woman, bent over her work. Quinn hesitated to interrupt, but curiosity had already gotten the best of her.

She knocked on the front door and waited. Anise opened the door, peering around the edge. When her eyes met Quinn's, she broke into a brilliant white smile. "Hello, my friend," she said, flinging the door to its full width. "Come in, come in. Let me get you a drink, or some *churros*, maybe?"

"I hate to disturb you," Quinn said, declining the offer with a shake of her head. "If you have a few minutes, I thought I'd run something past you." She sat at the table where Anise indicated.

"Of course. I need a study break, anyway. This paper I'm writing is a bugger." Anise leaned forward on one elbow and pushed a strand of hair behind an ear.

Quinn considered how best to proceed. "I've got a strange question. What do you know about people with borderline personality disorders?"

Anise squinted. "O-kay," she said, dragging the word through more than two syllables. "I won't ask about your motivation. Or whether you have a particular person in mind. I will say, however, that the borderline diagnosis can be quite serious."

"Really?" Quinn asked. "How does a person become a borderline? Does it run in families?"

"It can be genetic. Also may come from environmental problems during childhood, like abuse or trauma. The symptoms don't usually show up until puberty, when they come on like a speeding freight train."

Quinn tried but failed to picture Mrs. Oliver and her twin sister as adolescents. Double the trouble, if they both had the disorder. "What are the typical symptoms?"

"Oh, anything from impulsivity and anger to promiscuity and bad judgment. Patients often have trouble trusting or relating to others. They fear abandonment yet push people away. You've heard the expression, 'Running hot and cold?' A borderline might be friendly, even loving, one day and distant or cruel the next."

Quinn thought about Mrs. Oliver's generous gifts, the invitation to lunch, Ana's bracelet, and putting a tracker on her car. Her behavior had certainly been erratic. And sleeping with the gardener *might* qualify as impulsive. "If someone is diagnosed, would it be a life sentence?"

"That depends," Anise said. "Most people improve as they mature, but behaviors can be exacerbated by drugs or alcohol."

The martinis at Mrs. Oliver's place at Gaido's, when she ate with Mr. Becker popped into Quinn's mind. The picture of a very disturbed woman coalesced.

"Of course, there is treatment. Psychotherapy, sometimes drug therapy. Patients can achieve a modicum of relief if they're willing to work hard at it. If not, they might succumb to depression, or even suicide." Anise paused to wrap her hair around a clip. "If you know someone in this situation, Quinn, you need to get them help. I can give you the names of places he or she can go to for support."

Before Quinn could respond, a text beep came in on her cellphone. Josh, ready to be picked up. "I need to go. Thanks so much. Ordinarily, I'd appreciate that list, but the person I'm thinking about—well, it may be too late for her." Mrs. Oliver's twin was dead, and Mrs. Oliver was missing.

"Oh, I'm sorry," Anise said, bowing her head, as if in prayer. "I hope it wasn't a suicide."

Quinn gave her neighbor a heartfelt hug. "No, not a suicide."

Chapter Forty-nine

At home the next morning, before driving Josh to work and going to the funeral home, Quinn took the dogs out. While they frolicked in the back yard, she planned her day. Fortunately, Holly was mastering the art of peeing and pooping outside, and she confined her chewing to the dog biscuits and chew toys Quinn gave her. Quinn put the big bottle of bitter apple in her car to return to Mrs. Reid.

As much as she missed her own car, Quinn enjoyed dropping Josh off in the morning and picking him up in the evening. Bookending the workday with togetherness gave her a celebratory fizz. Less swollen now, his ankle allowed him to do more walking and standing. "Soon I'll be driving *you* to work and back," he said, kissing her goodbye.

Quinn couldn't envision that. Her schedule at McFarland's gave her much more flexibility. This morning, for example, Josh started shift at eight, but she didn't start until ten. That gave her time to run errands, like taking the anti-chewing spray back to Mrs. Reid's. Quinn had written a thank you note and stuffed the product and the note into a gift bag lined with colorful tissue paper. Due to the early hour, she would drop it on the doorstep, so as not to wake any people or puppies who slept late.

When she turned onto the street that encircled the neighborhood, Quinn came upon a pair of police cruisers parked in Mrs. Oliver's driveway. *Hmm…has Mrs. Oliver returned? Or are they looking for clues in search of her?*

Quinn drove around the curve to the Reid house, where she pulled into the circular driveway near the front door. Leaving her motor running, she jumped out of the car with the gift bag and tiptoed to the door. All was quiet until she set the bag down, and then a torrent of yapping filled her ears. Sorry to have caused the commotion, Quinn returned to her car and drove off.

By now the sun shone in a cloudless sky, and when Quinn returned to the street in front of Mrs. Oliver's, she braked and stopped. Maybe one of the squad cars belonged to Sergeant Schmidt. She ignored the crime scene tape and approached the front door almost as stealthily as she had the Reids', listening for signs of activity. Hearing none, she peered into the front windows. With no policemen in sight, Quinn eased around the driveway at the side of the house, leading to the garage. Perhaps something was going on in the back.

She inched around the garage, where voices and more police tape drew her. Sergeant Schmidt stood at the doorway to a storage shed, talking to someone inside. "Whatever they were looking for, it must have been valuable to cause all this mess."

Quinn froze. Should she return to her car and drive away before Schmidt noticed her, or should she make her presence known? Before she could decide, Schmidt ducked under the tape and headed for the front, carrying a large, sealed paper bag with a tag on it.

"Quinn. What are you doing here?"

"I—I was in the neighborhood and spotted the cars. I hoped it was you. I wanted to ask you when my car might be released."

The officer's eyebrow shot up, but his tone remained friendly. "I'll have to check on that. Shouldn't be too much longer." He kept walking toward his car, glancing at Quinn every few steps, as if thinking about saying something else, maybe waiting for her to speak.

"Any news about Mrs. Oliver?" she finally asked, as he opened the squad car and set the bag onto the seat. "I heard she's disappeared."

Schmidt rubbed his forehead and leaned against the car frame. "You know the rules. We shouldn't talk about ongoing investigations."

Keeping all traces of sarcasm out of her voice, Quinn said, "Except when you ask me to help?"

Perhaps the question hit its mark. Schmidt's face reddened, and he glanced around. "I can see why that doesn't seem fair. Maybe it wouldn't hurt to tell you a little bit." He took in a long breath and blew it out. "We don't know where she is. We found a lot of soil in the shed behind the garage. We'll try to match it up to other evidence we have. Looks like someone buried something under a whole lot of gardening dirt. And somebody knew it was there and dug it up. Could be important, not just in finding Mrs. Oliver, but in solving her sister's murder."

Schmidt pulled a pair of aviator sunglasses from his shirt pocket and put them on. "And I hope that satisfies your curiosity, because that's all I can say."

Quinn stared at the evidence bag sitting on the car seat, and something clicked in her memory. Elizabeth Lavender and Julio Martinez both got soil on their feet and on Mrs. Oliver's bedsheet.

They might be the ones who unearthed whatever was buried in the shed. And maybe that had gotten them killed.

Chapter Fifty

Quinn crossed the threshold of the embalming room at three minutes before ten, with the sense that the day was already getting away from her. Remembering yesterday's visit from Mary Hallom, she called her reliable transport guy, Zeke, and asked him to pick up the body of Julio Martinez from the medical examiner's office.

Not looking forward to working on Martinez after several days post-mortem and post-autopsy, she nevertheless vowed to do her best to honor the man's life with her services. When she was learning the ropes, her mother taught her that lesson. "If you take a moment to humanize the client at the beginning of a job, you elevate your work "

Despite Mary's warning that Quinn was in the crosshairs of Francisco Martinez, she readied herself to prepare his brother's body. Having Jack or her mother do the job would be a cop-out, and, besides, the deceased's family never knew which of them did the actual work. Julio, according to Mary, was a decent person. Quinn didn't foresee a problem working on him.

Within minutes, Rory and Zeke, the transporters, showed up at the back door, ready to unload the body. Quinn exchanged pleasantries with the two cousins.

"Second time's the charm, eh?" Zeke said, as he opened the back of the hearse. Rory assembled the gurney and rolled it over.

Quinn crossed her fingers. "Hope so. I hate asking you to go back and forth with the same person. Wasting our time."

"We don't mind, Quinn. You might say it's been a double pleasure." Rory flashed a mouthful of gleaming teeth that added warmth to his freckled face.

They rolled the bagged body into the room and transferred it to the stainless-steel table, where Quinn's equipment stood ready. "Appreciate the quick service."

"No problem. We'll drop off the paperwork to the front office and get out of your hair now." Zeke patted Quinn on the top of her head, a well-worn gesture of affection from the days when he was in high school, and she was in elementary.

After they left, Quinn took a break. Her stomach reminded her that she'd skipped breakfast, so she sauntered to the coffee room, where her dad's pot of joe filled the air. This was the room where her dad's buddies, including Chief Ramrez, met a couple of times a week to solve all the problems of the city, if not the world. Today the room was empty, so Quinn microwaved water for tea, and rummaged in the freezer for a cinnamon roll.

Her parents' voices emanated from the office. She stood outside the closed door, breakfast in hand, debating whether to interrupt them or not. Family and business didn't always mix well. Before she could make up her mind, the door creaked open, and her father hustled through it, headed for the embalming room.

"Dad. What's up?" Quinn said. A peek inside showed that Zeke had already left. Her mother was flipping through paperwork and didn't look up.

Her father spun around. "Hey. You surprised me. I'm on my way to you right now. Something important's come up."

"Do you want to talk here?" Quinn pointed to the office.

"No, let's go to your area. I don't want to disturb your mother."

Quinn didn't even try to match the stride of her dad's long legs, since she didn't want to spill her hot tea. They reached the embalming room, and her father opened the door for her.

"Go ahead and eat your breakfast," he said. "I can wait a few minutes."

Figuring the news would kill her appetite, anyway, she shook her head and set the tea and roll on her desk. "What's going on?"

"Is this Julio Martinez?" Her dad pointed to the body bag on the table.

Quinn nodded. Between Mary's warning and her dad's expression, she knew there was trouble.

"We can't touch him. His family's reneged. You'll have to call Zeke and Rory to come pick him up." McFarland's voice, usually modulated, came out loud enough to wake the dead.

"Have a seat, Dad." Families backed out from time to time, nothing to fret about. Quinn rolled her chair next to her father's, so their knees touched. "Do you want me to send him to the county?"

"No." He stood again and began pacing. "This isn't a case of indigence. Something else is going on. We received a call from the sister, Maria. She said the head of the family wants the body taken immediately to Carnes."

Jay Carnes, though a competitor, had been a lifelong friend of Jack's and ran a reputable business. "Why is that a problem?

We get clients from them sometimes, too. They'll do a good job. And besides, Mary told me yesterday to steer clear of the Martinez family as much as possible."

"The problem isn't what she said, but how she said it. At the end of the call, she said, "'*Estoy orando por usted y su familia.*'" Her father stopped pacing and looked her in the eye. "Maybe she thinks I don't understand Spanish, but I take that as a threat."

I'm praying for you and your family. Given the crazy situation with the two murders, the drugs placed in her car, the poisoned hot dog in her yard, and Mrs. Oliver's disappearance, Quinn had to agree. "I'll send the body over right away." She couldn't help feeling sorry for Julio Martinez. At the moment, his body had become a hot potato.

Chapter Fifty-one
TRISH

I would have loved to flee to New York, take up residence in Liz's shabby apartment, and slip into her world again. Nothing simpler or more expedient. But now that Liz is dead, prudence dictates otherwise. Dead people don't reappear. Not even I can change that, and I might screw myself by trying. For all I know, Sergeant Schmidt keeps in touch with someone in the New York PD, and they're watching her place and mine.

Dave Becker always says, "The innocent have nothing to fear," and he's encouraged me to stay put. But in this case, Becker doesn't know everything. I wonder if he would stay put if threatened by Francisco Martinez. Even the Martinez siblings, Julio and Maria, don't believe I'm safe.

As to my innocence, who in this world is completely free of sin? Even with good intentions, sometimes we fall into situations where we must stray from our own morality in order to survive. I don't consider myself a bad person, but following the straight and narrow path in life has not been my strongest suit, even as a teacher.

Anyway, I've bandaged my wrist, conveniently hiding my one identifying mark, the *pi* tattoo. I'm sporting a new subtle dark brown pixie cut, totally different and easy to manage. Using some of Liz's costume and makeup tricks, I've transformed myself into a nice-looking middle-aged lady. I can play the part just as well as Liz, maybe better.

If anyone's looking for me, and I imagine they are, I'm right here under their noses, less than fifty miles away. This way I can keep watch on the local news, specifically, my own situation, but I'm ensconced in a modest condo, owned by Blackie's empire. I can't leave a trail on my credit cards and need to conserve my cash. So what if I share space with a woman who takes her clothes off for a living? I'm the last one to be judgmental. She's gone at night and sometimes in the daytime, too, so my privacy is preserved.

If the police find me, I'll just say I was aiming for a change of pace. If the Martinez bunch find me—well, without the gun Blackie gave me for insurance, I'm a dead duck.

Chapter Fifty-two

Quinn's brother burst into the embalming room while Quinn was on the phone with Carnes Funeral Home, making arrangements for Julio Martinez. Now recovered from last year's kidney transplant, Jack served as the "face man" of McFarland's.

"Hi, little sis," he said, smelling of sausage and plopping a kiss on her cheek. "What're you doin'?"

Quinn put a hand to her other ear as she listened to the Carnes voicemail. After the beep she left a message, asking for a callback. "Trying to transfer the Martinez body to the competition."

"Already taken care of," Jack said, inserting a toothpick into his mouth. "I sat next to Jay at the Rotary breakfast this morning. He's sending his people to get the body, so we don't have to."

"I wish somebody'd told me," Quinn said, immediately regretting the whiny tone. "Never mind. My day is starting out a little crazy."

"Yeah. I saw Josh's car out back. Any idea when the police will release yours?" He leaned his hips against the table.

"Later today, maybe. More importantly, I hope they find evidence of who put the drugs in my trunk. Did I tell you about the poisoned hot dog in my back yard?"

"Someone tried to kill your *dogs*? What the hell?" Jack removed the toothpick from his mouth and made a show of throwing it in the trash can.

Quinn's lips curved into a half-smile. "I knew it. You love Calvin more than me."

"What? Of course not. It's just—anyone who would hurt those adorable animals…the thought kills me." Jack pushed the two rolling chairs together and motioned for Quinn to sit. "Listen, I'm trying to put two and two together. I've picked up bits and pieces from things Mary has said or done since the rooster raid. She doesn't talk, but sometimes I hear stuff."

Not for the first time, Quinn wondered what it would be like to live with a police officer. The endless stress from dicey situations might keep her up at night. On the other hand, having an officer of the law close by could provide a sense of security and a connectedness to what the "good guys" knew. "Tell me."

"Well, this guy, Francisco Martinez, he heads up a whole network of criminals. Not just the cockfighting, but drugs, prostitution, trafficking. There's a love-hate going on between him and your guy French, I mean Blackie. Right now, with Blackie in jail, Martinez is dominating."

"Interesting, but not surprising. I don't see what any of that has to do with why Martinez would set me up for drugs."

"I didn't either," Jack said. "Until late last night, when I saw a text pop up on Mary's phone while she showered." He leaned forward and lowered his voice to a whisper. "You need to promise me you won't tell anyone I looked at her phone. She could get in a lot of trouble for that, and so could I."

Quinn crossed her heart with a forefinger. "So what did the text say?" Her breath caught in her throat.

"Well, it wasn't a complete sentence—just four words— and I think you'll see why I took notice. 'Lavender and Martinez poison—formaldehyde."

Chapter Fifty-three

Quinn couldn't stop thinking about the poison used to kill Elizabeth Lavender and Julio Martinez. Trying not to succumb to paranoia, she hated that of all the poisons in the world, the murderer chose the one most likely to be found in a funeral home. And the person at McFarland's most likely to use formaldehyde, would be Quinn.

After Martinez' body was picked up, Quinn had no other work to do. She offered to make the bank deposit, and her dad suggested she take the afternoon off. The prospect of an open afternoon put wings on her thoughts. She took advantage by swinging home to change into running clothes and leashing Calvin for a proper run.

She cringed from the puppy dog eyes from Holly. "One day soon you'll be a big girl, and I'll take you for a run, too."

The weather gods had blessed the runners with a gorgeous January day—sunny and breezy; cool, but not cold. The faint roaring and briny aroma of the Gulf reached all the way to Quinn's house, mid-island.

Quinn warmed up by stretching her calves, and she laughed out loud when Calvin did the same. The little guy cherished runs even more than she did. "Ready, Cal? Let's go." They took off at a slow pace, increasing their speed after about two minutes.

Enjoying the way muscle memory kicked in, Quinn concentrated on her breathing—cool air in, warm air out. Her pounding of the pavement, so rhythmic, created a happy tune that resonated all the way to her soul.

The intensity of her runner's high, almost pushed the thoughts of murder and drugs and formaldehyde away. Someone evil enough to kill twice had targeted Quinn as a scapegoat. Perhaps impatient for Quinn's arrest, the killer had loaded her car's trunk with cocaine, further discrediting her.

Clop, clop! Quinn's thoughts pounded in her head with an uncomfortable clarity.She came to the end of her usual route, but her muscles and her brain pushed her to keep going.

What did I do to deserve all of this? Who would want to harm my reputation, and why? Perhaps a follower of Blackie's? Only one answer surfaced. If arrested and charged, Quinn would lose credibility, rendering her testimony against Blackie useless.

Francisco Martinez appeared to have a beef with Quinn, too, though over what, she couldn't fathom. Josh saved his life, and in return, Martinez spit on him. Did he fear Quinn's bringing down of Blackie would spill over onto him?

Quinn glanced at Calvin, whose panting and tongue-lolling signaled fatigue. She looked around for a place to rest before heading back, and she realized she was standing outside of Ana's parents' house, a place that held many memories—some good, some bad, and some traumatic. Maybe, unconsciously, she had intended to come here all along.

While these washed over her, a Chevrolet Malibu entered the driveway, and Mrs. French stepped out. Without noticing Quinn, she clicked open her trunk and began lifting bags of groceries and carrying them to the porch.

"Let me help you," Quinn said. Calvin sat on the grass while Quinn grabbed a couple of bags and followed Ana's mother.

"Oh, hi, Quinn. What brings you to this neighborhood? You've been on my mind lately. Did you receive the ID bracelet?"

Quinn had almost forgotten about the bracelet Mrs. Oliver had brought her. "Yes. Thank you very much for thinking of me." She pointed at her westie. "Calvin and I are taking a much-needed run."

"That's lovely. Can you and Calvin come in for a minute? I have something I'd like to show you."

Quinn had mixed feelings as she entered the house where she had spent a lot of time as a young girl. The kitchen and breakfast room hadn't changed a bit. A portrait of Ana at the age of ten or so hung over the mantle in the living room. A short sob, more like a hiccup, escaped Quinn's throat. She wondered how the Frenches could bear to look at that portrait now that Ana was gone.

Mrs. French filled a bowl with water for Calvin, and he lapped practically the whole thing in seconds. "Can I get you some water, Quinn?"

"No, that's okay." The sunlight flooding through the back window warmed the kitchen too much, suffocating Quinn and making her want to flee. "What did you want to show me?"

"Sit right there, and I'll get it." She left the room and returned with a diary. "I've been going through Ana's things for a year now. She left so many treasures. I thought you might want to see this." She opened the diary to the page marked by a narrow gold ribbon. "Take a look."

Quinn sat, not trusting her balance. "Today I did something terrible to Quinn. I took away her boyfriend. Now she's not speaking to me. I guess I deserve it. I wanted Brad, but I never wanted to lose Quinn."

Tears clouded Quinn's vision, and she wondered what cruel motivation Mrs. French had to remind her of Ana's treachery. Ana's betrayal had caused years of heartache.

"Keep reading," Mrs. French said, motioning to turn the page.

"Even worse," Ana wrote, "Brad probably still loves Quinn. I got him under false pretenses, and I hurt him just as much as I hurt her. I am a wicked, wicked person."

An odd coldness flooded Quinn's body as she read, as if she were a voyeur, invading someone else's life. Ana's words had been written half a lifetime ago. Had she known of Ana's angst, perhaps things would have turned out differently. Now a thick scab had crusted over the pain, and Quinn had moved on.

"Do you think—" Tears coursed down Mrs. French's cheeks. "Do you think that's why Ana was murdered? As punishment for being wicked?"

Quinn realized the reason Mrs. French had brought her in and shown her the diary. She craved the comfort that only Quinn could offer. "No," she said, her voice a hoarse whisper. "Ana didn't deserve to die. And she got her wish, because I've forgiven her."

The two women hugged, and Quinn went on her way, jogging with Calvin into the waning afternoon. On the way home, Quinn pondered whether people's worst moments merited exacting punishments. Was someone targeting her with poison, drugs, and framing her for two murders because of some inherent evil inside her? "No, Ana," she said aloud. "Sometimes, for no reason at all, life can be really shitty."

Chapter Fifty-four

After the long run and visit with Mrs. French, Quinn took Holly for a walk and returned to shower and get dinner started, before picking up Josh from work. When she stepped out of the shower, a *ping* sounded on her cell phone.

The voicemail from Sergeant Schmidt said, "We're finished with your car. You can come pick it up, or we can drop it off. Let me know when."

Eager to have her car back, Quinn called immediately. "I'm at home now. Is that convenient?"

"You wanna come pick it up, sure. If you want us to deliver, it'll have to wait until after nine p.m." Schmidt's typical gruffness came across as a growl.

"Nine is fine," Quinn said. "I don't have anyone to drop me before that anyway." She wanted to ask whether they'd found any evidence in the car, but she recognized his "don't-bother-me-with-questions" tone. Maybe he, or whoever brought the car, would open up later.

While she browned hamburger meat for a spaghetti sauce, Quinn thought about the ID bracelet given to her by Mrs. Oliver. Why would Ana have saved the gift more than nineteen years? Would guilt have prompted her to keep a souvenir of their friendship? And why would she have taken it to her office at the strip club? Even new, the piece of costume jewelry hadn't been valuable. She might have spent ten dollars on it, engraved and all.

Quinn supposed she should be flattered that the token of their friendship meant that much to Ana. The diary entry she'd seen earlier reinforced the idea. Still, there was something odd about the way the bracelet was packaged. If she remembered correctly, Quinn had purchased the bracelet at a kiosk. After being engraved, it had been returned to a clear plastic rectangular box, which Quinn had wrapped for Ana.

Leaving the spaghetti sauce to simmer on a low flame, Quinn dug through the contents of her bottom bureau drawer. She pulled out the box given to her by Mrs. Oliver and took it to the kitchen, where the overhead light was strong.

This package definitely outclassed the one Quinn remembered wrapping for Ana in the sixth grade. This box, covered in black suede-like fabric, had a gold tone clasp and a maroon velvet lining. The inexpensive bracelet sat inside like a poor relative attending a holiday feast. Who had put the bracelet in this fancy case, and why?

Quinn pulled at the maroon rectangle set inside the box. Perhaps she might find a message or some answer underneath. The insert lifted easily, and Quinn stared at an empty space of gray cardboard. Disappointed, but not surprised, she started to replace the velvety insert, when a thin strand of silver caught her eye. A thread, or, more likely, a hair—and possibly Mrs. Oliver's. Quinn left the hair just as she found it and took the whole package back to her drawer. Probably Mrs. Oliver had transferred the bracelet to one of her own jewelry boxes to make a nice presentation, but Quinn couldn't ask. Mrs. Oliver had vanished, and maybe for good.

Josh was delighted when Quinn picked him up from work and told him her car was being delivered. "Just in time. My ankle's much better, and I can drive myself now."

"Are you sure?" Quinn asked. As much as she wanted him to be healed, she hated giving up the twice-a-day transportation arrangement.

"Absolutely. Watch." Josh walked from the car to the front door without limping or favoring a foot.

"How did you heal so fast? I thought sprains take a long time."

"Bad sprains do. This was a 'good' sprain, I guess. Or maybe my vitamins helped. Anyway, I'm good to drive starting tomorrow."

The dogs competed for Josh's attention as soon as he entered the house and turned off the alarm. He scooped them both into his arms and allowed massive licking to begin.

After dinner, Quinn and Josh cleaned up, took the dogs out, and sat on the rear porch with her back spooned into his chest, while they waited for the car delivery. "I've been thinking about the cocaine in your trunk," Josh said. "And the fact that the car sits out on the driveway all the time. Maybe we should clean out the garage and put your car there every night."

"And what about your car?" Quinn asked. "I don't see how that helps anything. If somebody wanted to get into my trunk, which I doubt will happen again, plenty of opportunities exist outside the funeral home or at the grocery store. This happened to my car in broad daylight."

"True, but it's such a major hassle. You know, your car's going to need a lot of cleaning when you get it back. Possibly repairs, too. The police aren't gentle when looking for evidence."

The night air was chilly, and Quinn snuggled into her husband's arms. "We'll deal with that when we have to. Right now, I'm concentrating on the big picture."

"Which is what?" Josh asked.

"Mainly, why. And what might be next. Planting evidence to make me look like a drug dealer is one thing, but I found out something worse today." Without revealing her source, Quinn explained that both Elizabeth Lavender and Julio Martinez were poisoned with formaldehyde. "I'm thinking that the same person who planted the coke chose the main ingredient in embalming fluid, in order to cast suspicion for the murders on me."

Josh stood and clenched his fists. "That's nuts! The police haven't questioned you, have they?"

"Not yet. They may get around to it, though. I'm hoping they've found something in my car to implicate someone else. I read something once that since the use of DNA for police work, criminals have almost no chance of avoiding being caught. If a person was present at the site of a crime, his DNA is there, no matter how careful he's been."

Josh began pacing. "I don't know. If that's true, then how come there are so many unsolved cases?" He opened the door to let the dogs in. "It's too cold out here. Let's go inside."

A few minutes later, Sergeant Schmidt, dangling the fob to her car, knocked on the front door, causing the dogs to burst into a chorus. Quinn opened the door and invited him inside.

"I can't stay. Tom's out there, waiting to drive me back to the station. And the missus has dinner ready at home." He turned to leave, but after a few steps, pivoted in place. "Hope the car's not too much of a mess."

Quinn couldn't remember Schmidt's ever mentioning his wife before, or maybe she hadn't paid attention. "Don't worry about the mess. I can take care of that, but I was hoping you could tell me if you found anything."

Schmidt's face cracked into a one-sided smile. "I knew you'd ask. The car was amazingly free of prints. We thought the whole thing was going to be a bust, but at the last minute we found something."

Quinn took in a loud breath. "Please tell me."

"Not for publication, but we found a hair. We've sent it out for testing."

"A hair?" Quinn thought of the hair at the bottom of the jewelry box. If he needed one for comparison, she could provide it.

"Yep. One long, straight silver hair."

Chapter Fifty-five

Quinn's car was indeed a mess, but she drove it to work the next day anyway, and Josh drove his own. This small return to normalcy comforted Quinn, and she hummed a happy tune as she entered the embalming room. Zeke and Rory had brought in two bodies overnight, so today she'd probably work overtime. So much for taking her car to the dealership after work.

She gathered her materials and equipment, thinking of the poisonings when she set the canister of embalming fluid on the countertop. Before she could don the protective clothing and her iPod buds, she received a text from Jack, who was at a community breakfast meeting for one of the organizations in town.

Wait till you hear what Jay Carnes told me about Martinez. Glad we aren't doing that funeral.

Quinn texted back, Oh, no. TTYL. Turning back to the task at hand, she put on her PPE and popped in a stick of spearmint gum. She took a moment to introduce herself to the silent person on the table. "I promise to treat you with tenderness and respect," she said aloud. *For all I know, this lovely lady can still hear me.*

While she cut an inch-and-a-half incision at the collar bone, she thought about being a PA, how it would be to treat a living human being who could respond. In a lot of ways, the job would differ from this one, but the ultimate principle, to provide the best care possible, would be exactly the same.

At noon, her dad burst through the door, breathless. "Big news. You should sit down." He rolled the desk chair to the table where Quinn stood.

Quinn's heart pounded. Her father wasn't prone to dramatic announcements. Instead of clawing at him for information, she took off her gloves and mask and forced herself to sit.

Her father did something else he hadn't done in years. He squatted next to her and peered into her eyes. *What? Is something wrong with Mom? Jack?* She hoped her interview for PA school hadn't gotten back to him before she could share the news, herself.

"I just got a call from Marty Ramirez. Lionel French is dead."

"Blackie." Quinn whispered, erasing her personal fears about people she loved. Still, this was shocking news. "What happened?"

"Not sure. The sheriff's office is investigating now. Found him unresponsive in his cell this morning. They suspect foul play." Grabbing her hand and using it to stand, he said, "I wanted to tell you myself."

"Blackie, dead? Hard to believe." A million images flipped in her mind like pages of an old, yellowed photo album. Blackie had caused a lot of trouble in her life. She couldn't summon any sadness over his death, but a dam-bursting flood of relief coursed between her shoulder blades. "I won't have to testify."

"That's right. You can't try a dead man." Her dad took her hand again. "I know it's shocking. Glad you're off the hook for the trial. How about taking a break? There's chili and cornbread in the coffee room."

Quinn debated working through lunch, so she could finish earlier, but the surprising news merited digesting, and the thought of her mother's chili made her mouth water. "Do you have time to sit with me while I eat?"

"Of course. I haven't eaten yet, either." Her dad helped her cover the body and waited while she removed her garb and cleaned up.

They crossed the living room and passed the office, where Quinn's mother sat at the computer, talking on the phone. She waved them inside and held up a finger.

"Let's see what your mother wants," her dad said, ushering Quinn into the small office and pointing to the chair at the second desk. Quinn took the seat, and her dad leaned against the file cabinets, crossing his legs like a stork, propped against wood pilings.

When her mother hung up, she turned to Quinn. "How soon do you think you can finish those two bodies? Both families are local and ready to roll."

"I'm planning to stay late. I can get them done tonight." Quinn hoped Josh would be home at a decent time for Holly's sake.

"That's wonderful, darling. We are so lucky to have you around. Not only are you an excellent embalmer, but you don't mind putting in extra effort when needed." She rose and planted a kiss on the top of Quinn's head.

The compliment churned like buttermilk inside of Quinn. She wanted to share her hopes for PA school with her family, but the guilt of leaving them in the lurch prevailed. Finding a skilled and reliable embalmer was no easy task. People weren't vying—or dying—for the job.

Left to her thoughts while her parents chatted about the upcoming funerals, Quinn picked at a cuticle and luxuriated in the fact that she was finally free of Blackie. Maybe, since she wouldn't be testifying, whoever had been harassing her would now leave her alone.

"—Quinn and I are going to have some chili now. Join us?" Her father moved toward the hallway.

"No, you go ahead. I had some earlier."

***

The aromas of chili powder, cumin, garlic, and onions wafted through the first floor, but another, less appealing, one, too. Disinfectant? Furniture polish?

Her dad led the way into the coffee room. When they got there, he reheated the chili.

Hunger caused Quinn's stomach to growl, and she helped herself to a big bowl full. She topped the dish off with a warm cornbread muffin. "Mom's outdone herself," Quinn said, as she tasted the first bite. "Not too bland, not too spicy." Sitting across from her father, Quinn threw a questioning look. She hadn't forgotten his hints at other topics for discussion.

"Sorry to be so mysterious," he said, sniffing the air and coughing. "Let me start with Mrs. Oliver."

Quinn coughed, too, and her intake of breath betrayed her conflicted emotions. "What about her?"

"We never had a chance to deliver her sister's remains before the woman disappeared. Marty says the police are looking for her, but they have no leads."

"Maybe Mrs. Oliver will come back and claim them before the hundred-and-twenty-day period is over."

"That would be ideal, but I can't count on it. I've sent the certified letter, but, of course, Mrs. Oliver isn't there to receive it. I wondered whether you had any ideas at all about where she might be. Did she drop any hints when she took you to lunch?"

"None that I can think of." The re-packaged ID bracelet with a single hair flashed through Quinn's mind. "Mrs. Oliver could be anywhere. Held captive or hiding. Wherever she is, I hope she's okay." Quinn broke off a piece of cornbread, set it on her tongue, and gobbled it down. "As for the sister, I hope we won't have to bury her in a mass grave, but I don't think there are any other relatives."

"Speaking of relatives, there's one more thing I wanted to talk about." Her dad's brown eyes misted. "Quinn, Mom and I are the third generation of McFarlands here."

Uh-oh. Here it comes. Quinn braced herself for the next revelation.

"My brothers and sister didn't want to run the business, so it was an easy decision to leave it to me. Sometimes we've had challenges, and sometimes things have gone well, but mostly I've been grateful for the privilege of carrying on the tradition and good name."

"You sound like something's coming to an end," Quinn said, putting down her spoon.

"Not an end. More like a beginning. Mom and I want to do some traveling while we can. You and Jack are perfectly capable of taking over in our absence. We'll stay in touch, wherever we go, so you can consult with us as much as you want."

The chili and cornbread churned in Quinn's stomach. This was not good news for her.

Oblivious to her feelings, her father carried on. "Of course, we would raise both yours and Jack's salaries significantly. And we'd have to hire some new folks to help with the funerals and other services."

Quinn's tongue stuck to the bottom of her mouth. "H-have you spoken to Jack about this?"

"Not yet. I wanted to talk to you both at the same time, but your mother thought I should chat with you first. Now that you're married, and he's about to marry, it's time to make the transition. But one of you needs to be in charge. In fact, Mom and I are planning to move out of the upstairs, so one of you can move in. We love you both equally, and don't want to give preference to one over the other." He paused to take a long swig of water. "Do you have any thoughts about that?"

Quinn had a lot of thoughts, but she wasn't ready to share them yet. "Let me talk to Josh about it and get back with you." She threw her arms around her daddy's neck and held back a sob.

Chapter Fifty-six

After lunch with her father, and shaken by the triple pieces of news, Quinn returned to the embalming room to finish working on her very patient patient. Putting on the protective clothing and equipment took less than a minute, but when Quinn reached back to the counter for the embalming fluid, her hand came up empty.

She had opened a new sixteen-ounce bottle before her father interrupted her an hour ago. She'd set it on the counter, in the exact spot where she always put the fluid, so she could reach for it without looking when she needed it. Mystified, she searched all over—on the shelves, in the cabinet where she stored other inventory under lock and key. The bottle had vanished.

Quinn checked the outside door to the parking lot, although she seldom kept it locked when she worked. Transports and deliveries used the entrance, so locking and unlocking didn't make sense. *Who would steal embalming fluid valued at something like fifteen dollars?*

The fact that formaldehyde was used to kill Mrs. Oliver's twin and Julio Martinez swept through Quinn's mind, leaving unpleasant dust motes. And then it hit her. That unlikely odor in the coffee room—formaldehyde. No wonder she and her dad had coughed when they inhaled.

Quinn dropped her scalpel and ran through the first floor of the funeral home. Formaldehyde would attack the respiratory system soon after exposure, and, without proper ventilation and protection, a person could die. Especially an older person who already had asthma, like her father. Her heartbeat matched the pounding of her shoes on the tile floor.

She flung open the door to the coffee room, gasping at the strong odor. Her father lay on the floor, clutching his chest and wheezing.

"Call 911," Quinn shouted in the direction of the office. She gulped a lung full of air and held her breath as she flew into the room and bent over her father. Still holding her breath, she summoned her core strength as she had learned in karate, and she hooked her hands under his armpits. Her lungs stung with the effort of dragging her father's tall, thin body across the floor and out of the room, but she had to get him out of there fast. Her eyes burned, too, and her tears dropped onto his face and chest.

By the time she had moved her father out of the room and shut the door, Quinn gasped and tried to steady herself. Her mother and brother appeared in the hallway, and her mother fell to her knees next to her husband. "EMS is on the way." Her mother's voice held a tinge of hysteria. "What's happened?"

Quinn took her father's pulse and listened to his labored breathing. "Formaldehyde. Bring me dad's inhaler," she said to her brother. "Better yet, get his CPAP machine from upstairs." She estimated only fifteen minutes had passed since she'd left him in the room. His symptoms seemed severe for such a brief exposure. Her father rolled on the floor, coughing and gasping, and a red irritation had formed beneath his nose.

Jack returned with the machine and plugged it in. Quinn fitted the mask over her father's face. "Breathe, Dad. Slow and easy." Her hands shook. "Dad, you're going to be fine. Just breathe."

Quinn's mother, dressed in her usual business suit and heels, crouched on the floor next to her husband and held his hand. "John, John, oh, John."

"He's not gasping as much," Jack said. "That's good, Dad."

Quinn wasn't needed to tend to her dad, so she turned her attention to containing the formaldehyde. "Don't anyone open this door." She needed to return to the embalming room to grab a respirator. Without it, she might end up on the floor like her father. "Be right back."

By the time Quinn returned, the EMTs had arrived and started a preliminary assessment. "He's in shock," one of the EMTs said to Quinn, as he hooked her dad up to oxygen. A second person started an IV.

"We can follow to the hospital in my car," Jack said, guiding his mother by the elbow. "C'mon, Mom."

"No, I'm going in the ambulance with your dad."

Quinn wanted to go, too, but someone had to clean up the formaldehyde before someone else was affected. As the person who worked with the toxin, she qualified for the job. As soon as everyone left, she called Josh. When she explained what was happening, he promised to meet the ambulance at the emergency room.

Tamping down her own anxiety about her father, Quinn donned the respirator and a pair of gloves, opened the door to the coffee room, and flung open all the windows. A search for the source took less than a minute. An open bottle, missing its cap, stood like a witch's curse in the cabinet under the sink. Her father had been washing the dishes right above the fumes. A few good whiffs had sufficed to knock his system out of whack.

Hopefully, they had found him in time. Having him wear the CPAP mask may have calmed his breathing, but there were no guarantees that his lungs weren't compromised. Every embalmer knew that toxicity from formaldehyde could cause severe pulmonary damage and even death.

Quinn moved quickly to transfer the caustic substance to a glass jar and seal it with a sturdy lid. Unlike the embalming room, where formaldehyde was stored and used, this room lacked a strong ventilation system. Quinn flipped on the blower on the small stovetop hood. The breeze created between the exhaust system and the open windows would have to suffice.

She pulled the emergency spill kit from the refrigerator and cleaned the countertop, sink, cabinet, and floor with ammonia and water and sprinkled kitty litter to soak up the mess. Afterwards, she discarded the rags, gloves, and paper towels into a tightly sealed garbage bag. As she worked, she pondered the situation. All the bottles of formaldehyde in her storage cabinet looked exactly like the one found under the sink. Assuming that the uncapped bottle was the same one she'd reached for behind the embalming table, how had it been moved from her counter to the coffee room in such a tight time frame? The only person she could think of who had the opportunity was Zeke, and she couldn't imagine any scenario in which such a trusted employee and friend would wish to harm anyone at McFarland's.

Only when she had finished scrubbing and airing out the room did Quinn consider that, intent on removing the hazardous fumes, she might have interfered with a crime scene.

Her gut clenched, thinking of her father, rolling on the floor and wheezing. The light reflected from his silverish hair, and his face reddened from the toxic fumes—this man didn't resemble the young, vibrant person Quinn knew and loved. She wanted to run to his side at the hospital, but that's not how things worked at McFarland's. Someone had to stay on duty.

Quinn trudged to the embalming room, where the silent body awaited processing. If anyone entered the building, or if the business phone rang, she would be notified. Suddenly tired from all the commotion and worried about her father, who might have permanent damage, Quinn plopped into a chair and closed her eyes. She would summon the strength to go on with her work, but first she needed to call Sergeant Schmidt.

Chapter Fifty-seven
TRISH

Life in this condo leaves a lot to be desired, but at least I'm safe for now. Suzette, probably not her real name, works at night and sleeps all day—when she's here at all. Perfect for me, since I'm not looking for company, especially that of a twenty-year-old stripper.

I've got earplugs for the TV, so I can entertain myself without disturbing her. Let me just turn on the local news.

Oh, shit! That hunky new anchor on the local news has announced the death of Lionel French, my friend Blackie. Not many details—just that Blackie has been in custody, awaiting trial on two counts of murder. Police are investigating. Sounds like a jailhouse murder. Poor Blackie, and poor me. I'm sure I'll never get my money back now. I'll be lucky if his empire doesn't blow up and expose my part in building it.

Blackie and I have had a love-hate relationship, starting with hate. No one likes being threatened with exposure. Just because I like a good roll in the hay, that has made me prey for someone like Blackie. His threats to tell Marvin and the school board? A good way to get me to do Blackie's bidding.

Of course, lately, since retiring from teaching, I haven't been as useful to Blackie as in the old days, finding young girls for his enterprises. No one has ever had a better eye for identifying the vulnerable ones, and what better vehicle for finding their weaknesses than personal writing assignments? I must say, Blackie's best prospects have been my former students.

Best of all, I've discovered a taste for living on the edge. That's how the hate turns to love. A little success, a lot of praise, and pretty soon I'm a trusted part of Blackie's empire—an investor, even. And things have been great, until last year, when Quinn goes and gets involved.

Thanks to Quinn, Blackie's faced double murder charges. And now, before he can get his day in court, he's dead. This is not good news for a lot of reasons. Over the years, Blackie's become somewhat of a protector. Now I have no gun, no Blackie, not even Julio—or Liz, for that matter. The only one left is that Francisco, and that is one scary dude with a long memory and a fiery temper. No love-hate relationship with him—that man only knows hate. I need to be careful, and so does poor unsuspecting Quinn.

Chapter Fifty-eight

After she called Sergeant Schmidt, who said he would come over immediately, Quinn received a text from Josh. *I'm with your dad. He's being assessed in ER. They'll keep him for observation, but he's breathing normally now.*

Quinn exhaled, releasing pent-up worry about her father. Knowing that Josh was there helped her accept staying behind. People who worked in death services, ironically, rarely thought about their own deaths. Her dad's revelation about plans to retire, coming right before being stricken by poisonous fumes, gave her a stark realization. Her parents were aging, and she needed to cherish her time with them.

So many thoughts competed for space, like planets refusing to stay in their orbits. Cocaine in her trunk, silver hairs, three deaths, Mrs. Oliver's absence, missing formaldehyde. There must be a commonality to tie these together, but for the life of her, she couldn't find one.

Blackie's sudden death would take getting used to. The dread of testifying in his trial refused to dissipate. Her head told her to let the tension go, but her heart told her she would never be free of Blackie's reach.

A loud knock on the embalming room's outside door shook her from this reverie. Before she could respond, the door flew open, ushering cool air and the boisterous Schmidt. "Sorry it took me a little longer than expected. How's your dad doing?"

Quinn reported what she'd learned from Josh's text. She didn't want to talk about it further right now. "Listen, I'm sorry I didn't call you before I cleaned up the toxin. I was so upset about Dad and couldn't think about anything except protecting others from the fumes."

"Don't worry. It happens." Schmidt took a seat without being asked. "Now explain what happened from the beginning."

Quinn began with the faint smell in the coffee room when she had lunch with her dad. "I should have recognized the odor, but the chili smell overpowered it, and I was distracted by the conversation. Part of which was the news about Blackie."

"Yeah. I thought of you right away when I heard. You're off the hook for testifying. But go on."

Continuing with describing her return to the embalming room, Quinn pointed to the counter where she had placed a bottle of fluid.

"You sure it was there earlier?" Schmidt jiggled his knee while glancing around the room, as if he might spot the bottle elsewhere.

"Positive. Part of my routine set-up."

"How much time elapsed between when you set the bottle there and when you went into the lunchroom?"

Quinn had already thought of that question. "Maybe a half hour at the most."

"Anyone else here with you, or come in? Did you leave the room at any time during those thirty minutes?" Schmidt's knee continued to bounce.

Quinn explained that Zeke had arrived with a body. They'd refrigerated it, chatted a bit, and then Zeke had left to take the paperwork to the office. "I went to the bathroom sometime in there—not sure whether it was before or after Zeke came in."

Schmidt stared at Quinn for several seconds. "Do you think Zeke might have taken the formaldehyde?"

Quinn shook her head. "I can't see it. Zeke's been with us since high school."

"Can you get him over here? Maybe we can have a little chat. Meantime, let's look at the coffee room."

Quinn called Zeke, who said, sure. He could be there in ten minutes. While they waited, she showed Schmidt the sink, cupboard, and place on the floor where her father had been overcome by the smell.

"Hmm, smells like ammonia now. That must have been frightening." He walked around the room, hands clasped behind his back. "What did you do with the items you cleaned up?"

Quinn led him back to the embalming room and to the outside garbage can where she'd placed the sealed bag. "You're welcome to take this, but I warn you. Unless rendered inert, the formaldehyde continues to be toxic."

Schmidt nodded and put the bag in the trunk of the squad car. At that moment, Zeke arrived in the small lot and jumped out of the panel truck. He greeted Quinn with a partial smile, flicking his eyes toward the police officer.

"What's goin' on?"

Quinn led the two men through the back door and into the living room area, where everyone could sit comfortably. "Sergeant

Schmidt would like to ask you a few questions about when you were here earlier."

Zeke sat up straight and bit his lip. "Sure. Happy to help."

Zeke led Schmidt through his step-by-step actions from the time he brought the body in until he left in the truck, a total of approximately fifteen minutes. "Did you see or touch any bottles of embalming fluid while you were here?"

"No, 'course not. Why would I?" Zeke's wiry eyebrows hovered over his eyes, giving him a wary look. "What I do here at McFarland's is strictly routine. I been doin' the same stuff for more'n twenty years."

"Did you enter the coffee room at any time today?"

"Nope. Dropped off the body, drove around to the front, parked the truck, went to the office, and handed them papers to Mrs. McFarland, same as always."

Schmidt paused. "Well, let me ask you this. Did you see anyone going into or coming out of the coffee room while you were in the front of the building?"

Zeke made eye contact with Quinn before answering. "Come to think on't, I did. Didn't think much about it, but there was a guy in a khaki uniform going into that room when I came out o' th' office. Maybe a plumber or heating guy."

Schmidt's knee sat perfectly still, and he leaned forward on his elbows. "Can you describe him?"

"Yeah. Kinda short and stocky. Lace-up shoes. Medium-dark complexion. Moustache." He closed his eyes a few seconds, and then opened them. "Maybe Hispanic."

"Old or young?" Schmidt asked.

"On the youngish side. I didn't get too good a look. Just a glimpse is all." Zeke sat back and rubbed his eyes. "Can you tell me what's happened?"

"At the moment, we're just asking questions. Nothing to worry about, but thanks for your input. You can go now." Schmidt stood and began walking back toward the exit.

Quinn walked Zeke to his truck and waited as he climbed in and started the engine. "Thanks," she said, patting the door.

As the truck backed out of the parking area, Schmidt asked, "Do you trust him?"

On another day, Quinn might have laughed. But today she recognized a serious question when asked. The answer spilled from her lips without a second thought. "Yes. I trust him."

Chapter Fifty-nine

After Sergeant Schmidt left the funeral home, Quinn called to check on her father, who, according to Josh, was resting comfortably at the hospital. Headachy and exhausted, she still had two bodies to prepare before going home. She took a new bottle of formaldehyde from the cabinet, wishing she could ban the image of her father, gasping and miserable.

She took two ibuprofens, put on the protective equipment again, and returned to the body, where she had already made a collarbone incision. The incision gave access to the carotid artery and jugular vein, the main "pipes" of the embalming process. She prayed for no clots as she inserted the canula into the artery.

Within a minute the stream of formaldehyde caused the woman's blood vessels to rise, and a pink tone suffused the toes. "That's beautiful," she said aloud. "Now let's work on those elegant hands of yours."

Quinn's favorite part of the process, the most artistic and analytical part, came next—the cosmetics. Setting the face and hands into their most natural positions gave her the opportunity to practice the skills she'd learned from experience. This woman, Mrs. Gardner, had waited on Quinn at the nursery where she purchased most of her orchids. They had laughed about the woman's name being perfectly matched to her job. The long, tapered fingers had made an impression on Quinn in life, and she aimed to position them just right.

As she worked on Mrs. Gardner, Quinn thought about Mrs. Oliver's sister's body, her hands, and the wrist tattoo. So much had happened since the day at the morgue when she'd identified her, and yet the case remained unsolved. Since Mrs. Oliver had disappeared and other, more personal attacks had distracted her, Quinn hadn't spent much time or effort pondering Elizabeth Lavender's demise.

Originally, she'd wondered whether the killer's intended victim had been Mrs. Oliver, and now that old chestnut rolled around in her head. Maybe the killer had threatened Mrs. Oliver, causing the woman to flee.

Now a new idea germinated. What if the dead body really had not been the sister, after all, but Mrs. Oliver? The woman who had taken Quinn to lunch and told her about Liz's sex life might have been Liz, playing out the switch.

If that were true, how could the tattoos be explained? Satisfied with the now-pink skin tone on the hands of her work-in-progress, Quinn analyzed the woman's face. In her experience, every question had an answer. Once she finished beautifying her two charges this evening, she would find out what she needed to know about tattoos—even if she had to get one, herself.

Chapter Sixty

After the crisis with her father and preparing two bodies for visitation, Quinn could hardly keep her eyes open. Jack FaceTimed her from her dad's hospital room. Though weak, her father smiled and told her not to worry about a thing. "I'll be home before you know it, kitten."

Quinn reassured him that all was well at McFarland's and promised him his favorite pot roast dinner to celebrate his homecoming.

After the televisit, Jack took the phone out into the hallway. "He's really doing okay, sis. Don't worry."

"Then why did you step outside to talk?"

"I wanted to tell you what Jay Carnes told me about that Martinez guy." He sucked in a breath. "You know, that's the same guy with the cockfighting ring, the one Josh operated on? He's out on bail, evidently one nasty dude."

Remembering that Martinez had spit on Josh, she could believe it. "Why? What did he do to Jay?"

"Strutted into Carnes with a big attitude, demanding priority scheduling and service. You know the type. The best coffin, the biggest floral arrangement, 'nothing but the best for my little brother,' but not wanting to pay. Jay said the guy looks scary, too. Has a big scar between his eyebrows and one eye that stares you down, while the other looks somewhere else."

Quinn shuddered, glad she wasn't dealing with this customer. "Did he threaten Jay?"

"Not overtly, but on top of dirty looks and arguments about money, Martinez was packing a big revolver. Jay said, 'Next time you want to send me somebody like that, don't do me any favors.'"

"I'm sorry to hear that. Jay's a great guy," Quinn said.

"Yeah. Well, in case he changes his mind and comes back to our place, don't even *talk* to him on your own."

***

On the way home from work, Quinn fantasized about a hot bath and a good night's sleep. Even feeding the dogs presented a challenge, and she had no idea what she and Josh would eat for dinner.

Before she could think about it, Josh called. "I'll bring home barbecue for dinner. We can make it an early night."

Quinn needed to talk to Josh about her dad's revelations about retiring. The longer she kept her PA school application and interview a secret, the harder it would be to share with her parents. But tonight wasn't the night for a lengthy talk, and Quinn gave herself a reprieve.

When she arrived home, she walked and fed the dogs, showered and put on her jammies, and vegged out in front of the TV until Josh came home with dinner. A few bites of barbecued brisket and potato salad, and she was ready to brush her teeth and go to bed.

"Sorry I'm so wiped out," she said. "I don't ever remember dragging like this. Today kicked my butt."

Josh pressed her cheek to his chest in a warm hug. "That's okay, Q. I've had a day, too." He trashed all the takeout containers and brought paper towels and spray to clean off the table.

"You're limping. Let me do that."

"I've got it," Josh said. "I'm not hurting, just tired."

The next ten minutes were a race to walk the dogs, shut down the house, turn on the alarm, and get ready for bed. Quinn lay spooning behind her husband and fell asleep before another thought could wend its way through her overloaded mind.

***

The next morning, Quinn jumped out of bed, her mojo restored. "I'm starving," she said to Josh, who was showering and getting ready for work. "I'll fry some bacon and eggs."

"Okay, but I'll take mine in a wrap to eat on the fly. I've got a surgery this morning."

Quinn didn't mind. She was used to Josh's demanding schedule and sometimes, like last night, she had to prioritize work, as well. Taking care of people, whether living or dead, required that kind of commitment.

As soon as Josh departed, Quinn's phone rang. She held her breath when she saw Jack's name. "Is Dad okay?" she asked, instead of saying hello.

"He's doing super. Up and walking around, doing breathing treatments. Might come home this evening." Jack's strong voice carried a chuckle. "The one to worry about is Mom. She didn't leave his bedside all night."

"Poor Mom. Do you need me to go to the hospital?"

"Nope. In fact, I'm calling to tell you to stay home this morning. You did a great job cleaning the coffee room, on top of two bodies. How late were you here?"

"I don't know. You know Mom's saying about finishing strong." Quinn's mind flitted to possibilities for filling the morning hours. "Are you sure you don't need me?"

"Yeah. I've got things under control here. Setting up those two funerals—all office work. Why don't you come in around one or two?"

Quinn thanked her capable brother. "Okay, I locked the supplies cabinet but keep your eyes and ears open." It felt strange not to share the conversation about her parents' retirement. She and Jack had always been close. But her dad had made it clear that he had approached her first, and she wouldn't question that decision. Jack would be the perfect one to lead the family business when her parents retired. Another reason to be grateful for him.

Late start workdays were a perk of her job, even though she had earned the time off by working late. This one afforded her the opportunity to hatch a plan.

Dressed in faded jeans, torn at both knees, a cropped satin shell, and a fake leather jacket, Quinn grabbed her car fob and headed to the Asylum tattoo shop on the West End.

A thirtysomething brunette with ink on the insides of both arms was unlocking the door as Quinn pulled up. "Come on in, early bird." Her eyes moved across Quinn's body, as if sizing up a space for her artwork. "We're running a special today—twenty dollars for the minimum."

"Seems reasonable. What's the usual price?" Quinn looked around the shop, taking in the list of rules, prominently placed. "No one under the age of eighteen can enter this establishment." *Interesting.*

"Sixty. What have you got in mind?"

Here's where things might get tricky. "Well, mostly I'm curious. I've never been tattooed, but I'm thinking about surprising my husband." *And, boy, would he be surprised.*

"Something small and sexy to start with?" the woman asked. She opened a binder with pages of drawings protected in plastic.

"Yes," Quinn said, swallowing hard at the picture of a tiny naked mermaid. "First, I have a few questions."

"Ask away. We get a lot of virgins in here, and we want to make you comfortable with the process. My name's Renee, by the way. What's yours?"

Quinn extended a hand. "Nice to meet you. Call me Candy." Quinn couldn't believe how easily the lie slipped out. "Well, I've heard it hurts a lot. Is that true?"

Renee leaned on the counter and looked into Quinn's eyes. "I'm not going to sugar coat, Candy." She paused to giggle at the pun. "Any time you puncture the skin with needles, some pain will be involved. Some compare it to a bee sting. A lot depends on the location on the body, the person's pain tolerance, and the sensitivity of the artist. I counsel people to stay away from bony places to start with. And I give breaks during the procedure."

"What about age? Would it hurt more, for example, for a baby than for an adult?"

Renee's forehead furrowed. "I wouldn't know about that. It's illegal to tattoo anyone under eighteen. In the State of Texas, that is—and most states."

Quinn wondered about the McDaniel twins, Trish and Liz. Had that law existed when they were babies? "So that's why, no minors on the premises."

"Yes, a matter of consent. Tattoos are permanent, so anyone getting one needs to be very sure." An eyebrow lifted, as if Renee doubted Quinn's—or Candy's—seriousness.

Behind her, bells on the outside door announced the arrival of another customer. "Be right with you," Renee said, pointing to the row of chairs at the front of the shop. She turned her attention back to Quinn and said, "Any more questions?"

"Yes. I have a question about the permanence. What if I don't like the tattoo? How hard is it to remove and get a different one in the same place?" Quinn's hypothesis about what Trish Oliver may have done hung in the air.

Renee's lips turned down. "Nearly impossible. We have customers sign off. Once that ink is in there, it's not going to go anywhere."

"What about making adjustments to the design? Could you turn a letter or number into a different one?" *A pi into an epsilon, for example?*

Huffing and squinting, Renee spoke quickly, eying the other customer at the same time. "You might be able to thicken the design, but the end result wouldn't look right. Better to pick the exact design the first time."

Quinn said, "Why don't you take care of the other customer while I look through this book? I'm not in any hurry."

Renee smiled and left Quinn to flip through the pages of tattoo options. Amazed by the detail and artistry in each of the small tattoos, Quinn imagined showing Josh a heart, an angel, a dragon, or a red rose on her butt. Other, more suggestive, designs depicted lips and tongues, sexy sayings, and symbols of genitalia.

Quinn only half-looked through the designs. Her theory about Mrs. Oliver, having changed places with her sister, had popped like a carnival balloon. The *epsilon* on the wrist of the body in the morgue had to be Liz.

Turning the page, Quinn came upon the design of a rooster, reminding her of the Martinez brothers. Renee had given the other customer a binder to look at, and she returned to Quinn's side.

"You aren't interested in a rooster tatt, are you?" she asked.

"Not really. I know somebody who has one like this on his neck, behind the ear." Quinn examined Renee's face for a reaction.

"That's interesting," Renee said, lowering her voice. "We don't judge here, but that tri-color rooster on the neck most likely indicates a gang member."

Chills ran between Quinn's shoulder blades, but she kept her voice even. "So, what you're saying is the design is important, but its placement on the body is equally important."

"That's right. Did you find a design that you're interested in?" Renee looked in the direction of the other customer.

Quinn understood. Her job depended on paying customers. Perhaps she sensed Quinn didn't qualify. "I was thinking this angel on my neck." She flipped back to the first page in the binder and pointed to the skin under her chin.

"That placement is what we call a 'job-stopper.'"

"What do you mean?" Quinn asked, although she had a good idea.

"A lot of jobs won't hire people with ink in prominent places. You should consider that before you commit."

"What kind of jobs are you talking about?"

"Oh, mostly the professions. Anything in the medical field, cops, lawyers, teachers. If you think you might ever go for a career like that, I'd discourage you."

Quinn bit her lip, more for show than anything else. "You know what? I'm gonna think about this. Talk it over with my husband. I don't want to do anything I'd regret." She closed the binder and clutched her car fob. "Thank you for your time."

"No problem, Candy. Whenever you're ready, we'll be here."

Chapter Sixty-one

When Quinn sashayed into the mortuary, wearing torn jeans and a leather jacket, her brother let forth with a long whistle. "Who's that city girl glamming up this scene?"

"Don't be silly. I'll change into my work clothes in a minute." Quinn looked around for her mom. "Mom still at the hospital? How's Dad?"

"Coming home in a few hours." Jack pushed back from the desk and computer. "Glad you're here, though. Mrs. Gardner's daughter is coming in half an hour to view her mother and talk about the funeral. I told her Mom wouldn't be here, and she asked for you."

"Me?" Quinn tried to remember a connection. "What's her first name?"

"Farrah. She said she was in high school with you."

"Be right back." Quinn dashed to the embalming room, where she kept a closet full of work clothes. As soon as she changed, she checked on Mrs. Gardner, who still looked as pretty and peaceful as she had the night before.

Quinn had blocked out a lot about high school, but the name Farrah rang a bell. A lot of years had gone by—whether she remembered the woman or not, Quinn would turn on the Southern hospitality so important to this business.

As soon as Farrah entered the lobby, Quinn recalled the statuesque girl with the slightly pigeon-toed stride. Beautiful in a wide-eyed, exotic way, Farrah had no features in common with her mother.

Holding her arms open as if to invite a hug, she said, "Hello, Quinn. It's been a long time. Of course, I've been away ever since graduation."

Quinn moved closer, opening her arms, as well. The brief hug established acquaintanceship, if not friendship. "I'm so sorry for your loss. I have fond memories of your mother."

Farrah's eyes grew teary. "She was a great mother. Dad died when I was a baby, so we had it hard. Don't know if you remember I'm an only child. Now I'm pretty much alone in the world, except for my boyfriend in Chicago."

Quinn thought of her father and his brush with formaldehyde poisoning. "Must be awfully tough. I'll help you any way I can."

"That's kind of you. Do you remember we were in Mrs. Oliver's English class together? And that reading club she started that you were president of?" A faint curling of the lips revealed a chipped front tooth that Quinn remembered.

"Yes. The reading club meant a lot to me," Quinn said.

"Probably the only good thing Mrs. Oliver ever did." Farrah wrung her hands and looked around.

Though startled by the comment, Quinn changed the subject and softened her voice. "Would you like to sit for a moment, or would you like to see your mother first?"

Sighing, Farrah said, "Mom," and Quinn led her to the small room adjacent to the embalming room, where private family viewings took place and stood by while Farrah looked at her mother's body.

After a few seconds, Quinn said, "I'll give you privacy. Let me know when you're ready to leave." Quinn tiptoed out of the room and waited on the other side of the door.

When she exited the room, Farrah's eyes had reddened, and she clutched a tissue, but she remained composed. The two young women sat in the living room to plan the funeral service. Afterwards, Farrah said, "I shouldn't have said what I did about Mrs. Oliver earlier. I hope I didn't offend you."

Gooseflesh formed on Quinn's forearms, and she hugged herself. "No offense taken, but why didn't you like Mrs. Oliver? She seemed okay to me."

"Maybe you don't know. Very few did, and no one talked in those days. Mrs. Oliver pinpointed girls and groomed them."

Quinn fought to keep her voice low. "Groomed them for what? The sex trade?" Thoughts of Blackie and his enterprises stabbed her in the gut. "My God," she whispered. "How do you know?"

Farrah's eyes met Quinn's in a cold stare. "I know, because I was one of them."

Chapter Sixty-two

After Farrah left the funeral home, Quinn retreated to her desk in the embalming room. Ever since Elizabeth Lavender's death, people had been telling Quinn negative things about Mrs. Oliver, but none had been as serious or as shocking as Farrah's story.

A heart-pounding nausea welled up inside, and memories of a dark house with chains on the bed taunted her. How any woman could be a part of subjugating other women upset Quinn to the core, but a teacher who used her occupation for criminal purposes—that sparked the hottest outrage.

Poor Farrah. The scenario fit together perfectly—an only child, pretty, but with low self-esteem—easy prey for a canny teacher who knew what she was looking for. Farrah's absence and lack of connection with anyone in town for all these years made sense, too. The perfect target.

Quinn hadn't probed for details. Obviously one of the lucky ones, Farrah had been able to extricate herself from whatever exploitation Mrs. Oliver had gotten her into.

Shuddering, Quinn thought about her brush with sex trafficking, courtesy of Blackie. Even her homey little island fell prey to underground criminal activity.

Mrs. Oliver had admitted, the day she gave Quinn the bracelet at lunch, that she and Blackie were friends. Then she had tried to convince Quinn that putting the tracker on her car was a means of protection.

Now Quinn had no doubt that Mrs. Oliver was not a friend. The gifts, the lunch, the cookies, the warning that her car had been moved—none of these had been heartfelt or genuine. Quinn's head buzzed with doubt, anger, shame at having been deceived, even back in high school. While Quinn thought of Mrs. Oliver as a kind and caring teacher, who had helped her deal with the trauma of rejection, the woman was running criminal activity from the classroom. How she got away with that for years is a mystery, except that people kept more secrets in those days and were less likely to believe such evil could occur in a school.

Quinn knew she should report this information to Sergeant Schmidt, but how could she do so without repeating what Farrah had told her in confidence? Schmidt would have to talk to Farrah directly, and dredging up those terrible memories at a time when the woman was about to bury her mother—that constituted cruelty.

Talking in confidence to Mary might be an option. But what did she expect Mary to do? Not report the information to her superiors? Quinn couldn't put her sister-in-law-to-be in a dicey position like that.

Josh would say, "I told you so," or maybe he would only think that. He'd been suspicious of Mrs. Oliver from the beginning, and he had never approved of Quinn's involvement with the woman or her sister's death.

In a few days, after Mrs. Gardner's funeral, Quinn would urge Farrah to talk with the police. She'd offer to go with her, if need be. But in the meantime, someone was threatening Quinn and her family. Two people had been killed already, and Quinn couldn't sit by, waiting for the third.

The breath of fresh air Quinn had won from Blackie's death had transformed into a dark cloud of dread. What she'd learned yesterday about the rooster gang and today about Mrs. Oliver's participation in sex trafficking mingled in her mind. To get to the bottom of the malicious tricks she and her family were experiencing, Quinn must find Mrs. Oliver, without telling anyone and completely on her own. And she had a few ideas about how to do that.

Chapter Sixty-three

The rest of the day at work, Quinn met with the family of the other deceased person she'd prepared, and worked to plan the two funerals. She stayed long enough to welcome her parents home from the hospital and make sure they had everything they needed. Her dad's thin, sallow face told of the ordeal he'd suffered, but he produced a dazzling smile and wrapped Quinn in a bear hug.

"I worried about you," Quinn said, squeezing back.

"Don't worry, kitten. It'd take more than a few fumes to do me in."

No one said anything about how the open bottle of formaldehyde was placed under the sink. Quinn didn't want to spoil the joyful homecoming for her parents, but she couldn't rid her mind of threats and criminals, even as she'd planned for flowers, music, a pot roast dinner, and a welcome home banner.

At home that evening she focused on keeping Mrs. Oliver and the Martinez gang out of her thoughts and conversation with Josh. Instead, she broached the safer subject of her parents' retirement. "I feel like a traitor, leaving the family business, but even worse for keeping my plans a secret." She lifted Holly from the cushion next to Josh and plopped down in her place. Snuggling into his warm chest, she sighed. "I wanted to wait until everything was official, but maybe that's not fair. What do you think?"

Josh kissed the top of her head. "I think," he said, taking a few moments to choose his words, "I think you need a change of perspective."

Not sure how to react, Quinn sat back and looked into Josh's gray eyes. "What do you mean?"

"Put yourself in your dad's shoes for a minute. Why would he confide his plans to you before sharing openly at a family meeting? Maybe he's conflicted about having to make a hard choice between his son and his daughter."

"And if I opt out, Jack can inherit the business with no hard feelings. So, I'd actually be doing everyone a favor."

"Something like that." Josh moved a curly lock of hair behind her ear. "You aren't opting out of the family, you know. You'll still be around to pinch hit if needed, but, more importantly, if you don't participate in ownership of McFarland's, that gives Jack and his family a double share of the profit."

Something fragrant and sweet, like a bouquet of roses, bloomed inside of Quinn. "I never thought of that before. The business has given our family a good standard of living, but we're one family, not two."

Quinn began pacing around the small living area. "Jack deserves to take over the business. He's always connected more with the role of death services, and he's already representing McFarland's in the business community."

Josh's lopsided grin encouraged her. "Don't forget that you will be following your dream. Your parents will most likely celebrate your success. A win-win for everyone."

Quinn leaned over her husband and gave him a soft, sweet kiss. "How can I ever thank you for helping me look outside the box? I'll have the conversation with Dad tomorrow."

Standing and stretching, Josh slipped his arm around her waist and squeezed. "That's what husbands are for, Q. Now you don't have to walk around, harboring a guilty secret."

Glad that Josh couldn't see the heat rising in her face, Quinn cringed at his last words. If only that were her only guilty secret!

Chapter Sixty-four
TRISH

Well, finally, Quinn has her car back! It certainly has taken the police a long time to process the car after my brilliant moves. See there, Mommy Dearest, Liz is not the only gifted actress in the family. I've convinced Quinn that I am protecting her, that watching her car go back and forth to the docks and reporting to her was an act of generosity.

Meanwhile, that sweet little round disc remains in Quinn's car, despite the so-called thorough cleansing by Sergeant Schmidt and his cronies.

How have I managed this ingenious feat? I owe it to you, Mommy.

Remember that time Spike tore up the carpet in the back of our new car after Liz dropped her burger and fries there? Clumsy of her, as usual, and we all worried what Daddy would say when he saw the damage. But you knew just how to repair the tear so no one would ever know. You brought out your sewing kit, the plastic one with two dozen spools of thread, a ripper, a dozen needles of all sizes, and sharp scissors. The same kind you bought for Liz and me one Christmas.

I watched you work on that tear, holding my breath so long I had to gasp at the end. You trimmed the carpet fibers ever so slightly to make them even, and you stitched the ragged tear with matching thread and an ultra-fine needle. The end result was perfect. I doubt anyone would ever notice that anything untoward had occurred on that carpet, so smooth was your handiwork.

Now I've channeled your skills, taking them to a more important purpose. After stealing Quinn's car and placing a kilo of coke in the trunk, I've driven the car into my garage and closed the door for privacy, sliced a small hole in the carpet behind the driver's seat, placed the tracker inside, and stitched the opening with matching thread. Good enough to escape detection by the police, and I can keep my eye on Quinn, a double benefit.

Like Jane Austen says, "Now I must give one smirk and then we may be rational again." The tracker is performing like a worker-bee, and I'm following Quinn's movements same as before. Of course, that girl isn't going anywhere interesting—just back and forth to the funeral home most of the time. She hasn't even gone to the hospital to visit her dear old dad.

A little birdie's told me all about the formaldehyde under the sink. A little stronger, and McFarland's might have had to operate without its big boss. I wonder if Quinn would have the stomach to work on her dad's body like she did my sister's.

Don't get me wrong. I don't have anything against Quinn—or her father—except *she* puts herself in other people's business. Her shenanigans with Blackie have hurt a lot of us in the pocketbook, though, and I, for one, and Francisco, for two, don't take kindly to losing income streams. Also, Blackie and Francisco have competed and teamed up for many years, like brothers from other mothers, so I'll bet Quinn's high up on Francisco's shit list. Somewhere I would never want to be.

Chapter Sixty-Five

Quinn had never thought much about GPS trackers until Mrs. Oliver put one on Quinn's Toyota. Then questions started percolating in Quinn's mind, and she had to read all she could about trackers. Amazed by all the little discs could do to provide visual, audio, and positional information, she had made the decision to leave Mrs. Oliver's tracker in place. Knowing that it was there gave her the ability to lead her former teacher around, a kind of reverse tracking.

Of course, Mrs. Oliver had assured Quinn that the tracker was for her own protection. *What a lie!* And then, when someone had taken her car to the docks and loaded the trunk with a kilo of coke, Mrs. Oliver had reported that the car had been moved. *Some protection. I won't believe anything from that lady's mouth ever again.*

On her way to work, Quinn stopped by the police station to ask Sergeant Schmidt for an update. Located in the same complex as the county courthouse, the station exuded the ambience of strength and authority. Quinn harbored a few bad memories from last year, when she had been processed in one of the small rooms there, but today she pushed them aside.

On duty at the front desk, smelling faintly of coconut and vanilla, sat Quinn's favorite clerk, Ms. Frances. "Well, hi dee do, Ms. Quinn. I saw in the newspaper that you got hitched. Congratulations."

"Oh, thank you, Ms. Frances. Seems like a long time ago. Sergeant Schmidt in?"

"Yas'm. He just breezed through here a few minutes ago. I'll buzz him to say you're here."

Schmidt's voice boomed through the phone intercom. "Send her back."

"You know where to go," Ms. Frances said, pointing behind her.

Quinn glanced around as she strode past the people already crowding the facility. She'd never seen the place empty, even in the middle of the night. Schmidt's office, furnished with a utilitarian desk and chairs, gave the impression of sparseness, but not emptiness. The desk and shelves were cluttered with folders and notebooks, and both filing cabinets held open drawers. Schmidt's winter jacket hung on a hook on the back of the office door.

Schmidt stood. "Hey, Quinn. I was just about to call you." He invited her to sit in the metal chair opposite his desk. "Ninety percent accuracy that the hair in your trunk belongs to Mrs. Oliver. 'Course the margin of error could cover the possibility that it was the twin."

"I don't think the twin was messing with my car." Quinn couldn't imagine a scenario in which Elizabeth Lavender would give a flip about an embalmer's car, and, besides, Liz was dead well before the car was taken. "I'm sure Mrs. Oliver did it."

Schmidt huffed and grinned, an unpleasant gum-showing expression unsuited to the conversation. "Why? I thought you and Mrs. Oliver were big buddies for years."

"Yeah, well, I guess I misread the situation. She obviously has it in for me, and probably McFarland's, too. The lady is very hard to figure out—one day, friend; the next day, enemy." Quinn bit her lip to keep from spilling what she knew about Mrs. Oliver from Farrah. "I have another question for you, regarding my car."

"Shoot." Schmidt leaned forward in his chair. "Whaddya want to know?"

"When you processed my car, did you find Mrs. Oliver's tracker?"

Clapping a hand to his forehead, Sergeant Schmidt cried out. "I forgot all about that bug! Let me look at the report." He clicked keys on his computer and read for several seconds. "Nope. No mention of a tracking device. What the hell happened to it, I wonder."

"Maybe Mrs. Oliver took it back when she stuck the cocaine in the trunk—assuming she's the one who did that." Quinn had no doubt, but she didn't want to overplay her hand. "I guess the tracker served its purpose. Now I can breathe easy, knowing that my teacher isn't spying on me."

Schmidt walked around the desk and plopped down in the chair next to Quinn's. "I'll tell you a little secret. Comes from experience with police business, to which you are no stranger." He grunted a little before going further. "We're still working on the deaths of Mrs. Oliver's sister and her gardener. Mrs. Oliver's absence complicates matters, but we'll find her. I'm not happy about the whole hair-in-the-trunk issue, either.

"You've had too many situations recently—the poisoned hot dog, the tracker, the cocaine, formaldehyde fumes--What I'm trying to say is don't breathe easy when it comes to Mrs. Oliver. Stay on your guard, and if you see anything suspicious, call me immediately."

Chapter Sixty-six

Quinn had no plans to breathe easy, despite what she'd said to Sergeant Schmidt. Convinced that Mrs. Oliver was behind some, if not all, of the bad things going on around her, Quinn had kicked up her vigilance radar for anything related to Mrs. Oliver. And she didn't plan to sit around waiting to see what the evil woman would do next.

Meanwhile, she needed to talk to her parents, or at least her father, regarding her application to PA school. She didn't want to put that off even one more day.

When she arrived at McFarland's, things were quiet in the embalming room. No new bodies, no missing bottles of formaldehyde. She kept on walking through the living room and toward the office. The scent of lemon furniture polish contributed to the homey ambience, and a pang of familiarity struck her. These rooms were just as much her home as the apartment upstairs, where she'd grown up. She would miss being in this environment every day.

Bolstered by Josh's support and the knowledge that she was doing the right thing for herself, as well as her family, Quinn straightened her shoulders and set out to find her father. If her mother happened to be in the room, that was okay, too. She'd forgiven her mother's *faux pas* the last time she tried to tell them. Joy McFarland would never change, and, Quinn had to admit, her mother's delight over her marriage to Josh was overall a good thing.

Quinn found both parents in the office, poring over paperwork and whispering, even though no one else was in the room. "Have I caught you at a bad time?"

"No, no. Come on in," her dad said. "We're just going over the books from last year." He sighed. "Planning for retirement is not for sissies."

Quinn gulped air. "Well, that's what I wanted to talk about, too." Despite rehearsing this speech several times, she found herself tongue-tied. "I'm sure you remember when I was a kid, I wanted to be a doctor. I convinced myself that performing procedures on dead bodies was part of the medical profession, but it's never really been enough."

Her mother's eyes narrowed, but Quinn plowed ahead. "I decided several months ago to apply to the medical school in the physician assistant program. I have an interview coming up, and if all goes well. I'll start school in the fall."

The words hung in the air like droopy crepe paper streamers from a long-ago party. Her parents exchanged glances, but neither spoke.

"This probably comes as a shock. I'm sorry I didn't tell you earlier that I'd applied, but honestly, I never expected to get in, and I didn't want to upset you unnecessarily."

Her father leaned forward and managed a smile. "Congratulations, honey. We are very proud of you, aren't we, Joy?"

Joy's eyes misted, probably not from happiness, but she nodded and reached across the desk to touch Quinn's forearm. "I remember years ago how you wanted to study medicine. But I thought you'd put aside that dream in favor of carrying on the tradition of McFarland's. Do you really want to defer your life and your marriage for several years to get a job that probably won't pay you more than you're earning now?"

Quinn's heart hammered. Her mother's not-so-oblique reference to grandchildren ticked Quinn off. She hadn't expected her mother to approve, but the exchange bothered her more than she'd expected. "I know you're thinking about the business, who will do my job. I'm concerned about that, too. But we have several months to work on that, and I promise to help you find someone."

Remembering her conversation with Josh, Quinn switched gears. "Besides, Jack is perfectly capable of leading the business on his own. You can hire an embalmer for a lot less than I'm earning, and that means more profit for Jack."

Quinn's dad rose from his chair and crossed to his daughter. He put his arms around her shoulders and gave her a hug, whispering in her ear. "Don't worry about us. You have to find your path, and we'd never stand in your way. Last year we thought we'd lost you, and all we wanted was our daughter back, healthy and strong. We never gave a thought to losing our employee. McFarland's will get along fine. You follow your dream."

Quinn burst into tears and pressed her face into her father. She muttered thanks and turned to her mother for a stiff hug. Things would be different come next fall. Jack would be married, she'd be in school, and people would continue to need death services.

Somehow, Quinn knew everything would work out the way it was supposed to. Or did the word, "naïve," in the dictionary still have her picture next to it?

Chapter Sixty-seven

Now that her secret was out about PA school, Quinn could concentrate on finding Mrs. Oliver and bringing her rampage to an end. When the teacher disappeared, Quinn had tried to forget about her. But the formaldehyde incident made it clear that Quinn and her family were still being targeted by someone evil, and the hair in her trunk, along with Farrah's statement, convinced Quinn that person was Mrs. Oliver.

Waiting for the police to act had gotten her nowhere. The time had come to find Mrs. Oliver and confront her face to face.

Taking advantage of another late-start morning at work, and feeling a bit like a cross between Nancy Drew and Mata Hari, Quinn checked the app on her cell phone, which gave her regular reports of GPS coordinates, the location of Mrs. Oliver's car. They varied a little from one report to the next, but most of the time they designated a spot on the mainland about forty minutes away.

Quinn had recognized the location as the neighborhood off the main highway behind the upscale gentleman's club, Heaven's Door. Not surprised that Mrs. Oliver's Cadillac stayed near Blackie's establishment, Quinn set out with her cell phone and her purse, wearing powder blue sweatpants and top, running shoes, and a can of pepper spray in her coat pocket.

The cold engine took several tries, but once started, it moved smoothly through the neighborhood.

A thick fog enveloped the car, slowing the trip over the causeway to a crawl. Despite the morning hour, Quinn turned on her fog lights, primarily to make her car visible to other vehicles. The defroster threw warm air on the windshield, doing little to improve driving conditions.

As she cut a swath through the gray mist, Quinn recalled how she'd exited Rudy & Paco's and tacked her own tracker into the metal under the fender of Mrs. Oliver's car, while her teacher sat at their lunch table. She owed Jan for sneaking her out the fire door and back inside. When this was over, she'd have to invite Jan and her husband over for drinks and dinner one night.

The lunch at the fancy restaurant had served a purpose for Quinn, but in retrospect, what purpose had it served for Mrs. Oliver? The tracker she had put on Quinn's car had already been in place.

Bestowing the gift-wrapped bracelet from Ana couldn't have served as justification for the luncheon—there had to be a more malevolent motivation.

Quinn reviewed the conversation at the table that day, certain neither probing questions had been asked nor compromising information revealed. The bracelet must have been tampered with, the silver hair in the box a clue. Quinn hadn't tried it on. She hadn't even touched it, except for when she examined the box. Another to-do list item for later. She would take the package to the police station.

Jerking herself back into the here and now, Quinn exited the freeway and followed the U-turn toward Heaven's Door. Memories of things she'd experienced inside needed to remain dormant. Outsmarting Mrs. Oliver trumped everything else, and Quinn marshaled all her energy for the task. This time Quinn would have to provide the lesson, and she wouldn't accept any grade less than an A+.

Chapter Sixty-eight
TRISH

Well, whaddya know? Looks like I'm about to receive a visit from none other than Quinn McFarland. Quinn Brady, I mean. Of course, someone else might be driving her car, but probably not. And her car might be on its way somewhere else—like Heaven's Door—but probably not. Quinn's coming after me. That's the simplest explanation.

How has she found me, that little stinker? When might she have slapped a tracker on my car? She's smart, I must admit, even though she's naïve as hell. Somehow she's evaded all the trouble I've set in her way—the bracelet, the cocaine, the formaldehyde. Either she's savvier than I give her credit for, or she's plain ass lucky.

The question is, has she ratted me out to the police? Probably yes, since I saw her car went to the police station yesterday, but if she'd told them where I am, they would've been on my doorstep in a Gulf Coast minute. But that begs the question—why not? Hard to believe Quinn has more loyalty to her sweet little ol' English teacher than to Super Cop Schmidt.

Whichever, she can't evade what's coming to her forever. More importantly, what does she want, tracking me down on this foggy Gulf Coast morning?

Whatever she's after, I'm ready. She'll soon learn she's out of her league, messing with me. I can't be responsible for what happens next. I haven't told Quinn to chase after me. In fact, since the formaldehyde fiasco, I've decided to leave the girl and her family alone, let the string play out.

Now that Blackie's gone, Quinn isn't a priority, except for one thing, and that has to do with Liz. I'll play her little game of cat and mouse, only I'll be the cat, always the cat.

Hmpf. Here she comes, turning into the apartment complex. She's slowing down, looking for my car. I'll make things easy for her. Let me just put on this raincoat. I'm going to pretend to carry a sack of groceries into the condo. Let her think she's tracking me down.

I'll lead her up here and ply her with cookies. Just like in the classroom, I need to ask the right questions. And if she doesn't give me the right answers—well, I won't get ahead of myself.

"Yoohoo, Quinn, are you looking for me? How convenient. I'm looking for you, too."

Chapter Sixty-nine

Quinn turned into the complex where three multi-storied buildings formed a row, surrounded by sidewalks and parking spaces. The GPS on her cell phone squawked. "Your destination is ahead on your right."

Sure enough, there was Mrs. Oliver's Cadillac, parked in a handicapped spot near the entrance to the first building. A blue placard hung on the car's rearview mirror. Unaware of any handicap that her former teacher had, Quinn wondered whether this was the right car.

But at that moment, a flash of movement caught her eye. A brown-haired woman in a raincoat emerged from the nearby building, carrying a sack of groceries, and hurrying toward the car.

Not wanting to be seen, Quinn pulled into an empty spot opposite, where she could watch in her rearview mirror. Even through the mist, the shape and form, if not the hair color, of the woman matched that of Mrs. Oliver. *What is she doing? Who carries groceries to the car?*

Mrs. Oliver looked left and right before setting the grocery bag in her open trunk, closing the lid, and scooting into the driver's seat of her car.

Quinn held her breath, wondering whether her teacher would start the car and drive off. After a full three minutes without movement of the Cadillac, another thought entered Quinn's mind. *She knows I'm here. She's putting on a charade to lead me to her apartment.*

At that moment, the trunk of Mrs. Oliver's car flew up, and the woman climbed out of her car. She retrieved the bag of groceries, closed the trunk, and gazed around the parking lot, holding her free hand to her brow as a shade against the fog.

Whether she spotted Quinn's car or not, she crept toward the entrance of the first building. Quinn had no illusion this time that a visit to Mrs. Oliver would be purely social. Girded with that knowledge, and determined to head off any further plans to harm her family, Quinn decided to play along.

Before she left the safety of her car, however, she pinned her GPS coordinates and sent them to Mary Hallom. She wanted someone to know where she was, in case things became dicey. She could trust Mary not to panic or tell Quinn's brother or Sergeant Schmidt unless necessary.

With a mental apology to Josh for embarking on a potentially dangerous mission, Quinn kissed her wedding ring and touched the protective item in her pocket. She jumped out of her car and followed Mrs. Oliver into the small lobby of the building.

"Hello, Mrs. Oliver," she said, tugging on the sleeve of the woman's raincoat. "How about if I carry your groceries for you?"

The older woman turned around and touched Quinn's arm with her left hand. The wrist was bandaged and the touch heavier than necessary. A show of teeth and tongue masqueraded as a smile. "Why, Quinn. How lovely of you to check on me. Let's go upstairs to my temporary living quarters. I can offer you some fresh-baked cookies."

Chapter Seventy

The apartment smelled of chocolate, but also of those fruity room deodorizers that plugged into electrical sockets. Neither suggested a homey atmosphere. In fact, the combination living room and dining room held none of the appeal of a home—no artwork, no photographs, no pillows or throws, no TV, no books.

The latter distracted Quinn for a moment. She couldn't imagine her English teacher living somewhere without being surrounded by books. A long counter topped with fake granite separated the kitchen from the other space. Four barstools stood sentry, without any evidence that anyone had eaten there.

"Let me take your coat and handbag and have a seat, my dear," Mrs. Oliver said. "I believe you'll want tea with your cookies, if I remember correctly." She hustled to the kitchen, spryer than before and with an unnatural gleam in her eyes.

"No, thanks. Actually, I'm not hungry or thirsty, and I don't feel like sitting. Your hair looks nice." Quinn said, following her teacher into the kitchen. Her eyes fell on several racks of cookies, cooling on the counter, and some on a platter. Next to them lay the short story book Quinn had given Mrs. Oliver. Face down, it was open to a page about halfway through.

"Thanks. I decided my looks needed a refresh. And, yes," Mrs. Oliver said, touching the book's spine. "I'm enjoying your gift." She batted at Quinn's wrists. "I see you aren't wearing the ID bracelet I gave you. Too bad. I went to such trouble to get that for you. Anyway, your gift helps me pass the time while I sojourn in this little place."

"Quite different from your house." Quinn peered around, wanting to make sure they were alone. A closed door beyond the dining room probably led to bedrooms and a bath. If someone were in there, he or she must have been asleep. Now that she was here, she didn't know exactly how to start the conversation she wanted to have.

"Well, let me know if you change your mind about cookies," Mrs. Oliver said, taking a big bite out of one and humming. "Shall we sit at the dining table? That sofa's so low I can't get out of it."

Quinn sat and scooched in, not wanting to show the outline of the can of pepper spray in her pocket. Questions swarmed in her head, but asking them would make her vulnerable, so she held back.

"You probably have some questions for me," Mrs. Oliver said. She finished the cookie and licked her lips. "You wouldn't have come otherwise."

"Likewise." Quinn sat erect, her hands folded in her lap like an ingenue practicing party etiquette. "You go first."

"Okay." Mrs. Oliver's lips drew back, faking another smile. A cookie crumb sat on her bosom. "Congratulations on tracking me here. I assume you put a tracker on my car that day we were at lunch."

Quinn nodded. "What's that saying you used to quote all the time in class? 'Turnabout is fair play?'"

"Touche'. I see I've taught you too well." She leaned forward and put her elbows on the table. "Now, tell me. What's so interesting that you'd go to so much trouble to follow me here? Did Sergeant Schmidt send you?"

"Indirectly, you might say. The police found your hair in the trunk of my car with a kilo of cocaine. Maybe you can tell me why you went to all the trouble to implicate me and pretended to warn me that someone else had planted drugs there." As she spoke, indignation boiled inside, and her voice took on a sharp edge.

Mrs. Oliver stopped tapping her fingernails on the tabletop and exhaled with a whistle. "You ask a difficult question. You deserve a difficult answer. I hoped things wouldn't come to this, but here we are." She stood in place, her eyes boring into Quinn's.

Not wishing to be talked down to like a lowly student, Quinn rose, as well. Her heart beat double-time, waiting for the "difficult answer."

In a louder than normal voice, Mrs. Oliver began. "Ever since last year, when you went after Blackie, you stepped on a lot of toes. Toes of some very dangerous people. At first, I felt sorry for you. You'd been a victim when I knew you in high school, and I figured you didn't know what you were getting yourself into.

"I told Blackie to warn you off, and that would be the end of it. But, no—you kept on getting bolder. In the end, when Blackie went to jail—all your fault—that hurt a lot of people, me included." Mrs. Oliver lowered her voice to a whisper, a technique Quinn remembered from the classroom. "The coke in your trunk was meant to discredit you and your family business. When you came to testify in Blackie's trial, we hoped to negate the impact."

Quinn nodded. "I get that, but now there isn't going to be a trial." Quinn took a leap with her next remark. "I have reason to believe you were behind the formaldehyde poisoning that endangered my father's life. And that was *after* Blackie's death. Do you have a so-called reason for that one?"

"Look, Quinn. I'm not admitting to attempted murder, and you realize that this conversation alone puts you in jeopardy. I will say that you've butted into my affairs just a few too many times. My sister's death, my sister's sex life—none of this is any business of yours. You claim to be helping Sergeant Schmidt. Well, okay. That puts you in the category of police, and I can't let you abuse our relationship."

These last words brought a redness to Mrs. Oliver's face and an unhealthy sputtering to her voice. Quinn wondered whether the woman would stroke out before her eyes. Quinn considered replying to the comments, defending her collaboration with the police, perhaps, but she remembered a quote from *The Scarlet Letter*, which she'd read in Mrs. Oliver's class. "She could no longer borrow from the future to ease her present grief."

"You made yourself a target, over and over again. I tried to warn you. I even sent my sister's body to McFarland's, hoping you'd snap out of snooping on me and concentrate on doing your own job, but you kept coming at me, just like you kept after Blackie. And we aren't the only ones who've taken notice. Suffice it to say, you've made a lot of people angry."

Quinn dismissed some of Mrs. Oliver's rantings as the words of a deranged woman, however, the barb about assisting the police stung. She hadn't wanted to be involved in Elizabeth Lavender's murder investigation. She'd been pulled into helping Schmidt—how? Quinn couldn't even remember what tack he'd used to enlist her cooperation.

Before she could come up with a response, Mrs. Oliver lashed out again. "I can't let you get away with these things anymore, Quinn. I led you here for a reason, and you must see that I can't let you leave." Mrs. Oliver advanced into Quinn's space with her eyes blazing and her right arm raised. "You know too—"

Quinn ducked and slipped her hand around the can of pepper spray in her pocket.

A racket coming from the outside door caused both women to turn their heads and stare. A pounding and smashing announced the intruder, a young man built like a bulldozer, whose voice echoed in the open space. "Say your prayers, Trish Oliver."

His nostrils flared when he glanced at Quinn, and his eyebrows knitted themselves into the deep scar in the middle. Recovering quickly, he gave a one-eyed stare that shifted between the two of them, while his other eye wandered to the side. He said to Quinn, "How fortunate. I will kill two birds with one stone. But first—we need to talk." He brandished a revolver, indicating for them to move to the back of the kitchen, where there was no exit.

As he pressed forward, the collar of the man's shirt opened slightly. What Quinn saw confirmed the man's identity—on his neck was a rooster tattoo.

Chapter Seventy-one

Quinn's heart pounded, and her breath caught in her throat, as she gazed at the barrel of Francisco Martinez' gun. Assessing her chances for survival, she gripped the can of pepper spray in her pocket, unsure of when the right moment would be to set it off. Too soon or too late would be disastrous. She'd read the instructions, but now wished she had taken time to practice. She'd have one chance.

Mrs. Oliver stared at her, mouth opened, as if screaming, but with nothing coming out. Two against one could be an advantage, but only if the two women worked together to outsmart the man with the gun. In different circumstances, Quinn might have laughed at the irony of being thrown into combat on the side of Mrs. Oliver, who, moments before, had come after her with a threat. Now, there was no time to laugh.

"Empty your pockets, *senoras*. Now." His eyes glittered with evil—or maybe drugs. Martinez backed them into the small area where the stove flanked the two long counters. He poked his gun into Quinn's ribcage and then into Mrs. Oliver's. Quinn held her thumb on the button of the pepper spray as she pulled the small canister out of her pocket. Now-or-never, she ignored the gun pointed at her middle and aimed the spray at the assailant's nose.

A stream of pressurized aerosol burst forth, causing Martinez to drop his gun and grab his face. Quinn tried to push the screaming Martinez aside and flee, but Mrs. Oliver squeezed her shoulder with a vise-like grip.

"Let me go!" Quinn slapped at her teacher's hand. If Mrs. Oliver wanted to stay until the pepper spray wore off, that was up to her, but Quinn wanted out—now.

Meanwhile, temporarily blinded and pouring mucous from his nose, Martinez blocked both women from exiting the interior of the kitchen. "*Agua*," he said, his voice a sob.

"The sink's behind you," Quinn said, hoping Martinez would turn around. The effects of the spray would last for hours, unless he washed it off quickly. Even so, he'd be disabled about fifteen minutes.

Mrs. Oliver jerked at the strap of Quinn's shoulder bag, causing Quinn to whip around and shove her hand away. Martinez grunted, opened his arms, and planted his feet at the sides of the cabinets, effectively trapping the women inside.

Quinn considered ducking and crawling between his legs, but before she could manage the move, Mrs. Oliver squealed. "Don't let her get away." Surprised by her teacher's intent to hold Quinn back, even if it meant her own entrapment, Quinn doubled her own determination. She took a step backward into the stovetop. Maybe she could grab something to use as a weapon or a shield.

Quinn's movement, intended to be subtle, knocked a tray of cookies onto the floor. Perhaps shocked by the sudden clatter, Mrs. Oliver gasped and shouted, "The cookies." She bent to pick up the half dozen still-warm discs, but Martinez stopped her with a blind smack to the head.

"Leave them." His booming voice echoed in the small space, and he punctuated his order by crushing the cookies with his foot. An ankle monitor peeked out from beneath his jeans, reminding Quinn that he was out on bail from the cockfighting charge.

A coyote-like laugh burst from the man's mouth, as he struggled to hold Quinn in place. Desperate to change the balance of power, Quinn still had her arms. She swiped a cookie from a platter on the counter next to her. "Have a cookie," she said, stuffing it into his mouth.

Eyes and nose running, Martinez gasped, and Quinn thought he would spit out the cookie, but miraculously, he sucked in air and chewed. Looking for any advantage, Quinn hoped the cookies *were* poisoned. She glanced at Mrs. Oliver for a cue, but the woman's face had frozen into a hard stare. Quinn shivered. Stuck in this tight space with two dangerous lunatics, she needed to think fast. The only one she could count on was herself.

"Who are you?" Quinn asked the question, hoping to distract the monster in front of her, even though she was pretty certain about his identity. "Why are you doing this?"

"Shut th'fuck up," Martinez said, spewing crumbs. "I no needa talk to you." He pushed the rest of the cookie into his mouth and gobbled it down.

Mrs. Oliver suddenly sprang to life, picking up a second cookie from the same platter and sticking it in his mouth. "Good for you. Have another," she said. With an unexpected strength, she shoved him against the counter, grabbing his gun from the floor, and running out of the kitchen and through the outside door.

Torn between chasing Mrs. Oliver or continuing to hold Quinn, Martinez stood, paralyzed and still blinded from the spray. His face took on a greenish pallor, and, without warning, he let out a gurgling sound before vomiting all over Quinn's shoes and the floor full of cookie crumbs. He doubled over in pain and slumped to the floor, groaning.

Quinn didn't hesitate. She gathered her belongings and fled the apartment, dashing toward her car for safety. By now the fog had lifted, and Mrs. Oliver's Cadillac no longer sat in its handicapped parking spot. Quinn threw her smelly shoes in the trunk and took off.

Quinn drove around the block, where a 7-Eleven parking lot offered temporary asylum and a steady stream of customer traffic. Imagining herself as a heroine in a spy movie, she backed into a parking spot, watchful, in case of the need for a speedy escape.

Quinn panted as the number for Mary's cell phone rang—three, four times. When voicemail picked up, Quinn disconnected and called Sergeant Schmidt. Answering on the first ring, Schmidt said, "Quinn. What's up?"

Shaking her head at the thought that Schmidt was more accessible than Mary, Quinn blurted out fragments. "Mrs. Oliver—Martinez—apartment on the mainland—gun—cookies."

"Hold on. Take a deep breath and start over." Sounds of traffic in the background said he was on the go. "Wait a minute. Let me pull over."

When he indicated, Quinn summarized the events of the past hour and asked him to come. "Mrs. Oliver's driven off, but Martinez may still be in the apartment. I'm guessing he ate poisoned cookies intended for me." She gave him the address and directions.

"That's Texas City's jurisdiction," he said. "Listen carefully, Quinn. I need you to go directly to the Texas City police station for your own safety. They'll be expecting you. I'll meet some of their officers at the apartment, but you stay at the station until I get there." He gave her directions to the station and ended the call.

Still shaken, Quinn assessed her situation. The threat from Martinez may have been resolved, but Mrs. Oliver remained a danger. Quinn checked the tracker she'd placed on Mrs. Oliver's car, but no signal was coming through. Probably the woman had found and disabled the tracker by now. At large again, Mrs. Oliver presented a threat, but for the moment, she was out of the landscape.

Her Toyota turned over several times without catching. Now was not the time to have car trouble. Hands trembling, she pushed the ignition button again, and the motor roared.

Reassured by Schmidt's authoritative instructions, Quinn let out her breath and calmed down. Her biggest worry now was what Josh would say when he found out.

Chapter Seventy-two

While Sergeant Schmidt and the Texas City officers investigated the apartment where Mrs. Oliver had been living, Quinn met with Carrie Pye, a young officer, as petite as Quinn, and whose enthusiasm reminded her of her sister-in-law-to-be. They sat opposite one another at a small conference table in a cozy, but chilly, room in the Texas City police station.

Still in her stockinged feet, Quinn gave Officer Pye the run-down on the events of the past hour, Carrie looked up from the notes she was making and said, "For someone who's been through so much stress, you are incredibly calm—at least on the outside."

Quinn moved her hands through her curly hair. Her emotions ran the gamut from hyperawareness to shock to gratitude that she had escaped a deadly situation. She didn't feel calm, but she also accepted the inevitability of confrontation with Mrs. Oliver and the knowledge that the trouble wasn't yet over.

"I'm wondering about a few things you told me," Carrie said, leaning forward. "Why do you think Mrs. Oliver intended to poison you with the cookies?"

Quinn shuddered and crossed her arms for warmth. "There's been a series of incidents, harmful to my family or me, and I only recently connected them to Mrs. Oliver. The reason I went to her apartment today was to confront her." Quinn enumerated the various events, ending with the uncapped formaldehyde in the coffee room.

"Do you know why she would do those things?"

"Not really. Something about my involvement in the arrest of Lionel French last year."

"*You* had something to do with *that*?" Carrie's eyes grew rounder, and she stared at Quinn as if she were about to ask for an autograph. "We were glad to get French off the street. He was the ultimate bad actor."

Carrie paused and sat up straighter. "I'm sorry. Just had to say that."

"No worries," Quinn said. "Anyway, Mrs. Oliver—and Francisco Martinez—have something to do with French's business. Neither one cares for me."

Carrie asked a few more questions, including whether Quinn wanted to call anyone to let them know she was safe. Quinn shook her head. Nothing would be gained by telling Josh or her parents. She wanted to wait until Schmidt and the other officers returned from the apartment, but that might not be for a long time. She had to be at work in another ninety minutes.

"Am I good to leave?" Quinn wanted to go home, shower, change clothes, and get to McFarland's. She'd figure out the rest after that.

There was only one thing she wanted to know before she left. "Is Martinez alive or dead?" The thought that he may have died from a cookie she'd given him bothered her, but at the time she hadn't had other options.

Carrie sent a text and waited. "I can't divulge information about an ongoing case." She paused when a beep sounded, and then she read the text. Winking, she said, "But, if I were you, I'd be more concerned with Mrs. Oliver than Mr. Martinez."

"You can go," Carrie said, standing. "As long as you're comfortable. We don't need to keep you here." She handed Quinn her business card. "You know the routine. Call if you think of anything pertinent."

The two young women shook hands and then hugged. As Quinn turned to leave, Carrie called after her. "Don't forget to be careful. Mrs. Oliver is still out there."

Chapter Seventy-three

On her way home, Quinn remembered having sent Mary the GPS location of Mrs. Oliver's apartment. She called Mary's cell phone but again went to voicemail. "Hey, Mary. I sent you some GPS coordinates. Just ignore them now. Let's talk soon."

Mary might get wind of the incidents in Texas City and put two and two together. Quinn regretted the earlier text, but she could count on Mary to be discreet—she hoped.

The bigger problem was what to tell Josh. When they were dating, Josh had made his feelings clear about her association with the criminal element. They had almost broken up, and she eventually promised not to keep secrets from him.

Not that she sought out dangerous situations—her connection to Blackie went back to her childhood and had never been in her control. The same could be said this time. The burden of the past—her friendship with Ana and the comfort shown her by Mrs. Oliver—restricted her life as surely as if she were tied up in chains. She knew what that was like, too.

Most of all, she regretted having been so naïve about Mrs. Oliver. It shouldn't have taken so many warnings for Quinn to realize that Mrs. Oliver was not the kindly teacher she appeared to be.

Bottom line—she needed to tell Josh what had happened this morning. She cleaned up, walked the dogs in the back yard, put some chicken in the slow cooker, and secured the house with the alarm system.

The afternoon flew by at work. Still weakened by the formaldehyde poisoning, Quinn's father remained upstairs. Her mother divided her time between the office and the upstairs living quarters. Jack was out at another community meeting, so Quinn spent a few hours setting up funerals in the office. Her heart and mind were elsewhere.

***

When Josh arrived home after his shift at the hospital, he shed his jacket, sniffed the aroma of chicken and dumplings, announced that he was starving, and threw his arms around Quinn's waist, lifting her for a long kiss. "How's my sweetheart?" He carried her to the sofa, where he eased them both into a cozy embrace.

Life doesn't get any better than this. Quinn responded with enthusiasm, but the dread of telling him about her morning tainted the moment. "I love you, Josh Brady," she said, winding her hand under his button-down shirt. "No matter what happens, never forget that."

Josh pulled back, resting on his elbows, and Quinn's hand fell to his waist. "Sounds ominous. What's going on?"

Quinn couldn't dissemble now. He'd be furious if she said nothing and later revealed her news. Better to pull the bandage off in one swift motion. She sat up and ran her hands through her hair. "I was going to wait until after dinner, but I need to share something important that happened today."

"Okay," Josh said, his grayish eyes clouding over. "Are you okay? Is it your dad?"

Quinn stared at her lap and gulped air. "Dad's fine, and so am I. It's about Mrs. Oliver."

"Oh, no. I thought you were going to stay away from that lady. She's toxic." The mood spoiled, Josh rose and paced around the sofa.

"Yes, even more toxic than we thought. I learned from the police that the hair in my trunk was hers. That whole coke incident was her doing, designed to cause trouble for me and McFarland's." Quinn perched on the arm of the sofa, where she sat, bent-legged, with one foot tucked beneath her.

"What about the other crap—probably responsible for that, too." Josh cut off the words and spit them out, as if they were made of wormwood. "The bitch probably killed her own sister. I don't know why they haven't locked her up."

"The hair in the trunk convinced me and ticked me off, and I decided I had to do something about her. I had the morning off, so I went to Texas City to confront her in person at her apartment."

"What? Wait a minute." Josh slapped the dining room table as he paced. "Her apartment? How did you know where she was staying?"

That was the problem with having married a smart guy. He always came up with the exact right question. "I put a tracker on her car the day we went to lunch."

"You've got to be kidding me, Quinn. You're not the police." His voice cracked, and Quinn thought he might explode.

"She gave me the idea. Putting a tracker on my car." Despite the defensive tone, Quinn knew this wouldn't win any points with Josh. "Look, I know you don't approve of my involvement with Mrs. Oliver. It's not like I'm enjoying any of this. I've been tossed into this crazy salad like a day-old radish."

"Seems to me like you're the one doing the tossing. So, what happened when you went to the apartment?"

"She came at me. Tried to get me to eat her cookies. Of course I didn't. But then that scary Martinez guy, the one who spit in your face, broke in and threatened to shoot us both."

Josh grabbed both of her hands and sat. "Dammit, Quinn. This is terrible. Start from the beginning and tell me everything."

Calvin jumped up on the couch and inched between them, as if sensing the need to mediate. Glad to release the dreaded story, but not expecting much, Quinn launched into the details of her morning.

When she got to the part about being held at gunpoint, Josh raised his voice, louder than she had ever heard it. "Do. You. Realize. You could have been killed."

"But I *wasn't* killed. Let me finish." Tears stung Quinn's eyes. Josh was right, of course. Sheer luck had saved her from being shot. When she explained how Martinez had crumpled in pain from eating the cookies, the whole thing sounded unreal, even to her.

"Where do things stand now?" he asked.

"The police went to the apartment. I believe Martinez is dead, but not sure. And Mrs. Oliver is who knows where." Quinn put her head in her hands and tried to breathe deeply.

Red splotches stood out on Josh's cheeks and neck, and, when he spoke, his voice was soft and even, his words clipped. "Wherever she is, she still has you in her cross-hairs—your family—us— even our dogs. I'm glad you told me, Quinn, but this situation is intolerable." He stormed around the tiny living room, slamming the wall as he passed the dining table. "I'm really pissed that you put yourself in harm's way again this morning after all we've been through in the past—all the promises you've made."

He spun around to the peg where he had hung his winter jacket and slung it over his shoulder. "I can't live like this—worried about your safety all the time. I'm going out to think."

"I thought you were hungry," she said, her voice a mere mewl.

Josh shot daggers at her as he opened the door. "Not anymore." The door slammed behind him.

Chapter Seventy-four
TRISH

I can't understand why things happen the way they do. I bake cookies, and I'm in the midst of formulating a plan to lure Quinn to my apartment, when boom! She shows up on my doorstep, as if by magic. She's carrying that sweet little shoulder bag with her, as well.

I'm sure she hasn't found the little item slipped inside the day we were at the Galvez. I would have heard by now. So, I'm very excited to have this opportunity—Quinn and her purse in my little temporary apartment. What luck!

But then ol' crazy Francisco Martinez shows up, gun in hand. He's ruining everything, I think, not to mention threatening my life and Quinn's in the process. I can't let him do this, but he's stronger than any twelve women, combined. I think of going after him with a frying pan, but before I can reach one, Quinn shoots him in the face with pepper spray, a little canister probably intended for me.

The spray disables him, all right, but Martinez remains in control, and Quinn and I are trapped. This isn't going to end well, I can tell. Quinn and I both struggle to get away, but, even blind, he pins us in the space between counters in the kitchen.

I've got to hand it to Quinn, however. She jams a cookie into his mouth and gets him to chew. Not just any cookie, but one from the platter I've set aside for *her*.

Holy mackerel! The most skillful fiction author couldn't make up something this convoluted. I give him a second cookie, and Martinez collapses on the floor, writhing in pain. I can't believe this tough guy is going down from a cookie. Serves him right, though, for killing Julio.

One of Blackie's henchmen says Francisco is Julio's murderer, and I believe it. Although the same person tells me Francisco probably killed my sister, and I know that can't be true.

Anyway, I have to move around again. I can't go back to the apartment. I've found and removed the tracker Quinn put on my car—under the front fender, passenger side. Shows how creative Quinn is—not! And I have to ditch my car, too. Breaks my heart, because I love this little Cadillac, but there's probably an APB out for it already.

I may also have to give up on trying to get my hands on Quinn's purse. Dealing with Quinn is just too risky. I swear that girl has nine lives like a cat. Besides, she's going to avoid me like the plague. Too bad for her that I'm still tracking her, though.

I imagine the police are having a field day with my cookies. When the lab reveals the toxic ingredient—formaldehyde—they will try to tie me to everything. Liz, Julio, Mr. McFarland, and Francisco. The circumstantial evidence will make me look bad.

I will say, I *am* bad at times, just like my mother's saying about the little girl with the curl in the middle of her forehead. Is that me or Liz, I forget. But I call myself misunderstood. I don't intend to hurt anyone, ever. I simply need to protect myself and everything I've worked so hard to acquire. Isn't that the American way?

Chapter Seventy-five

The only arguments Quinn could remember having with Josh had been about this same topic—her involvement with criminals and police matters. But Josh had never walked out on her before.

Quinn didn't enjoy the drama—far from it. She had spent almost fifteen years of her life, before Josh, as a sort of recluse, avoiding social situations, and careful about relationships. When her former BFF, Ana, was killed, she was forced into stepping up, and she was able to reclaim her life in the process.

Josh had been along for the ride, and his support had been part of their love story, but he'd made it clear that he worried about her safety. Had she broken her pledge to him by involving herself in Mrs. Oliver's issues? Or had she been drawn in insidiously by the police and Mrs. Oliver herself? Either way, Quinn feared her honeymoon was over.

The clock said eight-thirty-five. The chicken and dumplings had dried out in the slow cooker, and she hadn't heard a peep from Josh about coming home. A voice in her head told her to call or text him. Hadn't she always heard that the key to a good marriage was communication? She guessed she needed to work on this. A second voice told her to let him have his space.

Her stomach had more knots than a pretzel, and the inner debate twisted them even tighter. Calvin, with his sharp sensitivity to her moods, had curled up on the sofa next to her and put his head on her lap. Where was Josh? At the hospital? He'd slept there many nights when on call. At a restaurant or a bar?

By eight-fifty, a pounding had begun in her head, and she checked her phone for the umpteenth time. Still no word. Was he checking his phone, too? She composed a text of adjectives, hoping he would respond. *Lonely, hurting, empty.*

The ticking of the clock echoed in the quiet house while she waited for an answer. When it came, it said, *Upset and worried.*

At least they were talking. Quinn would give him some time. She picked herself up from the sofa and went into the kitchen, where she took two ibuprofens, fed the dogs, watered the orchids, and threw out the ruined dinner.

She needed to get herself organized and think through this situation with Mrs. Oliver. She sat down at the dining table with a pen and a stack of blank paper. She drew a K-W-L chart, just the way Mrs. Oliver had taught her to do in English class years ago. She labeled the three columns, WHAT I KNOW, WHAT I WANT TO KNOW, and WHAT I'VE LEARNED.

A pang of guilt stabbed her from the realization that this activity furthered her participation in the Oliver mess, exactly what Josh hated. She couldn't help herself. She was smack dab in the middle, whether she liked it or not. The only way she knew to get out was to run the course.

KNOW	*WANT TO KNOW*	*LEARNED*
Elizabeth Lavender poisoned (formaldehyde), strangled	*Who? Why?*	*Possible connection to Julio, dirt*
Julio Martinez poisoned (formaldehyde)	*Who? Why?*	*Possible connection to Liz, dirt*
Poisoned frankfurter in yard	*Who? Why?*	
Cocaine in my trunk	*Who? Why?*	*Mrs. Oliver To discredit me for testifying against Blackie?*
Blackie, killed in jail (foul play)	*Is there any connection to Lavender/ Martinez deaths? If so, what?*	
Formaldehyde in coffee room	*Who? How? Why?*	*Stranger seen by Zeke*
Francisco Martinez' attempt on Mrs. Oliver and me	*Why?*	
Martinez poisoned? (Mrs. Oliver's cookies)	*Were cookies intended for me? Why?*	

Mrs. Oliver's threat to kill me	*Why?*	

As she filled out the chart, Quinn realized how many unanswered questions she had. Also, the number of items threatening her own well-being, lined up like that, caused a lump to form in her throat. How could she expect repeated attempts on her or her family to stop until the perpetrators were apprehended?

Quinn's pen hovered over the last item on the list. Why did Mrs. Oliver come after her in the apartment? Quinn replayed the experience, frame by frame, starting with her arrival at Mrs. Oliver's apartment, being invited in. Mrs. Oliver had offered to take her coat and handbag, then offered her tea and cookies, which Quinn had declined. They'd sat at the dining table, where they exchanged harsh words. Mrs. Oliver kept glancing in the direction of Quinn's purse, hung by the strap from her chair.

Wait a minute! What was this fixation on her shoulder bag? Quinn ran to her closet to get the shoulder bag from the peg where she kept it. Admittedly, her purse served as a receptacle for junk. She threw things into it, rarely thinking about them again. She couldn't remember the last time she'd gone through the contents.

She set the bag on her dining table and unzipped both compartments. She dug through the pouches, not knowing what to look for. Tissues, wallet, sunglasses, lipstick, a brush, a small bottle of aspirin, loose change, spearmint gum, a photo of Josh taken when they'd just started dating. Not seeing anything out of the ordinary, she dumped everything out on the table and spread the items out.

Her heart thumping, she picked up objects and moved others around. After a few seconds she came across an article that took her breath away, something *she* hadn't put in there. She dropped the item on the table like a burning ember, and she grabbed her cell phone to call Sergeant Schmidt.

"Can you come to my house? I have something you need to see right now."

Chapter Seventy-six

Quinn never thought she'd be glad that Josh hadn't come home, but he would have gone ballistic if he'd seen a squad car parked in her driveway. Sergeant Schmidt hadn't hesitated about coming over, even without knowing why.

"I'll try to be brief," she said, ushering him to the dining room table.

He looked around, as if wondering where Josh was at almost ten p.m., but he didn't ask. "Don't worry. You wouldn't have called me after hours if you didn't think it was urgent. Tell me everything you think I need to know."

Quinn walked him to the dining table. She explained how she'd reviewed everything that had occurred at Mrs. Oliver's apartment that morning, and how she'd made the K-W-L chart, which she showed him.

He glanced over the graphic organizer and nodded but made no comment.

"When I got to that last bit, about Mrs. Oliver's coming after me, I remembered a little detail that I hadn't paid attention to at the time." She lowered her voice. "Mrs. Oliver kept eying my shoulder bag. I couldn't imagine why, but Mrs. Oliver doesn't do anything without a motive."

Quinn pointed to the pile of objects on the table. "I emptied my purse and went through everything before I figured out what she wanted. It was this." Quinn indicated, but didn't touch, a plastic card, sitting between her key fob and a pack of tissues.

Schmidt peered at the card, but also did not touch it. When he realized what it was, his eyes popped open wide. "Are you saying you found this in your purse? You didn't put it there?"

"That's right," Quinn said. "How would I have obtained a New York driver's license for Elizabeth Lavender? I'd bet everything in my wallet that Mrs. Oliver put it there."

Schmidt's voice became louder, and his eyes bored into hers with interest. "When did she have the opportunity?"

"Could have been any time, starting with the day we met with her at the Galvez. Or when I went to her house to ask her questions. Or even when we went to lunch at Rudy & Paco's." She ran her fingers through her hair. "I don't clean out my purse very often."

"Did you handle the card?" Schmidt asked.

"Not after I realized what it was. It's sitting on the table just the way I found it." Quinn handed him a tweezers and a paper lunch bag. "I knew you'd want to check for prints."

Schmidt carefully lifted the license and slid it into the bag. "You have no idea how important this is. I can't thank you enough."

Glad she could contribute something of value, Quinn pushed her luck. "You're welcome. Can you tell me what you found with regard to Franciso Martinez?"

"Well, it'll be in the news tomorrow morning. Martinez is dead."

Quinn shivered, even though she expected so. "Any idea whether he was poisoned?"

"Not yet. Autopsy pending. Cookies are being tested."

"Mrs. Oliver ate a cookie from a cooling rack earlier, and she was fine. But the cookies he ate came from a separate platter. I gave him the first one to distract him. Then Mrs. Oliver gave him another." Quinn remembered her shoes, which were still sitting in the trunk of her car. "Martinez vomited on my shoes, if you want to test them."

"Sure, I'll take them in to Texas City. They've got all the cookies, as well." Schmidt lifted the bag with the driver's license. "If you want to give me those shoes, I guess I'll be going."

"They're in the trunk of my car. C'mon, I'll walk you out." Quinn fetched another brown paper bag from her pantry and handed it to the officer.

When she opened the front door and stepped out into the quiet coolness, the darkness of the hour slapped her in the face. Her body was chugging like an ancient train far from its depot.

She used her fob to open the trunk. A sour odor flew out immediately. "Help yourself," she said, pointing to the tainted running shoes.

Schmidt turned his head before reaching in for the shoes, and at that moment the glare of headlights turned the corner, lighting up the yard. Josh hit the brakes and parked on the street, so as not to block the police car in the driveway.

Quinn's insides became a cauldron, roiling with emotions that she was too worn out to identify. If only Josh had arrived two minutes later. *He must be seething.*

Despite the circles under his eyes and a slower-than-normal gait, Josh held out his hand to shake the policeman's. The two exchanged pleasantries, and Schmidt took off, leaving the newlyweds alone in the front yard.

"I'm glad you came home," Quinn said.

Josh rubbed his face before putting his arm around her shoulders. "Me, too. Let's go inside. I'm exhausted."

Within minutes, and without conversation, they had walked the dogs, brushed their teeth, and slipped into bed. Quinn snuggled into her husband's warmth and listened as his breathing softened into sleep.

She rolled over and let her mind replay the events of the day, eventually landing on the driver's license in her shoulder bag. Schmidt had said, "You have no idea how important this is," and before she drifted off to sleep, Quinn figured out why.

Chapter Seventy-seven

The next morning was Saturday, Josh slipped out of bed, showered, and started making pancakes for breakfast. The sweet aroma of maple syrup pulled Quinn from a dream. Time to face the reality of a regular day and unresolved issues from the previous one.

Quinn cleaned up and did a minimum to make herself presentable before padding barefooted into the kitchen. "Mmmm, smells great." She opened her arms for a hug, and smiled when Josh put down his spatula and stepped into them. He wrapped his arms tightly around her and rocked from one side to another.

Quinn wished the hug could last forever, but after a minute, Josh let go. "Breakfast is ready. Let's eat while it's still hot."

"And, we need to talk," she said, setting the table and pouring the already-brewed coffee into mugs. When they had both taken first bites and sips, Quinn said, "I love you, Josh Brady. I understand why you were upset."

Josh ate a few more bites and washed them down with coffee. "I love you, too. I'm feeling better with the sun shining outside and after food and rest. But the issue remains. What was Sergeant Schmidt doing here after ten o'clock last night?"

Quinn put down her fork and took her husband's hand. "I'll tell you everything I know." She began with where she had left off yesterday, when Josh had left the house. "First, I gave myself a pity party. Our first argument as a married couple, and I felt helpless to do anything to make things better for either of us."

She toyed with her silverware and napkin and searched for the right words. "Josh, I don't ask for these things in my life. I'm not an adventure-seeker."

Josh's eyes crinkled, and his lips turned up slightly. "You say that, my love, but every time we turn around, you are caught in the middle of intrigue. If you truly aren't doing anything to invite it, and I believe you aren't, you have the rottenest luck. Somehow you end up in the same spheres with nasty criminals and the police who chase them."

"True enough," Quinn said, "but you also had an unpleasant meeting with Francisco Martinez through no fault of your own. Sometimes these things happen."

"So, tell me how Sergeant Schmidt ended up here last night."

Quinn recounted how she'd found the New York driver's license. "There was only one way Elizabeth Lavender's license could have gotten in my purse. It had to have been put there by Mrs. Oliver."

Josh sat straighter. "How strange."

"Yes, and it explained a lot about why Mrs. Oliver repeatedly tried to get her hands on my handbag. She wanted to retrieve it before I found it." Quinn took a big swig of coffee. "I needed to get rid of it right away, so I called Sergeant Schmidt, and he came over to get it.

"While he was here, he told me Martinez was dead, and the cookies were being analyzed for poison. I offered to give him my shoes, which Martinez had vomited on. That's what we were getting out of the trunk when you drove up."

Josh grinned, and his voice warmed. "I'm glad you've turned everything over to the police instead of trying to investigate, yourself."

"Of course," Quinn said. "Sergeant Schmidt said the driver's license was a very important find, and he was grateful."

"Why do you think it was so important?" Josh asked.

Quinn smiled. "I do have a theory, if you have time to hear it."

He reached for her hand and squeezed. "I have all the time in the world. It's Saturday."

Quinn texted her mother to make sure she wasn't needed. Together, she and Josh walked to the sofa, where they cuddled, the pups at their feet.

"Okay, tell me your theory, Detective Brady," Josh said, twining his fingers through her hair.

Quinn inched away, so she could look him in the eye. "You remember that Mrs. Oliver and Elizabeth Lavender are identical twins, right?"

When Josh nodded, Quinn continued. "They had switched places throughout their lives, including this last time, when Liz was here, and Mrs. Oliver was in New York for the holidays. When we returned from Jamaica, the police thought they had Mrs. Oliver's body at the morgue, but when I went to ID the body, I recognized the *epsilon* tattoo on the wrist, and I knew the deceased was Mrs. Oliver's twin."

"I'm following you." Josh's arm now rested on the back of the sofa, and he stared at her with interest.

"Mrs. Oliver flew in from New York when the police notified her of her sister's death. She appeared to be bereaved and clueless as to how this could happen." Quinn stared at her hands. Her next words would represent a leap in logic. "The police most likely checked plane records to confirm that Mrs. Oliver was in New York when her sister was killed. But what if Mrs. Oliver flew to Houston as Elizabeth Lavender, using her sister's ID, killed her sister, and flew back using the same ID? She'd pass inspection at the airports as Elizabeth, and there'd be no record of Trish having left New York. She'd have a perfect alibi."

Josh's eyes widened, and he said, "But she couldn't let the police find the driver's license, so she had to park it somewhere the police wouldn't find it—in your purse."

"Exactly. But she also couldn't risk having *me* find it and put two and two together, either. So, once she felt safe from detection, she kept trying to get hold of my purse to snatch it back."

"Holy shit, Quinn. You're saying Mrs. Oliver may be a murderer. And you may have the evidence to prove it."

"*Had* the evidence. The police have it now."

Josh stood and took both of Quinn's hands in his. "There's only one problem, my beautiful wife. Mrs. Oliver doesn't know that."

Chapter Seventy-eight

Having a day off with Josh at home was the perfect gift after the stress of the previous day. They hung around the house, cleaning, cooking, washing his car, walking the dogs, and taking a long afternoon nap together. Ordinary things made special by the reconciliation of their argument and Josh's acceptance of Quinn's situation.

With Josh by her side, Quinn felt a little less like a renegade. That did a lot for both their attitudes and moods, but it did nothing to lift the tension from Mrs. Oliver. If the woman had killed her own sister, she might kill again, and her threats against Quinn and her family could not be ignored.

While Quinn prepared a triple-sized batch of chicken and dumplings, enough to take some to her parents and some to Jack and Mary, Josh popped into the kitchen from the back porch, where he'd replaced a rotten step. "How can we find out more about Mrs. Oliver?" he asked.

Quinn planted a kiss on her husband's scruffy face. "So glad you asked. I've been thinking about that same thing. I wonder if she has a presence on social media."

"One way to find out." Josh opened the Facebook app on his phone. "Oh," he said immediately. "It helps to have a Facebook account."

"I've never felt the need," Quinn said, looking over his shoulder, "but maybe it wouldn't hurt. I can always take it down." She opened the app on her own phone and filled in profile information, using her maiden name. Once she set up her password, she wandered around the site, familiarizing herself with the format and options.

She searched for Trish Oliver and found five, two living in Texas, but neither the right person. Then she searched for Patricia McDaniel Oliver and found six Patricia Olivers. One of these had a gray-haired avatar for a profile picture. The profile stated, "Lives in Texas, former English teacher, booklover." This had to be the right person.

Mrs. Oliver had no photos, but over a hundred friends, more than Quinn expected. Skimming through the photos of Mrs. Oliver's friends, Quinn found several names of people at Ball High School. This was definitely *her* Mrs. Oliver.

Posting a greeting on Mrs. Oliver's Facebook page or sending a private message might open communication with the former teacher, but Quinn was unable to do either of those, because she wasn't a "friend."

"Go ahead and click on 'add friend,'" Josh said. "I'll bet she'll accept, and then you can talk."

Quinn couldn't believe Josh was encouraging her to communicate with Mrs. Oliver, after being so vehemently opposed before. "Okay, did it." She supposed, if she were going to be on Facebook, she would have to find more friends, but before she started looking for people she knew, she searched for Elizabeth Lavender. The name came up with the word, "actress," next to it.

A profile photo of the actress was a dead ringer for Mrs. Oliver. The slim, silver-haired lady was pictured on the set of *Her Last Waltz*, in the arms of the dashing Sinclair Wilson. In contrast to Mrs. Oliver's page, this one was full of photos and more than a thousand friends. If Lavender truly suffered from borderline personality disorder, that hadn't stopped her from having friends and followers.

The vitality of the woman on the stage in the photograph stung Quinn's eyes. She wondered whether someone would take down the profile, now that Liz had died.

While she scrolled through the photos on Elizabeth Lavender's page, a *ding* drew her attention to her notifications. Trish Oliver had accepted her as a friend. A few seconds later, another *ding* told her she had a private message.

"Hey," Josh said, slapping Quinn's hand in a high five. "Mrs. Oliver's not wasting any time connecting."

Quinn both dreaded and couldn't wait to open the message. She held her breath and clicked.

Well, a double surprise! I didn't know you were on Facebook, and I didn't think you'd want to be my friend after yesterday.

Quinn started to compose a reply, but Josh tapped her wrist. "You don't have to respond right away. Better to think this through and plan your strategy."

"I agree," Quinn said. "In fact, I want to run this past Sergeant Schmidt before I do anything."

Josh's lop-sided grin spread across his face, and he kissed the top of her head. "Music to my ears, Q. Music to my ears."

Chapter Seventy-nine

Having Josh drive her to the police station in his car and meet with Sergeant Schmidt made a huge difference. The burden of keeping secrets removed, Quinn enjoyed the extra support and social media assistance.

Sitting across from Schmidt in his office brought back unpleasant memories of her dealings with Blackie and his crew. She'd hoped to put those thoughts to rest for good.

"Does Mrs. Oliver have any idea that you've found the driver's license? Or that you've communicated with me about it?" The sergeant leaned forward on his elbows, coming so close that the sandalwood of his aftershave tickled Quinn's nose.

Quinn and Josh exchanged glances, and she said, "I don't think so. I haven't spoken to her, except through a friend request." She pointed to the screen of her laptop, which she'd brought along. "I wouldn't tell her, anyway."

"Nor should you. The only thing keeping her from disappearing entirely is that driver's license." He sighed and sat back in his chair. "Grateful for your assistance, Quinn. As long as she thinks she has a chance of retrieving that license, she's going to want your handbag."

"Josh and I realize that. That's why I went on Facebook to communicate with her."

"Smart thinking," Schmidt said, glancing at the laptop screen. "But I'm glad you came here before responding. I don't have to tell you the stakes are sky-high. Mrs. Oliver has turned out to be as plugged into the drug and trafficking underworld as Blackie and Martinez. Her money's dirty, and her morals're even dirtier. We've got to figure out how to get her back here without putting you in the hot seat like last time."

"Can you tell me the significance of the driver's license?" Quinn asked, winking at Josh and wondering if his explanation would sync with her theory.

Schmidt rose and relocated to a corner of his desk, closer to the couple. "Ordinarily, no. We can't discuss evidence in a current case. But under the circumstances, you may need to know. I ask that you keep this information strictly confidential."

"We will," both said at once.

"A woman using the New York driver's license of Elizabeth Lavender flew from New York to Houston the day before Lavender's body was found and flew back to New York the evening the body was found."

Josh squeezed Quinn's hand. "I thought so," Quinn said. "Lavender couldn't have flown after she was killed, and the only person who could get away with using her license at the TSA screening would be her identical twin."

"So, you think Mrs. Oliver killed her sister and returned to New York as an alibi?" Josh asked.

"Hold up," Schmidt said. "We can't draw that conclusion just from the sister's driver's license. Mrs. Oliver might have had other reasons for flying back and forth. This is circumstantial evidence, at best."

Quinn said, "But the fact that Mrs. Oliver *hid* the driver's license in my shoulder bag—and so desperately wants it back—incriminates her further, doesn't it?"

Schmidt nodded. "It does. And we are following up on other leads. Not able to share."

"So, basically, I'm Dorothy in *The Wizard of Oz*, wearing the ruby slippers that the Wicked Witch of the West must have."

"Good comparison," Josh said. "The witch dies before she can get her hands on the slippers, however."

"Okay, let's talk about this Facebook message. Assuming Mrs. Oliver's going to press me for another opportunity to get to my purse, how do you think I should respond?" A shiver ran through Quinn.

"A good assumption. First, we're going to put the bait back in your purse." Schmidt's lips pulled back into a grimace that exposed his upper gums.

"What do you mean? I thought you needed the driver's license for evidence." Quinn shifted in her chair.

Schmidt went behind the desk and opened a drawer. "Yes, we do. But we've got a passable replica. I can't tell the difference between them." He handed the copy to Josh, who showed it to Quinn.

"Looks authentic," Josh said, "but I don't see where you're going with this. I thought you didn't want Quinn involved."

"I don't. Quinn's *shoulder bag* needs to be involved, but not *Quinn*." Schmidt clasped his hands, almost prayer-like. "I'm working on borrowing an officer from Texas City who looks enough like Quinn to be a stand-in."

Quinn thought of the officer who interviewed her. "You don't mean Carrie Pye? She's the same size as me, but that's where the resemblance stops." Hot waves of understanding pulsed through her veins as the situation melted into place. "Mrs. Oliver would never be fooled by Carrie."

"You'd be surprised at the disguises and other tricks we have up our sleeves. First, let's see if Carrie is available, and then we'll go from there." Schmidt rested his clasped hands on his desk. "But don't feel left out, Quinn. We'll definitely need your help. In fact, let's respond to your new Facebook friend, Mrs. Oliver, right now."

Chapter Eighty

Mrs. Oliver's Facebook message-- *Well, a double surprise! I didn't know you were on Facebook, and I didn't think you'd want to be my friend after yesterday*—opened the door for reconnection. Given the circumstances, Quinn's response had to be crafted carefully, friendly, but not too friendly. Quinn was glad to have Josh and Sergeant Schmidt in a team effort, but both insisted that the wording should come from her.

"Mrs. Oliver was your English teacher. She may suspect writing that doesn't sound like you," Schmidt said.

Quinn sat at the conference table in Schmidt's office, scratching out sentences on a legal pad. The strategy was to plan a back-and-forth conversation that would lead to a meet-up. After a lot of practice, feedback, and rewrites, Quinn typed in her response: *Decided to join the social media world finally! Yesterday was hard. Why are you so upset with me?*

Since the anticipated conversation might stretch over a period of days, Quinn wrote out possible responses by Mrs. Oliver and subsequent messages back. With the two men looking over her shoulder, the task weighed her down. She thought of a World War II book she had read in which a spy wrote a message to Hitler. At the same time, Quinn enjoyed the intellectual puzzle of analyzing how her former teacher might think and react.

While Quinn worked, Sergeant Schmidt received a flurry of calls, texts, and other interruptions, including the confirmation that Carrie Pye would impersonate Quinn in a sting operation with Mrs. Oliver.

When she and Josh left the police station, they had a solid plan. The only wild card was Mrs. Oliver.

An hour later, Quinn and Josh had delivered the chicken and dumplings to her parents and her brother, and were sitting down to eat their own dinner, when Quinn's phone *pinged*. Quinn jumped at the sound and clicked on the Facebook Messenger icon.

Upset with you? I'm grateful. You probably saved my life yesterday with your pepper spray. We should talk.

A happy warmth rose to Quinn's face. Her aim had been to have Mrs. Oliver propose a further conversation first. She copied Mrs. Oliver's message and sent it to Sergeant Schmidt, along with the planned response from her legal pad. She was itching to reply.

"Hold off," Josh said. "Waiting for Schmidt's input is a good thing. Better to make her wait a while. Too easy, and she may become suspicious."

"You're right," Quinn said. "Besides, this dinner deserves to be enjoyed."

After dinner and clean-up of the kitchen, Josh and Quinn leashed the dogs and took them for a walk around the neighborhood. Cool, but not cold, the January air and the quiet streets soothed them. "I almost feel relaxed," Quinn said. She pointed to Holly, who had squatted to pee on the grassy lawn of a neighbor.

"Good girl, Holly," Josh exclaimed, slipping the puppy a treat from his pocket. He took Quinn's hand and gave it a kiss. "May be too early to relax, Q. You still have to keep up your guard with Mrs. Oliver."

Later, after showering and getting ready for bed, Quinn returned to the phone. Schmidt had okayed her response to Mrs. Oliver's message.

Quinn opened the Facebook app. The strategy included making more friends on Facebook, so Quinn searched for random people she knew. She sent ten friend requests and then opened Messenger. She typed a response to Mrs. Oliver: *What do you suggest?*

Quinn didn't want to think about Mrs. Oliver anymore tonight. Despite the tense situation, this had been the best day she'd spent with Josh since their honeymoon. The love and support he'd shown had filled her up like a pot of warm honey, and as they crawled into bed, she was sure it would overflow.

Chapter Eighty-one

The next day, Sunday, Quinn went in to McFarland's to help out with Mrs. Gardner's funeral. She didn't mind occasional weekend work. She and Jack had collaborated to give her parents another day's rest after her dad's ordeal. Besides, she wanted another opportunity to interact with Farrah.

When she arrived at the mortuary, she received rave reviews on her cooking. "Truly delicious," her mother said. "And it was wonderful not to have to cook last night."

Quinn warmed to the compliment. "Your recipe. How's dad doing?"

"Miraculously, almost back to normal. Your dad's itching to come downstairs, but I managed to keep him in his lounge chair, watching a Jimmy Stewart movie."

"Okay, I'll get to work then," Quinn said. Wearing a new funeral outfit, a black skirt and jacket with faux leather trim, an espresso-colored silk blouse, and black high-heeled pumps, she felt normal for the first time in days.

Before adjourning to the chapel where the service would take place, she checked to make sure all the bottles of formaldehyde sat in the locked cabinet, just as she'd left them two days ago. On her way out of the embalming room, she brushed her fingers against the stainless steel table, unable to erase the thought that if Francisco Martinez had had his way, *she* might lie there today. Her years of working in death services had taught her that age and health often had no correlation with time of death. Much of the time, staying alive boiled down to luck.

Quinn couldn't block out the desire to log into the Facebook app on her phone to check for a message from Mrs. Oliver. She'd promised herself not to do that, though. She needed to keep her head in the job at hand, and she also didn't want to appear too eager. Tonight would be time enough.

Reining her thoughts in, she marched into the lobby to welcome Farrah and her friends for the wake and service. Jack was already there, wearing a spiffy black suit and shiny loafers. He handed out prayer programs with Mrs. Gardner's photograph on the front.

Quinn entered the chapel, where Farrah introduced her boyfriend from Chicago. Quinn explained she would remain in the chapel with them throughout the service, in case Farrah needed anything, and she would accompany them to the cemetery in her own vehicle. "Don't be bashful about asking me for whatever you need. We want this to be as uncomplicated for you as possible."

Quinn stood in the background, observing the many friends who had come to pay their respects both at the chapel and at the cemetery. Again, she marveled at Farrah's composure, her ability to overcome the challenges of her past. When the funeral ended, Farrah approached Quinn. "I'm grateful to you and your family. My mother's been in the best hands with you."

"Our honor to take care of your mother, Farrah. Thank you for giving us the opportunity." Quinn pulled a piece of paper from her skirt pocket and slipped it into Farrah's hand. "When things settle down for you, please call Sergeant Schmidt and tell him what you told me about Mrs. Oliver. So important in preventing future tragedies from happening."

Farrah nodded and put the paper in her own pocket. Then she gave Quinn a hug.

Later, when Quinn walked out into the waning sunshine on her way home, she felt more alive than before. Whether from surviving Martinez' threat—or Mrs. Oliver's—or from helping Farrah with her mother's funeral, Quinn breathed in the brisk air and listened to the chirping birds. She'd read somewhere that birds sing their most beautiful songs in the late afternoon, before they go to sleep. She stopped to watch a little gray Northern mockingbird, throttling out a melodious tune from the branch of a pecan tree. And she was grateful.

***

The dogs greeted her with yaps and pirouettes, followed by Josh, who had just showered after a day on the golf course. "How'd everything go?" he asked, scooping Quinn into his arms and spinning her around like a ballerina. His steamy kiss created the perfect finish.

"Mmm. I need to spend more Sundays away from home if that's the way I'll be greeted."

"Let's take the dogs out. I have something really exciting to tell you." Josh opened the back door and motioned for Quinn to go first. On the way out, he scooped a stack of envelopes from the kitchen counter.

They sat on the top step, and Josh nuzzled Quinn. "You won't believe this. We were so busy yesterday, we forgot to pick up the mail from the chute." He handed over the letters.

Quinn flipped through the bills, solicitations, real estate ads, and a letter from the University of Texas Medical Branch. "UTMB!" Quinn ripped open the envelope and scanned the letter quickly. "We have scheduled you for an interview—"

"Woohoo!" Quinn raised her arms in a victory pose, and her pups circled around her. The interview would be in three days. She threw her arms around Josh's neck and squealed.

They brought the dogs in and gave them their treats, and Quinn said, "I've been dying to see if there's a message from Mrs. Oliver." She laughed. "Never thought I'd be a victim of FOMO."

"Fear of missing out," Josh said. "Not finding the humor."

She grabbed her phone and clicked on Facebook. The Messenger icon had lit up with a red number one.

Mrs. Oliver had sent the message at one-fifteen this afternoon. *Can you meet off island, sometime tomorrow? Only you and me. Just to talk. I promise. You name the time. I'll pick the location.*

Quinn showed the message to Josh before copying and emailing it to Sergeant Schmidt.

While she waited for his response, she paced around the living room sofa. She had a prickly feeling about the invitation from Mrs. Oliver. No matter how skillfully Carrie Pye was fixed to resemble Quinn, something told her the plan was destined to fail.

Chapter Eighty-two
TRISH

I need that driver's license back—no two ways about it. I probably shouldn't have slipped it into Quinn's purse. Totally impulsive of me. I can and will get it back, even if I have to harm somebody.

But this incident with Francisco Martinez has taken the starch out of me. To be honest, so much has happened in such a short time since switching places with Liz—my head is spinning. I've always believed in having a plan—a lesson plan, a roadmap, a script, or whatever—but my life appears to be careening out of control. Even when I come up with a strategy, something happens to foil it.

Case in point—I invite Quinn to lunch, hoping to get into her purse, but every time she leaves the table, she takes her stupid shoulder bag with her. I step back and plan another occasion, but before I can execute it, Quinn arrives at my apartment unannounced.

Great! So, I figure out a way to take impromptu advantage, but then Francisco Martinez shows up, ready to kill me. I take back all the times I've wished that I'm the actress and Liz is the boring teacher. Right now "boring" sounds heavenly.

I count myself lucky to be alive, and I hate to complain, especially when I think of Liz. Her death weighs heavily on me, and sometimes I think that I'm the one who's died. In a way it's true. Here I am on the lam with none of the creature comforts of the home that Marvin and I have shared. I'm living in a no-tell motel, driving a rental car.

My wrist still hurts, and I've twisted my back, running away from the apartment in Texas City. I'm getting too old for these physical confrontations.

I tell myself I deserve better. The only thing holding me back is that damned driver's license sitting in Quinn's purse. If I can get it back, my alibi is secure.

According to Dave Becker, Marvin's left me enough money invested in legitimate stocks and bonds, even without the principal or returns from Blackie's empire. As long as Trish Oliver's name stays squeaky clean, she can make a new start anywhere. Unfortunately, I can't say the same for Elizabeth Lavender.

No point in crying over past mistakes. What's done is done, but getting that driver's license back is still possible. I must try.

Out of the blue, Quinn sends me a Facebook friend request. I can't believe my luck, but I can't trust it either. Quinn is no dummy, and that father of hers is friends with the police chief. I need to tread carefully.

Like I say, I need a good plan, and fortunately, I have one in place. Also, I'm still tracking her Toyota, and she doesn't know it. If she goes anywhere near the police station, I will be the first to know. I'm going to try one more time to retrieve Liz's driver's license. If that doesn't work, I'll be gone with the wind, one of my favorite books. Scarlett O'Hara, don't fail me now.

Chapter Eighty-three

While getting ready for dinner, Josh expressed congratulations again on the UTMB interview, but a worry line in his forehead told a different story. Finally, he said, "I'm concerned about this last message from Mrs. Oliver. Did you hear back from Schmidt?"

"Not yet," Quinn said, as she put kibble in the dog dishes and filled the water bowls. "I agree. She's stirring the pot, and the soup is warming. The meeting will be the boiling point."

"Interesting way to put it," Josh said. He peeked in the oven, where leftover chicken and dumplings warmed. "Another five-star dinner. Shall I pour some wine?"

Before Quinn could answer, her cell phone rang. "It's Schmidt. I'll put it on speaker."

"Good evening." The policeman's voice boomed into the house, causing Calvin's ears to perk. He ran to Quinn's side, as if to protect her. "Thanks for the email. I appreciate being kept in the loop."

"Of course," Quinn said. "Josh is here, and you're on speaker."

"Hello, Josh." He paused. "Listen, it's a good thing that Mrs. Oliver wants to meet. She thinks it's her idea, her show. We absolutely will accept the invitation; however, she can't be the one to designate the location. We have to be in control of that."

"Okay," Quinn said, and Josh nodded. "How do we make that work? That's not one of the responses on my legal pad."

"Tell her you can arrange to meet her at a convenient time for her, as long as it's after business hours on a weekday. The later the better. Darkness can be our friend in covering Carrie's face a bit." Schmidt paused to tell someone to return in a few minutes. "But also tell her you have a location in mind, neutral turf, guaranteed to be private."

"She'll never go for that. She'll think it's a set-up," Josh said.

"Possibly," Schmidt said, "but she wants the meeting, and Quinn won't meet unless the conditions are right."

"What's the location?" Quinn asked, her mouth dry. Even though she wouldn't be there, the arrangements filled her with trepidation.

"Not sure yet, but wherever we choose, we'll have the advantage."

"Do you want to give me the exact wording for the Facebook message?" Quinn asked.

"Yeah, I'll send it in an email as soon as we hang up. Go ahead and send the message. Let me know when you get a response." Schmidt's words came faster, as if preparing to end the call. "Oh, one more thing. Carrie needs to get together with you tomorrow, Quinn. She's going to analyze your voice, gestures, walk—everything—so she can be you."

Josh said, "Huh. Hate to tell you this, Schmidt. All the observation in the world can't accomplish that. There's no one in the world like Quinn."

Chapter Eighty-four

Quinn had to hand it to Sergeant Schmidt. His response for Mrs. Oliver was anything but straightforward. *I'll let you pick the time. The place? How about Dawn Donuts on Stewart Road?*

Schmidt said, "We know she won't agree to this. She asked for an off-island location, and we're ignoring that. The donut place is a known police hangout. We're asking for the extraordinary but will settle for the ordinary. Trust me."

Knowing how controlling Mrs. Oliver was, Quinn imagined the woman's fury when reading this message, but Schmidt had asked to be trusted, so she sent the message before going to bed.

The next morning, there was still no answer from Mrs. Oliver. Stringing the communication out like this increased Quinn's anxiety. She'd prefer to get the whole thing over with, but she couldn't take matters into her own hands at this point.

Josh left for work, and Quinn started getting dressed, when she received a call from Carrie.

"Good morning, Quinn. I hope it's okay if we meet today. I've got instructions to borrow some of your clothes and take your shoulder bag"

"I'm leaving for work in a few minutes. I don't see how I can come to the station in Texas City."

Carrie said, "Oh, no. We don't want your car anywhere near the police station. Someone might be watching, and we don't want to tip our hand." Her voice was whispery, not at all like Quinn's. "I'll come to you, not in uniform and riding in an unmarked car."

Quinn thought about having Carrie come to McFarland's, but she didn't want to alert her family to the situation. Also, meeting at the house would provide more opportunities for trying on clothes and hair style, so Carrie could mimic Quinn. If the purpose weren't so serious, this could be fun.

"Would it be okay to come to my house this evening?" Quinn asked. "Say, seven o'clock?"

Carrie agreed, and Quinn gave her the address. Before they hung up, Quinn was already thinking about which clothes to suggest. Whatever items she chose, she might not ever see again. She also needed to prepare for the interview. So many things crowded her mind these days.

When she arrived at work, she saw her brother in the office, poring over paperwork. "Hey, Jack," she said, "how's everything going?"

"I'm glad you're here," he said. "Have a minute to talk?" He pointed to the other chair in the small office, and when she sat, he closed the door.

"Uh-oh," she said. "What's going on?"

"Mom and Dad told me about their retirement plans. I know they talked to you separately." He leaned his elbows on the desk and pressed his hands into a tent-shape by his lips. "Are you sure about stepping back from the business?"

"I'm sure. I've got an interview at UTMB in two days, and I'm fairly certain I'll be accepted. I've wanted to work in the medical field all my life."

Jack frowned, and his voice took on a plaintive key. "I'm gutted. What can I do to, you know, entice you to stay?"

Quinn's stomach curdled, and her tongue stuck to the bottom of her mouth. "Where is this coming from, bro? You're sounding like Mom."

"Sorry. I guess I always thought we made a good team. So many changes, happening too fast. You're married. I'm getting married. Mom and Dad retiring. I can't imagine this place without you."

A pang of sorrow hit Quinn in the chest. She hated to disappoint her sweet brother, who'd always been there for her. But she had come too far to abandon her dream now. "I get it, believe me. The easiest thing would be for us to work together at McFarland's. Our comfort zone. There are a zillion reasons that would be a good idea." Quinn stood and put her hands on Jack's shoulders. "But there are an equal number of reasons to the contrary."

"I can't think of any," Jack said, his eyes resembling Calvin's when begging for a treat.

"Family businesses don't always run smoothly. What if we disagreed, or one of us made a poor business decision that would hurt both families? What if the business didn't bring in enough for two families? Or Josh got a great job in another city? A lot of things could go wrong, but one of them is this—if I don't go to PA school now, I probably never will. I'm almost thirty-one. I don't want to give up my dream and regret it. Or resent you and our parents for tying me down.

"I'll be here to train the person who takes my place. I'm not leaving town, either. If you got into a pinch on a weekend or something, I'd be here to help out." As confident as she presented herself, Quinn had a niggling doubt that her family relationships would remain the same when she left McFarland's. She couldn't dwell on that now.

Standing, Jack turned around to face his sister. His eyes shone with emotion, and he bent to hug her tightly. "I understand, baby sister. Maybe this is really for the best."

Quinn hugged back. Her brother's understanding felt like a balm washing over her. One big step closer to helping real-live people. Now all she had to do was pass the interview and be accepted.

Chapter Eighty-five

Josh had to work late that night, so when Carrie came over at seven o'clock, they had the house to themselves. Except for Calvin and Holly, who leaped in circles when the doorbell rang and welcomed Carrie as if she were the Queen of England.

"Come on in," Quinn said, ushering her into the living room. "Would you like something to eat or drink?"

Carrie set a small suitcase on the floor and flashed a toothy smile. "Actually, one of the things I want to do while I'm here is watch *you* eat and drink. We can do that now or later."

"Okay," Quinn said, thinking this would be an even more thorough session than expected. "Let's start with my closet."

"I can make that easy for you. I only need one outfit—something you have worn in Mrs. Oliver's presence recently, something she will recognize as yours."

The strategy made sense. The clothes she wore to Rudy & Paco's were too dressy. That left what she wore to the Galvez, to Mrs. Oliver's house, or to the Texas City apartment. The latter would be the most expendable. Quinn had washed the clothes. "Sergeant Schmidt has the shoes I wore with this outfit," she said, as she pulled out the powder blue sweatshirt and pants and the light coat she'd worn over it. "I purposely wore this coat, because I wanted pockets."

"Perfect," Carrie said. "Mind if I try them on?" Not waiting for permission, she stripped off her jeans and sweater and stepped into Quinn's clothes.

Quinn held her breath. Carrie modeled the outfit, with and without the coat. "Not bad," Quinn said. "We really are the same size."

The women compared shoe sizes, and Quinn described the running shoes she had worn to Mrs. Oliver's. Carrie had a similar pair in her own closet that she could wear.

Clothing settled, but still wearing Quinn's outfit, Carrie opened her suitcase and pulled out a selection of short, brunette, curly wigs, all made from human hair. "Let's see which of these comes closest to your 'do." She put her own reddish hair into a ponytail at the top of her head and pinned it as flat as possible.

The wigs resembled each other, except for fine differences in the tightness of the curls. Carrie walked around in each one, giving

Quinn several minutes to assess it. "Wow, these are really natural-looking," Quinn said. "I can't believe you have three so similar."

"We must have close to fifty. You'd be surprised how important clothes and hair are in identification activities. Most people don't look any further than those before making up their minds that a certain person is the right one."

Quinn could believe it. In the third wig and wearing her clothes, Carrie might even fool Quinn. She said as much, and Carrie cautioned her not to be so sure. "We still have makeup, elocution, posture, walking, and eating to work on."

For the next hour, the women examined each other in minute detail as Carrie copied every gesture, mannerism, idiom, tone of voice, and facial expression. While they were at the dining room table, drinking glasses of water and eating sandwiches made of leftover chicken, Josh came in. He did a double-take when he saw two women, both looking like his wife.

The real Quinn greeted him with a kiss. "Let me introduce you to my alter ego, Carrie Pye."

Josh shook hands with Carrie and shrugged after staring from one to the other. "I'm amazed. I wouldn't be able to tell the difference, especially from a distance."

The women high-fived and smiled at each other, the same smile. Carrie said, "Well, Mrs. Oliver may come pretty close, so let's hope we're good enough to convince *her*."

Satisfied with Josh's assessment and their own, they pronounced the mission accomplished. Carrie changed back into her own clothes, put the wig and Quinn's garments into her suitcase, and prepared to leave.

"Oh, one more thing," Quinn said, as she walked Carrie to the door. "What about my car?"

"Good catch," Carrie said, smiling. "As soon as we have the time and place nailed down, we'll figure out a way for us to come pick up your car. The new Quinn won't be completely authentic without Quinn's car."

Chapter Eighty-six

A flurry of Facebook messages flew between Quinn and Mrs. Oliver before they agreed on a time and place to meet. Of course, Quinn was only the intermediary. Mrs. Oliver actually negotiated with Sergeant Schmidt and the combined police departments involved.

The final arrangement was to meet on the patio at Maceo's, a famous island restaurant and spice shop known for authentic Italian cooking. Tomorrow at closing time, which was five p.m. The owner and workers at Maceo's nurtured warm relationships with the police, and they cooperated fully with the plans.

Sergeant Schmidt ran all the details past Quinn. Even though she wouldn't be present for the meeting, Quinn knew Mrs. Oliver best, and he wanted Quinn's predictions on how everything would go down. He also insisted that she remain in the police station during the operation for safety's sake.

Quinn refused, thinking the precaution ridiculous and unnecessary. At home she had her dogs and a security system she could arm. Sometimes the police over planned, in her opinion. If anything untoward happened, she could call 911.

"I won't fight you," Schmidt said, "but I'm going on record that protecting you is part of our plan." He continued in a matter-of-fact voice. "Carrie-Quinn will borrow your car and arrive at Maceo's around four-thirty, wearing a wire under your clothes. She'll sit around, chatting with people until around four-forty-five, when she'll order and pay for a muffuletta and a cream soda. She'll take it out on the patio, offering to clean up after herself when she's finished eating."

The real Maceo's employees would leave then, but two police officers would take their places inside the restaurant, where they could listen to the conversation between Carrie and Mrs. Oliver.

More officers, both from the island and from Texas City, would be scattered outside, across Market Street at DTO, and even a few blocks away. Carrie was prepared for as many scenarios as the team could come up with, including handing over the duplicate driver's license to Mrs. Oliver—but not without extracting an explanation of why she wanted it.

A confession would be nice, but the police would settle for anything that gave them a lead or evidence in the murder of Elizabeth Lavender.

Quinn continued to fear that Mrs. Oliver would see through the disguise. "She's known me practically all of my life." Quinn barely touched the dinner Josh had brought home from The Gumbo Diner. "It's not like she's got cataracts, either. The woman is sharp and pays attention to detail."

Josh put his napkin down on the table. "All right. I remember one time when I was anxious about a transplant surgery, and you told me I had to trust the process. Good advice, so back at ya, Q. There are no guarantees, but the plan is good. Carrie's disguise might have fooled *me*. You have to give this its best shot."

"I guess," she said, pushing her plate away. "Carrie will have my car, so I'll be here with the dogs, wondering what's happening." She didn't tell him the police wanted her to stay at the police station.

"Forgot to tell you. I'm coming home mid-day tomorrow. I don't want you to be alone."

Quinn was gratified, but also a little suspicious. Maybe Josh wanted to make sure Quinn didn't do something rash or impulsive, like show up at Maceo's. "Thanks, honey. I really can handle being home by myself. I know time off is hard to come by."

"Already taken care of. I switched with another guy. I'll be working both days this weekend."

By the weekend, hopefully, Mrs. Oliver would be taken care of, Quinn's PA interview would be over, and maybe she would reward herself with a new orchid plant and a new thriller to read. She could take the pups to the dog park, go to a movie, or even clean out closets. These normal activities drew her enthusiasm more than any material wealth. She could almost taste the freedom.

She clasped Josh's hand in both of hers. "I'm glad you arranged to take off. Maybe we can work on the shelves for the garage tomorrow afternoon. Those boards have been sitting in a pile since before the wedding."

"Good idea," Josh said. "After the shelves I want to get your car in the garage. Nothing like manual labor to take your mind off ol' Mrs. Oliver."

Chapter Eighty-seven

The next day, Josh dropped Quinn at work early and drove his car to the hospital. The object was to leave her car with a tank full of gas. He planned to pick Quinn up and go home shortly after three.

Quinn hoped she could accomplish everything at work by then. As it turned out, a body had come in overnight, and she was able to start working right away.

She was so intent on making the perfect incision, Quinn didn't hear her father enter the "beauty parlor." He coughed, and she startled. She removed her ear buds and flipped off the blower. "Hi, Dad. How're you feeling?"

"Okay. Lucky to be alive." He pulled up a chair next to where Quinn stood. "I haven't talked to Marty to find out if they've got any leads on who caused this. Makes me edgy. Maybe whoever it is will come back."

Quinn sympathized with her father, but she didn't want to dig too deeply into this topic today. "I have a suggestion if you want to hear it."

"Of course, kitten. I'm always open to your ideas." He crossed one leg over the other and leaned back. "Tell me."

"I know mortuaries need to be welcoming places, and some doors need to be open at erratic hours. That might've worked well back in the day. But the world is different now. We should hire a security company to help restrict traffic from unknown people. People like Rory and Zeke could have permanent access codes, but others could be given temporary codes to get in for a specific date and time. And the system could be suspended during a funeral."

Quinn enjoyed talking to her father, but she needed to get on with this embalming, so she could go home with Josh at three. Her nerves jangled enough without worrying about being late. "I remember Grandpa saying we owe it to ourselves and our customers to protect the premises where their loved ones lie."

"That's true," her father said, standing and putting his chair back under the desk. "Thanks. I'll look into it right now." He kissed her on the cheek. "I'm sure gonna miss you when you leave us, Quinn."

"Let's not even think about that now," she said. "I'm here for several more months, at least. And I'll always love you and be ready to help you with anything you need." She gave him a hug before putting her mask back on. "Oh, one more thing. Okay if I leave as soon as I finish here? I've got a project at home to finish." *Not exactly lying.*

"No problem, sweetie."

Grateful to have such a loving boss and such an easy conversation, Quinn concentrated on introducing the embalming fluid and observing how the chelating of proteins brought color into the body. The cosmetic effect offered a glimpse of what the person looked like when alive. It gave her a sense of accomplishment every time, although she imagined work on a living human being would be much more fulfilling.

Her thoughts drifted to the body of Elizabeth Lavender, not embalmed, but cremated, and stored on a nearby shelf. No funeral, no mourners, no one coming to pick up her remains. Could Mrs. Oliver really have flown in from New York, pretending to be her twin, poisoned and strangled the poor actress, perhaps drowned her, too, and flown back to New York?

Quinn had read examples of killers who dismembered bodies and ate steak dinners afterwards, their consciences apparently untroubled. But those were crazy people, not retired English teachers who read books, baked cookies, and appeared to be solid citizens. It had taken Quinn a long time to recognize Mrs. Oliver as crazy.

If Mrs. Oliver murdered her own sister, what was the motivation? Quinn couldn't imagine any circumstance under which she could intentionally harm her brother. Weren't twins supposed to be even closer than siblings?

Mrs. Oliver had come at Quinn, supposedly because of the role Quinn had played in apprehending Blackie. Maybe Liz had done something similar—confronted her about her activities—knowingly or unknowingly. The game of switching places may have sparked intense jealousy or anger in an already-unstable woman. The game then turned deadly.

However the emotions had unfolded, Quinn hoped that this afternoon would bring closure to the many questions that plagued her. Most of all, she prayed to be free from the twisted relationship she had with Mrs. Oliver. At this thought, she whispered aloud, "Amen."

Chapter Eighty-eight

Quinn finished her work in plenty of time for Josh to pick her up at three. By this time, the anticipation of the police operation had her nauseated, keyed up, even though she wouldn't be physically present. She kept these symptoms to herself, however. She didn't need Josh or her parents or anyone else to know how anxious she was.

When they arrived at home, Josh parked on the street, not wanting to block Quinn's car in the driveway. They walked the dogs and changed into comfy sweats. Quinn did some stretching exercises to relieve tension.

"Okay, Q, how about we knock out these shelves in the garage?" Josh asked. "Might as well do something constructive, instead of waiting around."

"A man after my own heart," she replied, putting a pause on the fifty sit-ups she had almost completed. "Let's go."

The garage had never been used for parking a car since Quinn had owned the house. Detached and weather-beaten, the structure served as a storage facility. Not a well-organized one. Tools and equipment were piled up everywhere. Cans of gasoline for the lawn mower blocked access to the screen door, which needed re-screening. Copper piping and boxes of nails and screws and other hardware sat on the floor in one corner. A set of dining room chairs that needed new seats were stacked in another.

Josh had purchased materials for building shelves, peg boards and hooks for tools, and wood to build a workbench. He'd mapped out the dimensions, so eventually there would be enough space to park one car.

The area smelled of wood and dry leaves and machine oil. Spider webs decorated the corners and the rafters in the ceiling. "There's a lot of potential here," she said. "Once the shelves are up, this place might actually look like a garage, instead of a storage barn."

"I'll get started. Now that I think about it, why don't you go inside and wait for Carrie? I'll be fine till after she leaves." Josh made a makeshift table out of boxes and a sheet of thick plywood. "There's plenty of light in here. I should be able to keep working for several more hours."

Quinn checked the clock on the oven. It was one minute past four. Carrie was due at four o'clock. Only one minute late, but twinges stabbed Quinn's stomach anyway. She knew from the past how important it was for the police to stick to precise plans, as much as possible. She also knew how quickly things could go south when extenuating circumstances butted in.

Telling herself that a few minutes late did not constitute an emergency, Quinn did a few more sit-ups and ran in place. But when the clock said four-ten, a clammy feeling enveloped her, and she texted Sergeant Schmidt.

He responded immediately. *On her way. Accident on I-45. Should be there ASAP.*

Josh came in from the garage. "Shouldn't Carrie have been here already?"

Quinn showed him the text. "I'm ready to hand off the fob the minute she's dropped off."

"That's right. She wouldn't want to leave a police car here. Even an unmarked would get attention in this quiet neighborhood."

At four-fifteen a car screeched to a stop outside, and Quinn ran out with the fob, while Josh stood at the open door. They both did double-takes when "Quinn" stepped out of the police car. Dead-ringer was an understatement.

With no time to waste, Quinn dropped the fob into her doppelganger's hand, and Carrie jumped into Quinn's car. She pushed the ignition, and the car gargled and grumbled, turning over, but not catching.

"What the hell?" Josh said, running to the passenger side of the car.

Carrie waited a few seconds and tried again with the same results. She threw up her hands and popped out of the car. "What's up? The car won't start."

A rock sat in Quinn's chest as she remembered having had car trouble the last couple of days. "I'm so sorry! This is horrendous, all my fault."

"Here, take my car," Josh said, exchanging his fob for Quinn's and pointing to his. "No time to waste fixing Quinn's."

"Thanks," Carrie said, in a voice that sounded a lot like Quinn's. She dashed to Josh's Audi and fired up the engine. She took off for Maceo's without another word.

Quinn's breath returned, but her insides remained tense.

"Why didn't you tell me about your car? We need to get that fixed." Josh put an arm around Quinn's shoulders.

"I completely forgot. What time is it?"

"Four-twenty, and we're off and running."

The ticking clock sounded in Quinn's head, as if she had swallowed it whole.

Chapter Eighty-nine
TRISH

I'm leery about this arrangement with Quinn to meet at the Maceo's patio. I understand her wanting to be out in the open after what happened at Blackie's apartment. I also get it that she needs to meet somewhere local. She probably needs to put in a day's work at the mortuary.

Which reminds me. I must go back there someday to pick up Liz. Not now, though. I have more important worries.

Now here's something interesting. I see by my little handy-dandy tracker that Quinn's car is not at the funeral home. It's been sitting in her driveway all day, like a fat princess waiting for a suitor. Maybe she took the day off to rest up for our little meeting.

Not a problem. It's always good to be ready, and this time I'm prepared to the hilt. Well, that's an incorrect metaphor, since I'm not carrying a sword. I should say, I'm loaded. At the first sign of anything hinky, I'm going to shoot my way outta here. Thank you, Marvin, for teaching me how to use your revolver.

As soon as I have that little ol' driver's license in my possession, I'll head for the ferry. Nobody will expect me to go to Louisiana. When I get to Lake Charles, I'll fly to Las Vegas, and from there to Italy. Nobody can stop me—not the police, not Quinn, not Francisco, not Liz.

The thought of all that freedom makes me dizzy. But I can't lose my focus. "I have miles to go before I sleep," as my favorite poet, Robert Frost, says. And right now, I'm sitting in the parking lot at Target, watching the clock and the coordinates of Quinn's car, standing still.

Chapter Ninety

Quinn could hardly contain her jumpiness. Being on the outside of this police sting felt wrong, even though rationally it made sense. She had as much adrenaline flowing now, as she had when confronting Blackie last year, only now, it had no place to go. She'd been calmer then.

"Come help me in the garage," Josh said. "We can keep busy while we wait to hear from Sergeant Schmidt." He squeezed her shoulders and planted a kiss on the top of her head.

"Carrie really did look like me," Quinn said. "I'm so pissed about my car."

"No harm done. She'll get there in the same amount of time in my car. Maybe a little faster."

"I know. Your car's 'the bomb,' and no other car can touch it." Quinn shook her head. "I'll meet you in the garage in a few minutes. I want to check on the dogs and lock up the house."

"Good idea. I'll be the guy with the hammer and nails."

Quinn grinned. "I think I'll recognize you with or without your tools."

Quinn couldn't believe her luck in finding Josh Brady. He was smart, kind, responsible, fun to be with, and just looking at him tingled her insides with a voltage that surprised her, even now. They seemed perfectly suited, except for one thing. Josh's low risk tolerance made hers fly off the charts.

But maybe Josh was changing. A year ago, he would have insisted that they have tight security while Mrs. Oliver met with "Quinn."

And maybe Quinn was changing, too. Being open with Josh, Jack, and her parents had given her a new outlook on relationships. The value of their understanding and support was extraordinary. From now on, she'd be more forthcoming with people she trusted. And more discriminating in deciding whom to trust, she chided herself, thinking of Mrs. Oliver.

Before she secured the dogs and the house and met the love of her life in the garage, she needed to do one more thing.

Chapter Ninety-one
TRISH

That phrase from the Congreve play that's always attributed to Shakespeare comes to mind—"Hell hath no fury like a woman scorned." Of course, I'm the woman scorned. But not by a lover, heaven forbid. I'm betrayed by that idiotic brat, Quinn McFarland. Brady. Whatever.

The key word here is "fury." My insides are roiling, boiling hot—like the cauldron in Macbeth, which actually *is* Shakespeare. Oh, to hell with the quotes. I'm not teaching English anymore.

I've been sitting here in the parking lot, watching the minutes tick by, and watching the location of Quinn's Toyota—*which hasn't moved*. This means one of two things: either Quinn isn't coming to meet me at Maceo's, or Quinn got a ride to the restaurant with someone else. Either way, I smell a trap, and I'm not biting.

Whoever's expecting Trish Oliver to show up there can wait till doomsday, for all I care. That driver's license is important to me, but not enough to walk into a police set-up.

Which raises the question: why have the police gone to all the trouble to lure me there, unless they have something on me? And that something is most likely Liz's driver's license. So, thanks, Quinn, for handing that little item over to Sergeant Schmidt.

I knew I shouldn't have trusted Quinn. As nice as I've been to her all these years. She hasn't deserved all the attention I've given her. Or gifts. I blame her for Blackie. Come to think of it, she was the first to stuff a poisoned cookie in Francisco's mouth, too.

Well, she isn't going to take Trish Oliver down, no siree. Quite the opposite. Before I ditch this God-forsaken place for good, I'm going to pay that mealy-mouthed bitch a little visit. And her husband and little dogs, too!

Chapter Ninety-two
TRISH

Only seven minutes from Target to that little shack where Quinn lives, mid-island, with her husband, the doctor. I have scoped it out in the past, and I know all about the neighborhood.

I drive my little rental car with the windows open. The cool air whipping my hair back from my face invigorates me, gives me energy. I need to be in tip-top shape when I face off against Quinn, being twice the age of my opponent.

I'm still filled with white-hot fury. I haven't come all this way in life to be outdone by a smartass child. I can run rings around her in the IQ department, for sure, but I need to play this carefully and quickly.

I have about ninety minutes before sunset, but not that long before the police realize I'm a no-show at Maceo's. They'll start an immediate search, and I won't be surprised if they start at Quinn's. I need to get there, get hold of my license, and get out. With any luck I can make the five-forty ferry and be on my way.

As I turn off Broadway to 45th Street, I reconsider. Why risk everything to make Quinn suffer? Wouldn't I be better to keep heading east and get a jump on the police?

No! I can't in all good conscience leave town without avenging Blackie—and in some ways, Julio, Francisco, and Liz. Quinn is the one who set all of the deaths in motion, and she needs to pay.

I pull into the alley in back of Quinn's house and coast, so my car is hidden from the street. I grab my gun and stuff it in my jacket pocket with my good wrist.

I get out of my car and close the door as quietly as I can, leaving it unlocked. My approach to the house is from the side of the driveway. Quinn's car sits there like Cinderella's coach, left behind from the ball. I'm wearing my best gym shoes and creeping toward the back yard, when I'm distracted by activity in the garage. I peek in ever-so-quietly. Quinn's husband is humming a tune in the corner, bent over a woodworking project. How convenient!

I scope out the rest of the garage, making sure no one else is around. I can easily shoot him in the back and run before anyone finds out, but I force myself to slow down. Killing the husband without Quinn to witness it would be a pyrrhic victory.

I need to act, while I have the element of surprise in my arsenal. I pull my revolver and hold it out, butt-end first. I start on tip-toes and speed up on the balls of my feet, rushing at the back of his head and smashing the gun against it with all my might.

The good doctor literally doesn't know what has hit him. One "oomph," and he collapses onto what may be wooden shelves. Out cold.

I look around for something to tie him up, chastising myself for not bringing more supplies. The garage is full of options, however. My eyes land on a couple of bungee cords peeking out of a cardboard box, and if those aren't enough, there are extension cords, too.

I have no idea how long he'll be unconscious, but I roll him over and tie his arms together at the wrists, in front of him, his legs at the ankles. That should keep him from attacking me.

I suppress my hysterical laughter. Plenty of time to cheer for myself later.

I consider gagging him, but at the moment, he's not saying anything noteworthy or otherwise, and I only have a few minutes to get to the main attraction—Ms. Quinn.

Chapter Ninety-three

Calvin howled, and Holly yipped, both running back and forth from the back door to Quinn. Their behavior ratcheted Quinn's already-high anxiety. Before joining Josh in the garage, she had gone on her phone to see if Mrs. Oliver had left any new Facebook messages.

Nothing there, but now that she and Mrs. Oliver had friended each other, she had access to Mrs. Oliver's short "friend list." She perused the names and profile pics, recognizing a few, but astounded by others who were unfamiliar, certainly not locals.

Calvin literally jerked her from the computer, butting her leg with his head. She darted to the back door and peered through the glass panel. "I don't see anybody," she said to the dogs. That didn't mean anything. The dogs' hearing could be trusted more than a single peek outside.

Her first instinct was to yell to Josh, but her voice wouldn't carry to the garage, unless she opened the door and shouted at the top of her lungs. Shouting wouldn't help if Josh needed her. She had to go to him right away.

A bolt of panic ran through her. Quinn couldn't move. Her feet were nailed to the floor. Anything could have happened while she'd sat inside, trolling social media. *I'm coming, Josh.*

Finally able to move, Quinn put up the doggy gate, set the alarm on stay, grabbed the key to the house, and headed toward the back door. At the last second she thought about going back to get her cell phone, but getting to Josh quickly was more important.

As she locked the back door and spun around, Quinn jumped a mile. Mrs. Oliver rushed toward her through the open gate, brandishing a gun and speaking in an eerily quiet voice. "There you are, just the person I'm looking for. Come on, now. Let's go into the garage, where we can all have a little chat."

"Where's Josh?" If he were still in the garage, there's no way he wouldn't be shouting, warning her. Quinn's heart drummed, and her pulse throbbed. Her mind flew to the martial arts training she'd excelled in. That had helped her in dangerous situations before. She took a deep breath to calm herself and pictured the oxygen travelling to all her cells, nourishing and strengthening them.

Karate and the mixed martial arts had taught her how to overpower an aggressor, but not one wielding a gun. In fact, she had learned *not* to try to disarm a person with a weapon, except as a last resort. The better strategy was to de-escalate the situation and escape, if possible. *But Mrs. Oliver came from the garage, so where is Josh?*

"Ah, your Josh," Mrs. Oliver's eyes burned with an incandescence—perhaps fueled by total insanity. "I'll take you to him immediately. You lead the way." Her voice remained a whisper, but the jab of the gun at Quinn's back spoke loudly.

Quinn sprinted across the patch of concrete leading from the back yard to the garage. She had to get to Josh. Then the two of them would handle Mrs. Oliver.

She stopped short at the open side door to the garage. The overhead light bulb illuminated his form, where he lay, tied up and silent. Her first impulse was to spin around and yell, "What have you done to him?" But that might provoke their assailant. Instead, she ran to Josh and fell to her knees beside him, placing her ear on his chest.

"He's alive. Taking a little nap, I think." Mrs. Oliver thrust the gun in Quinn's face. "Maybe he'll wake up in time to witness your punishment. That might be fun to see. Or maybe I'll shoot him while *you* watch. So many options."

Quinn's mouth went dry. "My punishment?"

"Don't pretend you don't know why I'm here. You've caused multiple deaths. Blackie, Julio, Francisco, Liz. For all I know you killed Marvin, too, even though he had cancer. Speaking of which, why are you here and not at Maceo's?"

Keep her talking. "I—I was just leaving for Maceo's now. A little late, but I was coming." Amazed at how the lie flew from her mouth, Quinn kept going. "I heard Blackie was killed by a fellow prisoner. I get it, you think me responsible for his being locked up in the first place, but how am I connected to the others?"

The dogs, locked inside the house, barked incessantly. Quinn prayed for someone to hear them and call for help.

Mrs. Oliver either didn't hear or ignored them. "I don't have time to answer your silly questions, Quinn. But I have a question for *you*. What did you do with my driver's license? Is it still in your shoulder bag, or have you given it to your buddy, Sergeant Schmidt for safekeeping?"

Quinn clutched at the topic as another possible way to de-escalate the situation. She forced a smile and tilted her head. "Your driver's license? What would it be doing in my purse?"

"Don't play dumb with me, you little bitch. I stuck it in there the day we had met at the Galvez. Now what happened to it after that?" Bits of foam clung to the corners of her mouth, and she waved the gun in the air.

At that moment, Quinn considered making a break for the exit, but she didn't want to leave Josh, and in her hesitation, the opportunity passed. Mrs. Oliver trained the gun on Quinn and walked backwards until she reached a chair, dragging it to within a few feet of Josh. "Sit here," she said, waving the gun.

After Quinn complied, Mrs. Oliver stepped close and stared into Quinn's eyes. "You know what? Never mind. I *know* you gave the license to the police. They used it to get me to agree to meet you at Maceo's at five o'clock."

"Five o'clock today?" Quinn glanced at the single north-facing window in the garage. Judging by the absence of afternoon sunlight, the police must have given up on Mrs. Oliver's showing by now. Maybe someone would contact her by text, but her phone was in the house. "How could I have met you, when I've been here?"

Mrs. Oliver's eyes moved toward the window, as well. "It's getting late, and I must be on my way. Your little innocent act doesn't fool me, Quinn. You can *have* that driver's license for all the good it will do you." She thrust the gun into Quinn's chest. "Now watch carefully. I'm going to show you how it feels to lose someone you care about."

Chapter Ninety-four

As Mrs. Oliver advanced on Josh with her finger on the trigger of the revolver, Quinn found herself out of options for de-escalating talk. She rose and positioned herself at Mrs. Oliver's side, as the older woman aimed at Josh's head. Using the outer edge of her foot, Quinn swept just above Mrs. Oliver's ankle in a low, horizontal arc. At the same time, Quinn used both hands to push against Mrs, Oliver's upper body, causing her to lose her balance and fall.

The woman cursed, and she hit the concrete floor on her side, but she still gripped the gun in her right hand.

Josh stirred, and uttered a few syllables, diverting Mrs. Oliver's attention for a second. Quinn took advantage of the distraction to leap onto the woman's midriff and wrench the gun from her hand. It skittered across the garage floor, out of reach for them both.

Completely infuriated now, Mrs. Oliver reached for Quinn's hair and pulled hard. Quinn grabbed the woman's opposite wrist and twisted, using her thumb on the back of the hand and her fingers wrapped around the palm.

"Damn you. My bad wrist!" Mrs. Oliver snarled through clenched teeth, breathing hard. "You're going to pay double for that." She rose on her elbow and lurched at Quinn's neck with her open mouth.

Quinn held onto the left wrist and pushed Mrs. Oliver onto the ground, face-down. She placed a knee in the center of the woman's back and, still gripping the wrist, extended the left arm, pressing the hand toward the shoulder in an arm lock.

"Let me go, you devil." Mrs. Oliver squirmed and panted hard, but Quinn's takedown left no room for resistance.

Poised in perfect balance over Mrs. Oliver's back, Quinn's body held control, and her left arm continued to hold the left wrist. She couldn't ease up, though, because the older woman still had some fight in her. If she pried herself loose, she might regain possession of the gun. Quinn couldn't allow that.

Josh groaned and rolled from side to side, his hands bound at the wrists and covering his groin. He opened his eyes and closed them. Not wanting to alert Mrs. Oliver to Josh's waking, Quinn remained silent.

Moments later, when Josh opened his eyes again, Quinn made eye contact and jerked her chin upward, using her free right hand to signal quiet. A slight nod, a grimace, and movement of his arms up and down communicated as well as words.

"Let. Me. Go, Quinn." Mrs. Oliver grunted from the side of her mouth. "I promise I won't hurt you or Josh. I'll get out of here right now, and you'll never see or hear from me again."

Quinn had no intention of letting up on her adversary, but as long as the woman wanted to talk, Quinn would accommodate her. "Let's talk about that driver's license you say you put in my purse."

Mrs. Oliver struggled in vain to lift her upper body from the floor. "Oh, you admit you know about it now? I'm sure you gave it to the police."

"For the sake of the argument, let's say I did. Why did you call it *your* driver's license?"

"It *is* my driver's license. Elizabeth Lavender. That's me. I need it back."

Quinn hardly could believe her ears. The woman had completely lost it. "Really? You're saying that *you* are Elizabeth Lavender? I thought Elizabeth Lavender was dead."

Josh shook his head and stretched his bound wrists over his head. His eyes were still glazed, and he probably had a concussion, but at least he was awake. If only Quinn could cut him loose without releasing Mrs. Oliver—she could use his help, even in his present condition.

With her right hand, Quinn mouthed the words, "You okay?"
Josh nodded.

Quinn lifted her chin to point toward the gun on the floor, not that he could retrieve it, but to make him aware. She still held control over Mrs. Oliver.

"Hey, Quinn. You're hurting my arm. And my back. Let me up, and I'll explain."

Quinn wasn't falling for another trick. "Get comfortable. We may be here like this for a long, long time." Quinn concentrated on her balance, a critical part of keeping the woman disabled.

Facing left, Mrs. Oliver couldn't see Josh or the fact that he was now conscious.

While this communication was going on with Josh, Quinn kept her teacher talking. "So, explain. How can you be Elizabeth

Lavender, when the body I identified and cremated had an *epsilon* on its wrist?"

"Oh, *that.* I guess I never told you that my identical twin and I were switched at birth." Mrs. Oliver's voice took on a different timbre—a higher pitch. "They put the tattoos on the wrong babies. Liz and I never bothered to correct them. It was our little secret, and all the times we've switched, no one ever noticed, not even Marvin."

Quinn couldn't believe her ears. This patter didn't even make sense. "You're full of it, Mrs. Oliver. There's no way you could have fooled that many people. Even identical twins have different quirks and mannerisms. You know what I think?"

"What's that sound? A rat?" Mrs. Oliver asked, squirming and trying to lift her head and turn to the right. "I've got to get out of here."

"Calm down," Quinn said. "You didn't answer my question. I think you killed your sister while she was pretending to be you. You switched driver's licenses to travel to each other's homes, so you had her license when you were in New York."

"Ridiculous." Mrs. Oliver squealed from the corner of her mouth. The word could have been uttered by a coyote.

"Something happened between you that caused you to fly to Texas, using your sister's ID. You killed her and flew back to New York, still pretending to be Liz. But you took back your own driver's license after she died, so you could travel home to make arrangements as Trish."

The light outside the window had dimmed during the time they'd been in the garage, and Quinn wondered what time it was. She estimated she'd been holding Mrs. Oliver for fifteen minutes, though it felt like more. Josh had drifted off again. Her strength was ebbing, and Mrs. Oliver's, not so much.

"What do you think of my theory, Mrs. Oliver? You're mighty quiet down there."

Mrs. Oliver tried to raise her head and shoulder, but Quinn clamped down harder. "I think you should stick to embalming bodies, Quinn McFarland. I should have killed you when I had that gun."

"I take that as a yes," Quinn said. "You might as well admit everything. It's just you and me, and we both know each other's secrets."

"That's true enough," Mrs. Oliver said. "And I doubt both of us will get out of here alive." She cackled like an old witch. "If I had to bet, I'd say *I'll* be the last woman standing. In fact, the minute your arm wears out, I'll jump up, take back Marvin's revolver, and that'll be the end of you and hubby."

Quinn's left arm had tired long ago, but now it was going numb. She didn't know how much longer she could hold on.

Mrs. Oliver stopped struggling. Perhaps she was conserving her strength so she could make good on her threat. Quinn didn't care. She doubled-down on restricting the woman's movements. "Might as well sing your heart out, then. Tell me how clever you are," Quinn said. "One last lesson from the master of all teachers."

She strained to hear any external sounds, but, aside from muffled howling of her dogs, and maybe from Duffy, the dog next door, all was quiet. Surely the police weren't still waiting at Maceo's. She'd hoped Sergeant Schmidt would come to her house directly from there, but where was he?

Chapter Ninety-five

Whatever Quinn had said to unlock Mrs. Oliver's tongue, the woman continued talking. Her voice rang louder and clearer than it had been since she'd shoved the gun in Quinn's back. "You want to know the whole story? Okay, I'll tell you. And then I'll kill you, as the saying goes."

After several seconds of raucous laughter, the baying of a she-wolf, the woman abruptly switched to a teacherish voice. "I have to hand it to you, Quinn. You must have had a good teacher once upon a time, because you figured out more than I would have given you credit for."

She tried to turn her head to the other side, but Quinn's clamp on her arm and shoulder prevented any movement. "I wasn't lying when I said Liz and I were switched at birth. We were that close—always intuiting each other's thoughts, even at the end. We loved each other fiercely, but we were competitive, too. And unfortunately, in each other's business more than we should have been.

"This last time, Liz got involved with Julio. You know, Francisco's brother and my landscaper. He was much younger, a very sweet and attentive lover. I appreciated his—uh, friendship—I slept with him, but kept him at arm's length, because of Francisco. But Liz didn't. She and Julio had a hot little romance going. I don't know if Julio thought I had warmed up to him, or if he realized Liz was a different person. Anyway, he spilled the tea, as they say."

Incredulous that Mrs. Oliver was, herself, spilling the tea, Quinn held back her comments. She didn't want to say or do anything to stop the flow. Instead, she kept her energy on holding the woman in position.

"Julio wasn't involved in any of the business deals I had with Blackie and Francisco, but he knew all about them. From time to time, he would warn me about certain—uh, unsavory—things that were going down. He didn't think a nice woman like me should be involved in criminal activities, even though I knew Blackie protected me. That is, until you stepped in."

Quinn's arm quivered. She didn't know how much longer she could hold Mrs. Oliver down.

"Are you listening, Quinn? The worst part of my story is coming soon. My sister was always bullheaded. When Julio warned her about illegal dealings, thinking he was talking to me, she went ballistic. She called me in New York and insisted that I remove myself from everything. If I didn't, she would call the police and report me."

At this, Quinn blurted out a comment. "Maybe it was an idle threat."

"You didn't know my sister. Self-righteous to a fault, and spiteful, too. She meant it all right, and I had to stop her."

Quinn realized this confession had put *her* in jeopardy, as well. Anyone who would kill her sister to keep her quiet would do the same to Quinn. Too late to turn back, Quinn laid more wood on the fire. "So you flew down here, killed your sister, and went back to New York to await the notification that she'd been murdered."

"I don't like your tone, young lady. Yes, I killed her. You would have done the same if you'd been in my situation. I had to protect myself."

Quinn grasped at anything to keep the conversation going. "I'm sure you did. By the way, I hear you're involved in prostitution."

"That's it, Quinn. Are you going to bring up everything little thing I ever did to anyone? Yes, since we're playing end-of-life True Confessions. I helped Blackie find girls. Not my idea, mind you. You might say I was between the proverbial rock and a hard place. But that's all in the past now."

"You might not say that if you were one of the girls. You ruined lives."

"That's enough out of you, Miss Moral High Ground." A surge of strength erupted from Mrs. Oliver's core muscles, and she let out a loud screech as her arm slipped from Quinn's grip and she rolled over on top of Quinn. "Aha!" Mrs. Oliver said. "And now, my dear, you will meet with the same fate as Liz. You can't say I didn't warn you." She put her hands around Quinn's throat and started to squeeze.

A booming voice coming from behind cut through the conflict in an instant. "Okay, I've heard enough. Mrs. Oliver, stand slowly and put your hands in the air. You're under arrest for the murder of your sister. You have the right to remain silent—"

Mrs. Oliver wailed like a grounded walrus, but she did as Sergeant Schmidt said.

Still shaky, Quinn rose to her knees and then her feet, turning around in surprise. While several officers restrained Mrs. Oliver,

Carrie Pye, still dressed as Quinn, rushed in to assist with Josh. She called for the paramedics, insisting that he not be moved.

While an officer cuffed Mrs. Oliver behind her back, she looked from Carrie to Quinn. An unnatural cackle burst from the woman's mouth. "Quinn, you surprise me. I never knew you had an identical twin, too."

Meanwhile, Quinn found some lawn shears and cut the cords on Josh's wrists and ankles.

"How long were you standing back there?" she asked Sergeant Schmidt.

He winked at Quinn. "Long enough to hear the whole story. Good job in getting the confession. I couldn't have done any better, myself."

Quinn shrugged off the compliment. Right now, the only thing she cared about was making sure Josh was okay. Everyone and everything else could take a number and wait in line.

Chapter Ninety-six

Nobody at the hospital could believe a woman in her sixties could leave such a big goose egg on the back of Josh's head, or render him unconscious for twenty minutes. "Shows you how extraordinarily strong Mrs. Oliver is," Quinn said.

"Fortunately, the skull is not broken," the ER doctor said, "and he's mentally alert, but we still need to check for possible brain injury."

"I'll be okay," Josh said. "The only headache I have is in the back of my head, no double vision."

"Sorry, Bud," the doctor said. "This time I'm the doctor. You're the patient."

The CT scan was negative for brain bleed, but the doctor admitted Josh for overnight observation. Quinn called Jack to arrange for him to take care of the dogs, so she could spend the night in the hospital room with Josh.

Mary stopped by the room when she went off-duty at the police station. After she hugged both Josh and Quinn, she unloaded a bag full of food from Mosquito Café. "Soup, sandwiches, and lemonade dream cake. After all you've been through today, you shouldn't have to eat hospital food."

Word had spread around the police department about Mrs. Oliver's capture and the confession she'd made to Quinn. "I gotta hand it to you, Quinn. After confessing her sister's murder to you, Mrs. Oliver's now admitted everything to the police—killing her sister, poisoning Francisco, setting up the formaldehyde poisoning at the mortuary, attempting to kill you and Josh, and a whole shitload of illegal activities she did in partnership with Lionel French, not the least of which was human trafficking. The only murder she isn't owning is Julio Martinez. Says Francisco offed his own brother, same as she did with her sister."

"Did she say she's really Elizabeth Lavender, and the dead sister is Mrs. Oliver?" Quinn asked.

"Yeah, she goes in and out of that fantasy. Or maybe she's trying to set herself up for an insanity defense." Mary patted Quinn on the back. "I thought you were Superwoman last year when you brought down Blackie, but this time you've outdone yourself. Maybe instead of PA school, you should join the force. You've got a real talent for crime stopping."

"Omigod," Quinn said. "My PA school interview is tomorrow morning. I completely forgot."

Josh interrupted from the bed, where he sat, wearing a lop-sided smile. "Sure you want to go ahead with the interview, Quinn? Being a PA might seem awfully boring after all this excitement." He rearranged the covers on his lap. "Not that I'm complaining, now that you've literally saved my life."

Quinn leaned over to give him a long kiss. "Thanks for the accolades, but I'm sticking with my plan to become a physician's assistant. I have a feeling there'll be plenty of excitement in taking care of sick patients. And if I have any boring moments, I'll remind myself to be grateful I'm alive and helping others live their best lives."

"Okay," Josh said. "I just don't want you to have regrets."

Tears stung Quinn's eyes as she remembered all the difficulties she'd experienced in her life—with Ana and Brad, Blackie, Francisco Martinez, and especially Mrs. Oliver. She'd do it all over again exactly the same way if she had to, to reach this point in her life. "Honey, as long as we're together, and my family and pups are healthy and safe, I guarantee I'll be the happiest woman in the universe."

Acknowledgments

Mrs. Oliver's Twist is my eighth book, and each time I have more gratitude for the people who serve as alpha and beta readers, research resources, interviewees, critiquers, encouragers, supporters, and friends along the way. No book is possible without these angels, and no words could express how much their assistance means to me.

I owe a huge debt of thanks to Captain Destin Sims of the Galveston Police Department, Jay Carnes of Carnes Funeral Home, Kevin L. Byron, Howard Rubin, Margaret Mizushima, Nancy Lund Shelton, Mara Ruff, Joey Brennan Miller, Bobbie Hurt, Jan Collier, Sara Ennis, and Renee Overton of the Aasylum Tattoo Parlor. Thanks also to my critique partners, Eleanor Shelton, Regina Fite, Phyllis H. Moore, Randall Jackson, Zelly Ruskin, Savy Guthrie, and Carla Seyler.

Last, but never least, is my partner in crime, ride or die, best first reader ever, Ed Richard. His belief in my writing and constant support make this writer's journey both possible and extraordinary.

Dear Reader,

If you enjoyed this book, please consider leaving a rating and review, so other readers can benefit from your opinion.

Follow me at *https://www.amazon.com/stores/Saralyn-Richard/author/B0787F6HD4?ref=* and on my website at *https://saralynrichard.com.*

Sign up for my monthly newsletter for news, specials, surveys, and other fun content at *https://saralynrichard.com.*

I am available for book clubs and other speaking engagements in person or virtually. Contact me at *saralyn@saralynrichard.com* to schedule.

S.R.

About the Author

Saralyn Richard writes award-winning mysteries that pull back the curtain on people in settings as diverse as elite country manor houses and disadvantaged urban high schools. Her works include the Detective Parrott mystery series: *Murder in the One Percent, A Palette for Love and Murder, Crystal Blue Murder*, and *Murder Outside the Box*; *Bad Blood Sisters, Mrs. Oliver's Twist; A Murder of Principal*; and *Naughty Nana*, a children's book. Her short stories have appeared in various anthologies, including *Eccentric Circles, LitBop, Provoked,* and *Taking Flight*. Her essays have won many contests and been published in magazines, such as *Bacopa* and *Past Loves*. An active member of International Thriller Writers and Mystery Writers of America, Saralyn teaches creative writing and literature. For more information and to reach out to Saralyn, see https://saralynrichard.com